PRAISE FOR

JACK OF HEARTS (AND OTHER PARTS)

An ALA Rainbow Book List Top Ten Title

A *Guardian* Best Book of the Year

A *B&N Teen Blog* Favorite YA Book of the Year

"*Jack of Hearts* might be **the most important queer novel of the decade**."
—*Gay Times*

"**Whip-smart**....Humane, **sex-positive** writing of the funniest, filthiest and most heartening kind."
—*The Guardian*

"*Jack of Hearts (and other parts)* is **the sex-ed class you didn't get in high school**—positive, frank, and inclusive, but also hilarious, heartfelt, and impossibly fun. This book is like a hug that also slaps you on the ass (in the consensual flirtatious sexy way)."
—Mackenzi Lee, *New York Times* bestselling author of *The Gentleman's Guide to Vice and Virtue*

"Told in a **ferociously original voice**, this subversive and **defiantly queer ode to living your truth** as an act of resistance arrives right on time."
—Caleb Roehrig, author of *Last Seen Leaving* and *White Rabbit*

JACK

 OF

HEARTS

(AND OTHER PARTS)

L. C. ROSEN

LITTLE, BROWN AND COMPANY
NEW YORK BOSTON

Text copyright © 2018 by Lev Rosen
Illustrations copyright © 2018 by Neil Swaab
Bonus Columns copyright © 2020 by Lev Rosen
Discussion Guide copyright © 2020 by Little, Brown and Company
Excerpt from *Camp* copyright © 2020 by Lev Rosen

Cover design © 2018 by Penguin Books
Cover copyright © 2020 by Hachette Book Group, Inc.

Little, Brown and Company
Hachette Book Group
1290 Avenue of the Americas, New York, NY 10104
Visit us at LBYR.com

Originally published in hardcover and ebook by
Little, Brown and Company in October 2018
First Trade Paperback Edition: May 2020

Little, Brown and Company is a division of Hachette Book Group, Inc. The Little, Brown name and logo are trademarks of Hachette Book Group, Inc.

The publisher is not responsible for websites (or their content) that are not owned by the publisher.

Image of stars © Elizaveta / Shutterstock.com; image of eggplant emoji and 100 emoji © Shutterstock.com / PremiumVector; image of crying emoji © Shutterstock.com / flower travelin' man; image of smiling emoji and winking emoji © Shutterstock.com / DStarky; image of peach emoji © Shutterstock.com / Sudowoodo

The Library of Congress has cataloged the hardcover edition as follows:
Names: Rosen, Lev AC., author.
Title: Jack of hearts (and other parts) / by L.C. Rosen.
Description: First edition. | New York: Little, Brown and Company, 2018. |
Summary: "An unapologetically sexually active queer character works to uncover a blackmailer threatening him back into the closet" —Provided by publisher.
Identifiers: LCCN 2017051339 | ISBN 9780316480536 (hardcover) | ISBN 9780316480529 (ebook) | ISBN 9780316522526 (library edition ebook)
Subjects: | CYAC: Gays—Fiction. | Bullying—Fiction. | Extortion—Fiction. | Sex—Fiction. | Advice columns—Fiction. | High schools—Fiction. | Schools—Fiction.
Classification: LCC PZ7.1.R67 Jac 2018 | DDC [Fic]—dc23
LC record available at https://lccn.loc.gov/2017051339

ISBNs: 978-0-316-48051-2 (pbk.), 978-0-316-48052-9 (ebook)

Printed in the United States of America

LSC-C

10 9 8 7 6 5 4 3 2 1

For Chris,
because if I didn't dedicate my next book to
him, my mom was going to be so mad

"ALL FOUR OF THEM WERE JUST GOING AT IT."

"I thought there were three."

"No, four. That's what Tori said. All hard, and I think the guy from St. Jude's was going down on the other one, what's his name, Zack, from Riverton Prep."

"I thought Jessica Lauter was there with Zack."

"She was."

"No she wasn't."

"I don't know, but if she was, she probably didn't leave with him, after that."

"Who was the other one?"

"I don't know. But Jack was, like, orchestrating the whole thing. He totally seduced them all in there and started the fourgy."

"What did Tori do?"

"What?"

"When she walked in on them?"

"Oh. I don't know. I guess she just closed the door."

"I would have watched."

"No you wouldn't have. Ava?"

"You wouldn't."

"I would!"

Laughter.

"I wonder how he does it."

"Who?"

"Jack. How he gets all that D. A fourgy in Hannah Ling's hot tub? It's like his life is a porno. Is it like that for all gay guys?"

"Like when he got fucked by the coach from Highbrook in the locker room during the homecoming game."

"Home wasn't the only thing that was coming!"

Forced laughter.

"He's just got a gift."

"It's 'cause he's so cute."

"Did Tori see his . . ."

"You can say 'cock,' Emily."

"Yeah. Well, did she?"

"She said it was huge. Like this big. I bet he was bottoming because the other boys were afraid of it."

"Well, and he's so queeny."

"Ava, you can't say that."

"Why not? Isn't he? I mean, he wears tank tops cut so low you can see his nipples. And makeup."

"But you don't say it."

"Fine . . . he's just totally a bottom. You can tell."

"Oh man, I wish I was a gay boy. I could fuck that ass of his, and we could go have orgies all the time."

"Kaitlyn! That's so pervy."

"No it isn't. He does it."

"Yeah, but he is a gay boy."

"Whatever."

My reputation for sluttiness is only partially deserved. Yeah, I was kissing that guy from St. Jude's, sure, and then I kissed that guy Zack, who maybe was a friend of Jessica Lauter's, but mentioned being president of his GSA, so I don't think he was there with her. Although, maybe, I guess? I didn't ask. He should have said something. There wasn't a fourth guy. There was a big mirror in the bathroom, maybe that's what Tori saw. But yeah, that's me. Jack. I don't love being called queeny, but I do have some fantastic tank tops and a love of eyeliner and black nail polish. I also have some great button-downs with mesh insets and tight jeans with tears so high up you have to go commando in them. I talk with my hands a lot, too. So, sure, call me "queeny" if you're feeling nasty. I won't hold it against you, as long as it's said with love.

I don't know if Kaitlyn, Ava, and Emily know that the vent in the girls' bathroom means I can hear everything they're saying from the boys' bathroom. But on Mondays, I like to come in here for my second-period break, smoke a cigarette (the only time I do, mostly), and hear about what I did over the weekend. It's scandalous.

So, true story: Yes, we were in the downstairs bathroom at Hannah Ling's party, and yes, I maybe kissed both of them, one after the other. Yeah, with tongue. And it was pretty hot. They were going to kiss each other next. But we all had our clothes on, and we weren't going to strip down and have a threesome right there. I mean, we would have gone back to my place, or someone's place or something.

But then Tori walked in and gasped, really dramatically, and the guy from St. Jude's blushed and took off and Zack started laughing. We made out a little more after that, but then he had to go home and study or something. I think he wasn't so into me as he was into the idea of the threesome, which is fine, because the feeling was mutual.

So I didn't even get laid, much less have my first three- or four-some, but somehow, it seems I had a hot-tub orgy. My rumored life is so much more fun than my real one. I bet rumor-me doesn't have a history quiz next period. Or if he does, he already has an A on it for giving Mr. Davidson a blowjob.

I toss the cigarette out the window and hop down from the counter where you can hear the best, check my hair and makeup in the mirror, then leave. I leave before they do, because I think if they came out of the bathroom the same time as me, they'd just explode with giggles or embarrassment or...something. Better to just let them have their fun.

I'm not big on confrontation. I walk by the guys who mutter "fag" under their breath. I know, it seems like I should be that guy who screams at them, calls them homophobes. But why start something? Just...try to be likeable. That's my motto. Not, like, pretend to be someone you're not, obviously. Just be likeable. Don't cause drama just because people who won't talk to you in class talk about you naked when they think you can't hear.

What is there to get mad about, really? They think I'm hot and want to lady-jack-off to the idea of me getting pounded by three guys. It could be worse, so I tell myself not to think about it. Private school in New York City is liberal and cool, generally. It's not like I'm in Arkansas, forced into the closet and getting beaten up every day for just saying the wrong thing, my wrist being too limp. I've seen the "It Gets Better" videos. I know what it can be.

I mean, I do wonder what it is about my sex life, even active as it is, that attracts their attention. Other people have sex without becoming the stuff of legend and gossip. I guess I'm just special. Lucky me.

At my locker, I take out my history book to cram, but a note falls out when I open the door. A pink piece of paper, folded origami style into a triangle. It lands on the floor louder than I think paper should land. I pick it up and unfold it.

7

I smile. A secret admirer? That's sweet. Or creepy, maybe? I look up and down the hall, but no one is looking at me, waiting to see my reaction. I look back down at the paper. Black marker. Bad handwriting. I doubt it's any of the other out boys in school. Ben is one of my closest friends and I am not his type. He likes bears—big hairy guys—usually older. I'm definitely not in that particular gay subset of wildlife (on Grindr, I unhappily checked the twink box, because I'm seventeen and hairless and slim—but muscled, from running track—why isn't that a box?). And Jeremy Diaz thinks I'm a whore who gives queers a bad name, and Don Caul is way too focused on getting into Yale to take the time to write a love note. Maybe some new freshman? Or maybe someone still in the closet? Is this Ricky Gavallino's way of finally trying to inch his way out? Oh god—what if it's a girl?

"Hey," Jenna Rodriguez says from behind me. I stuff the piece of paper in my pocket and turn around.

"Hey," I say. She raises an eyebrow at me, barely visible under the tangle of long half-bleached hair.

"What was that?"

"Nothing."

She purses her tea-painted lips like she doesn't believe me, but then shrugs, deciding she also doesn't care. That's why I love Jenna. If I want to keep something private, she doesn't pry.

"So, I had this idea," she says, sitting down. I sit down next to her, our backs against the lockers, her dark skirt pooling on the floor. "For the blog."

Jenna was kicked off the school paper for, in the words of Principal Pattyn, "pursuing an agenda of aggressive anti–Parkhurst School spirit." That was after she reported that Mr. Botts had crashed his car driving drunk one weekend. So she started her own blog—website, I guess—called The Private Line, writing about the stuff the school doesn't want us to know. All the schools, really—the private schools. It's not a gossip blog, like Famke Stein runs, with all the hookups and breakups and rumors. (I don't feature on it as much as you might think—Famke is way more interested in the more popular boys and girls. But I do have my own tag.) The Private Line is actual, newsworthy sort of stuff. Local news. Teachers getting fired for whatever, department budget crises. Her mom is a reporter—the kind that travels the world and visits war zones and interviews dictators, so Jenna holds herself to a high standard of reporting. But lately she's been trying to branch out. And for some reason, she wants me involved.

"Okay," I say, opening my history textbook to the chapter I didn't read last night.

"I want you to do a column."

"I'm not a reporter."

"I know," she says. "An advice column. Sex advice."

"Oh god," I say, bringing the textbook up to cover my face. "Why? What did you hear?"

"Well, I did hear you found a guy on Grindr who looks like Tom Blackwell's dad and you invited him to the tennis match last week and made out with him in the stands opposite Tom so he'd play a lousy game."

"I don't know Tom," I say, dropping the book. "I wasn't even *at* the tennis game." I know it's not the end of the world, but I wish I could fuck around without any commentary in the girls' bathroom. I guess I could stop listening…but that's not going to happen.

Jenna shrugs. "Just own it. Use it. For this column."

"No."

"Please?" she says in a slightly begging voice. "You can use it on your college applications."

"How is that going to look? 'Told people how to suck dick.' That's some serious Harvard material."

"Okay, so not a sex column. Like, a relationship advice column. We can call it Jack of Hearts." She makes a headline in the air with her hands.

"Right. And other parts."

"I like that," she says, hitting me on the shoulder. "We can call it that."

"I haven't had a boyfriend who lasted more than three weeks."

"So what? You know what makes people tick. You'd be good at it."

"I'd be a disaster." I turn the page in my history book without having read it.

"Do it once." Jenna clasps my arm with both her hands, her tawny fingers warm but her pewter-painted nails digging in sharply. "Please? I need a little spice. People aren't as interested in the backroom politics of the teachers' union as they once were. Famke's kicking my ass with that story about the Miller twins at Edgemont dating the same guy without him knowing."

I sigh. We both know I'm going to give in. "I just have to answer questions?"

"Yeah. I'll give you a stack, and you pick one out and you answer it. Easy."

"I'll do one," I promise. "But only because you're my friend. Not because I want to."

"You never know," she says, reaching into my bag and taking out my phone. She knows the password and has it open in two seconds. "You might like it." She hands my phone back to me—there's a new mail app on it. I tap it open to see I have a full mailbox waiting.

"You already have the questions?" I swipe through the emails. There's a little over fifty of them, but at least a dozen are just calling me a fag.

"I may have used the rumor mill to spread the idea that you were going to be doing this last week. . . . That way I'd know if there was interest before asking you to do it. And I set up a special server that anonymizes the senders' information. People feel more secure asking questions that way."

"Thinking ahead," I say, deleting the fag emails.

"A reporter's job. Anyway, I didn't filter them. So a lot are just like 'How do you know you're gay?' and 'Doesn't anal hurt?' stuff, but there are some good ones in there. But if you want to talk about anal, that's okay, too."

"Good to know what people think of when they hear my name," I say flatly.

"Live it up," Jenna says. "Better than not being known at all, right?"

"Sure," I say, though anonymity sounds delightful. I know lots of kids want to be famous, and yeah, I like attention, but I'd much prefer it for things I do—like dress amazing and say witty things—than *who* I do.

"It's like a public service," she says in the voice she used when she ran for class president freshman year. "They don't teach gay stuff in sex ed."

"I can take a few days with these, right?" I ask, shaking the phone.

"Take until Thursday. Email me your question and response. I want to post your first column a week from today—Monday. And then the second one the Thursday after that. Then we'll decide on weekly or twice weekly, depending on how people react."

"I'm just doing one," I say as firmly as I can.

She leans her head on my shoulder and rubs my knee. "No," she says. "You're not."

"Not what?" Ben asks, coming down the hall. He plops down on my other side and takes out his history textbook, looks at what page I'm open to, and opens his to match. "Oh, I read all this already," he says, flipping ahead. "You're in trouble, girl."

"Thanks."

"Jack is going to write a column for my blog," Jenna says. "Relationship stuff."

"Oh, I bet that'll be popular," Ben says, without a trace of sarcasm. Ben doesn't do sarcasm. Ben Parrish is like a beach ball—short, bouncy, round, and somehow always radiating happiness. The shaved head and round red glasses add to the effect. He also wears yellow a lot. His skin is really dark, so he pulls it off well.

"Right?" Jenna says, pushing me slightly in a "told ya" way.

"Is it going to be erotic?" Ben asks.

"No," I say. "It's advice. How is advice erotic?"

"Like, 'How to spice things up in the bedroom!' or 'Ten great kissing tips!' "

"No." I shake my head and turn to Jenna. "Right?"

She shrugs. "It's whatever you want it to be. Erotic is fine." She smiles, like she thinks that's what it's going to be anyway.

"Come on," I say, standing up, "let's go fail a quiz."

"Later, fellas," Jenna says, taking out her phone.

"I'm not going to fail," Ben says, walking next to me. "I studied."

"I studied...some," I say. I look sideways at him. "Hey, you didn't slip a note in my locker, did you?"

"A note?" Ben sounds confused. "What, are we in one of those old John Hughes movies we watched in our film history class?" He pauses. "Because I would love that."

"There were no gay people in John Hughes movies," I say. "Or black people."

"I could break ground! Or it could be a modern reboot. I look extra pretty in pink."

I snort as we get to Mr. Davidson's classroom. It's empty and the lights are out—class isn't for another ten minutes. I don't turn them on, just plop down in my seat next to the window and open my textbook again.

"Wait," Ben says, apparently oblivious to my attempts to cram that last chapter in before class. "Did someone slip a note in your locker?"

"Never mind, I need to study."

"Let me see!"

"I threw it out already." I don't know why I don't want to show him, but there was something so weird and intimate about it.

"Was it a love note? Like, a secret admirer?"

"Can I study?"

"Why would you think I would write you a love note?"

"It wasn't a love note. It was...nothing." I point at the textbook. "I don't want to fail."

"Mmmhm." Ben crosses his arms and juts his chin out at me.

"Fine, keep your secret admirer secret. But if you figure out who it is, you better tell me."

"I don't think I want to know," I say, before focusing on the history book again. The start of World War I. I know the whole wrong-turn-led-to-an-assassination story—that's fun. But the actual reasons for the assassination are a little fuzzier than they should be. Luckily, Ben lets me go over them for the next few minutes as the other students trickle in. Then Mr. Davidson comes in, makes us put our books away, and hands out the quiz. Quizzes aren't so bad. They're quiet, which I like. And I can focus on the questions I know the answers to—which is about the first half.

But then there's a question I don't know, and suddenly that pink note is burning a hole in my pocket. Who writes notes anymore? Is it sweet or creepy? Or both? I guess it depends on who sent it. I mean, if it were like, Dylan Vandergraff, then it's sweet, because I fantasize about him pretty regularly. He's got blond hair but darker stubble, and he's on the swim team, with thighs that could crack walnuts. I would love to be between those thighs. So if he wrote the note, then that's delicious, and he can call me cute all he wants, and we're going to live happily ever after.

But if it's someone else—and let's be honest, it probably is—then maybe it's less cute.

"Ten minutes," Mr. Davidson says. I turn back to the test and fill it out best I can. The perfectly folded triangle of the note presses into my leg like a branding iron.

2

Dear Jack of Hearts,

My boyfriend really wants to do anal. We've been together for a few months, and I totally love him, and it's not like we're virgins. But I'm nervous about the buttsex. Does it hurt? Is it even fun for girls? Should I do it just to make him happy?

—His Anaconda Want

I flip through the emails at lunch, snickering at a lot of them.

"What?" Ben asks every time I giggle, and then I show him the emails. He doesn't laugh as hard. Ben isn't a big slut like me. For one, there aren't many large hairy men willing to have sex with a teenage high schooler, and though I can pass for barely legal, Ben's round baby face makes him look like serious jailbait. But also, he's shy with boys. I respect that. Just 'cause I like sex and have a decent amount of it doesn't mean everyone else should. Everyone gets to use their naughty parts however and as often as they'd like. And Ben is saving his for his dream daddy. Except for those blowjobs he traded with that guy from The Mount Oaken School. But he regrets that, I think. Wanted it to be special. I'm not sure what constitutes a "special blowjob." Violins, maybe?

"Did you pick one yet?" Jenna asks. She pokes at her yogurt half-heartedly. She's wearing giant sunglasses. She always wears sunglasses in the cafeteria, which I don't blame her for. They put those LED overheads in two years ago, and the lights make the cafeteria glow radioactively, showing how filthy it is. White floors, white tables, silver counters, all just the wrong shade of dirty.

"I can do this one," I say, showing her the email from His Anaconda Want. "Tell her how to prep, clean up beforehand, use lots of lube, make sure he uses a condom, that kind of thing."

Jenna frowns slightly.

"What? I thought you wanted me to talk about anal."

"I just . . ." She tilts her head. "I think it would be stronger if it were more narrative. The safer sex stuff is great—it's important, and I think it should be in there. But can it be more personal? This isn't Dr. Jack's What They Don't Teach You in Sex Ed."

"Beyond Condoms on Bananas," I say, making a headline in the air like Jenna does. Ben laughs at that, though Jenna doesn't.

"I mean, maybe if you wanted to do a whole article on that—but if you're going to answer the letter, maybe try to make it more personal. Tell her about your first time."

"My first time?"

"With anal, yeah." Jenna takes a spoonful of yogurt. "Is that okay? I mean, everyone knows all about your various exploits, right? You're not telling them anything they don't know."

I nod and bite my lower lip. I look down at my own lunch of carrot sticks and hummus. "I just...I don't think anyone knows about that particular first of mine."

"So tell them," Jenna says. "Or make it up."

"Make it up?" Ben asks, shocked. "I thought you wanted honest journalism."

"I want a good story. Jack has good stories. But if he doesn't want to tell one, I get that. So he can make one up. Retell his own history. Control some of the gossip around him, for once."

"By lying?" I ask.

"You said yourself half the rumors about you are lies. Why not make them lies you want?"

"I don't know what lies I could tell," I say, thinking of the hot-tub fourgy. "They're already so crazy."

"So tell the truth," Ben says. "Then people will stop spreading those rumors. Which, for the record, I never believe."

"You should believe some of them," Jenna says. I laugh, while Ben blushes.

"I'll think about it," I say.

"You got all week, babe," Jenna says. "Do what feels right."

I turn back to my lunch and eat another carrot.

"Did he tell you about his love note?" Ben asks Jenna suddenly.

"No," Jenna says carefully, turning to me. I can feel her curious look through her sunglasses.

"It's not a love note," I say. They both stare at me in silence, and I sigh and take it out of my pocket. Maybe they can convince me to stop obsessing over it.

"You thought I wrote that?" Ben asks. He shoves my arm. "Girl, you wish."

"I just didn't know who it could be. Not that many out guys."

"The pink paper is from the attic art room," Jenna says, twirling the note in her hand. "So it has to be someone taking one of the advanced art classes—a junior or senior."

"Or someone who bought pink paper outside of school," I point out. I snatch the note back and put it in my pocket again. "It's cute, right?" I ask. "Or is it creepy?"

"Depends if you like who it's from," Jenna says, grinning.

"It's totally cute," Ben says. "Even if you don't like them, they like you so much they wrote you a note about it."

I can feel Jenna rolling her eyes behind her sunglasses. "For now," she says. "But you have to wonder about someone so... intimidated by you that they can't just ask you out. That's weird. There's cute-shy, and then there's, like, passive-aggressive romantic. That's not cute."

"Yeah," I say.

"Why be so negative?" Ben asks. "Maybe he's, like, the man

of your dreams and you don't know it. He's just waiting for you to show him a sign. You could fall in love!"

Jenna laughs a not particularly nice laugh.

"Ignore her," Ben says, waving his hand at Jenna. "She's just jealous 'cause no man is writing her love notes."

"Thank god," Jenna says.

"Oh, please. You're not thirsty?"

"I got laid last weekend at a college party," Jenna says, putting her yogurt down. "Smoke break?"

"Wait, what?" Ben asks. "Who?"

"Some college guy." Jenna stands up. I stand, too, and Ben follows us as we throw our trash away and head outside. It's a nice big campus with a quad in the middle, and technically we're not supposed to go off campus...but no one notices. There are two guards for the whole school, and they're never outside—they mostly hang out in their office, watching cameras. So we, and plenty of our classmates, stroll out through one of the big stone archways and then turn left and walk down the street a block to a small park. Behind us are skyscrapers, but in front of us there's a straight street, leading to the river, and you can see the water. We sit on the bench there and Jenna takes out her e-cig, which looks like an old-fashioned cigarette holder, and starts vaping her rose-scented stuff. I think about taking out my cigarettes and lighting one, but I resist. I already had my one for the week.

"Does the college guy have a name?" Ben asks.

"I think it was Will?" Jenna says. "Bill? Miller. It was Miller." She takes a drag, pauses. "That could have been his last name."

"You two are such whores," Ben says, laughing, then shaking his head in mock-disappointment in us. "Was he cute at least?"

"Oh yeah," Jenna says, taking out her phone. She opens a blurry photo of a guy pulling up his shirt to show off his abs. They're nice abs. Lickable.

"That's it?" Ben asks. "No face?"

Jenna shrugs. "I wasn't there to take yearbook photos."

Ben smirks, leaning back on the bench on the other side of Jenna. I cross my legs and look back at the school—it's built like a castle, on the far west side of the city. Past it is the Hudson River—it used to be a fort, I think, for ships. There's an old cannon on the roof that I supposedly got fucked on once.

"You guys are too jaded," Ben says. "No romance."

"Bitch, look at my wardrobe," Jenna says, waving a loose black sleeve. "I'm plenty romantic."

Ben laughs. "You know what I mean. Don't you guys want to find some guy to settle down with? Hold hands with? Go to prom with?"

"Do we have a prom?" Jenna asks, confused. "I thought proms were patriarchal bullshit and we were too progressive for that."

"We totally have a prom," Ben says. Jenna smirks. "You're just messing with me to avoid the question!"

"I'll hold hands later," Jenna says. "We're going to college in less than two years. I just want to have fun right now."

"Don't say 'college,'" I say, remembering the PSAT this weekend and rubbing my temples.

"Are you going to Brandon Summers's post-PSAT party?"

Jenna asks, understanding me. "Everyone is saying it's going to be a blowout."

"Will there be alcohol besides beer?" I ask.

"Def."

"Then I'll be there."

"Maybe your secret admirer will be there, too," Ben says.

"Oh, and we should go shopping before," Jenna says. "Like, right after the PSAT. Soho, or Bloomie's, or something. Just to decompress."

"I'm in," I say. "Ben?"

"Yeah, but we have to hit some men's stores. Not all of us have slim girlish figures." It's true—I have a tiny waist and narrow shoulders, and they make way cooler jackets for women.

"Deal," Jenna says, putting away her e-cig. "I better head back—I can't be late for journalism. See you later, fellas." She stands and walks off, waving without bothering to turn around.

"Seriously," Ben says. "Men's clothing. You have to make her. Promise?"

"Yeah," I say, grinning.

We walk back to school, where Ben waves goodbye before practically sprinting off to class. I take the more leisurely route, stopping by my locker first to switch out my books for English, which I have right after art.

Another pink note falls out of the locker when I open it. This one is larger, folded into a flower. I pick it up off the floor and look around. The hallway is empty. Class started a minute ago. I unfold the note and read it.

I saw you showing my note to your friends. Did you like it? I know, it wasn't so long. I have a hard time telling you how I feel. That's why I use these notes. But I do like you. I hope your friends could see that. Even if they don't, I'll make them believe. I'll be friends with them, too, for you, even though I don't like them. You're that special. I wish you would come home with me tonight.

I shiver and feel nauseous all at once. Okay. Not cute.

3

Dear His Anaconda Want,

*My first time getting it in the butt was kind of weird.
I think it's going to be weird for everyone's first time,
though. I was a freshman, and it was winter break,
right before everyone left on vacation—a big holiday
blowout party. There was this senior from another
school, and we were drinking and flirting, and
eventually we took off together. His parents were home,
and my mom was home, so he got us a room at a hotel
nearby. Ordered up some champagne to be fancy.*

*Now, before this, I'd sucked my share of dicks and had
gotten plenty of blowjobs, handjobs, every kind of job,
but the only buttsex I'd had was with this junior who*

*was in love with my cock and he'd just hopped aboard.
And he'd taken control then. Total bossy bottom. I'd
pretty much just laid back and enjoyed. So, as far as I
knew, anal was pretty easy—like porn easy.*

*Anyway, so this senior (I'm not naming names) and
I are having fun, kissing and sucking and 69ing and
what have you, and then he says to me, "I want to
fuck that pretty little ass of yours." And I was like,
"I don't know, I've never done that before." And he
smirked and said, "Sure, right." And I said, "No,
really." "Well, I paid for the hotel room," he said,
"so let's use it. I'll take it easy on you." But it was
pretty clear he didn't believe I was an anal virgin.*

*So he bends me over the bed and drizzles some lube on
my ass. I made him wear a condom, of course. And he
starts pushing it in. And WOW, that hurts. I tell him
to stop, it hurts, and he says he'll go slower. I say okay
because he's already in, and I'm thinking, I'm gay, so
this is something I have to learn how to do, right? So
he slows down and pushes in, and eventually it starts
to feel good—like, really good. He's hitting the right
spot, nerve endings are all aglow.*

*Eventually he finishes and pulls out, and the
condom, of course, is covered in shit. And he gets*

mad at me, like it's my fault. I didn't know about how to clean up down there. He makes me take the crap-covered condom off him and flush it, and then he showers alone. When he gets out of the shower he frowns at me and goes, "You're still here?"

Anyway, here's my advice to you: Make sure you want to do it, 'cause it's going to be uncomfortable at first, for sure. But it can be fun, too—even if you don't have a prostate, there are nerve endings and pressure. Just make sure you've taken a shit beforehand and cleaned after—preferably with soap and water in the shower. 'Cause if you gotta go while he's inside you, it's going to come out gross. When you're ready to get fucked, use lots of lube. A finger first. Go slow. Make sure he's still focused on keeping you turned on, too. It helps if you start out riding him, facing forward—then you have more control over how deep he goes, and you can still communicate what you need. Once he's in you, tell him to just stay there for a while so you can get used to it, then when you give the okay, he can slowly start fucking you. If you don't like it, tell him to stop. If you decide to switch holes, use a fresh condom. And be prepared—sometimes shit just happens. But if you take it slow, it can be really great.

—Jack of Hearts

Mom is never home for dinner—she's the director of the surgical department of a hospital downtown. A fancy one. She's technically a heart surgeon, too, but since she turned fifty, she doesn't operate as much.

So, as usual, I come home to an empty apartment—which for some reason Mom redecorated five years ago so it's all white and shiny and almost all the furniture and art is made from parts of old airplanes. So when it's empty, it feels really empty. Like an airport runway at night with no flights.

The notes are starting to make me think about them again, so I dive into homework, and then the column for Jenna, which feels like homework, but then it's seven thirty and I'm out of things to do. I take the notes out and reread them. The paper is soft construction paper, with that slightly fuzzy texture, especially along the perfect creases. Maybe they're a joke. Like a prank. Like the fag emails I got before I even knew I was writing a column.

So my secret admirer doesn't like my friends. Well, fuck him, right? I like my friends. Jenna is kind of a bitch, but she owns it and is crazy loyal. Ben is naive and a little needy, but he always sees the best in things and would probably jump in front of a bus for me or Jenna. Or maybe anyone.

I read the notes over again, once, twice, then crush them in my hand, ruining the folds. Then I get up, go to the bathroom, and flush them down the toilet. If another one comes, maybe I'll tear it up, leave little pink scraps all over the hall. That'll send a message.

My phone buzzes with a text.

> Got your column. Is this really what happened with Keith?

I'd never gone into details about it with Jenna. When she asked how the night had been, I'd told her about the hotel and sex, but nothing else.

> Yeah. I couldn't think of anything to make up

> Ew. He was kind of rapey

I frown. Is that what she got from the column?

> Nah, he was just drunk, horny, and didn't want me to blueball him

> If I'd said no, he would have stopped. He's not a monster...he was just being an asshole

> Okay, but drunk and horny is no excuse for that

> That we agree on

> He's a real turd. You sure you okay with me publishing this?

28

> Sure why not?

Jenna's "…" hovers in place, sometimes disappearing as she deletes.

It's just a different kind of intimate than I thought it would be

But it's good! Really good

I mean, the "shit happens" felt unavoidable, but it works

> Thanks

I'll put it up on Monday

> Cool—my full name isn't up on it, right? It just says Jack of Hearts, not Jack Rothman, right? I don't want to be googleable

Right—but people are going to know

> Yeah. But not be able to prove it. Just thinking of colleges

Gotcha. Should be safe

> If there's ever a problem, I can take everything down, too

>> Thanks

She responds with a GIF of a cat typing on a computer, which I take as a sign to let her work. I'm done with everything by now, so I put some water on the stove and turn on the TV. I've been cooking for myself since freshman year. I'm pretty good at it, too. At least, I like what I make. And if I don't, I just down some of Mom's really expensive wine with it, and then I like it a whole lot more. I'm fancy like that.

TV is either news, sitcoms, or crime shows. I choose a crime show. Mom will probably be home by nine and will want leftovers.

Here's my mom's favorite story to tell about me: When she was pregnant she used to call me—the fetus, whatever—Itall. She would say she was having Itall. Having it all. She almost named me Itall, too, or Yital, or some variation, but decided on Jack after her grandpa. Thank god. But yeah, now she has it all, courtesy of sperm donor 87469LNY, a tall, fit, Ivy League student, trying to pay his way through college.

Mom and I used to be closer. I had nannies, but we'd talk on the phone all the time and she'd be home earlier. But once I could answer the phone myself, get myself to school—once there wasn't this mediator between us—it was like there was this empty space instead. Like we can't talk without nannies to hold the phone up to my ear.

Pasta cacio e pepe. Butter, cheese, and black pepper. Easy recipe. Totally unhealthy. I tell myself that the PSAT stress I'll feel on the weekend will burn it off. Or the stress of those little pink notes. I try to focus on the crime show as I eat. A woman is claiming she was raped by a celebrity, but nobody believes her. Even the cops think maybe the sex was consensual and now she just regrets it.

The key rattles in the lock at nine thirty. I'm done with the crime show by then, and I'm doing practice PSATs.

"I made some pasta," I tell her as she walks in and takes off her jacket. She wears suits, complete with ties, to work. The ties were my contribution to her look. They give her more authority and make her more badass. She said it works, too—that doctors don't argue with her as much. She could be lying, but I like to think she's not.

"You're perfect," she says, dropping her briefcase on the kitchen counter. "I'm starving."

"On the SATs I would mark those statements as not similar."

"Oh?" she asks, taking the pasta out of the fridge and eating it right from the Tupperware without reheating it. "Why's that?"

"Because you're only starving right now, but I'm perfect all the time."

She snorts a laugh while she eats, which is pretty gross. My mom has loud snorts and a louder laugh for being so tiny. She's like me—thin, with a narrow face, high cheekbones, all that, but more so, like a little cartoon pixie or something, with a pointed nose and too-big eyes. Her short, curly hair is mostly white but

31

streaked with light brown, sort of backward from what it should be. Whatever donor-dad gave me, it seems like it just smoothed me out. Made my face more oval, my lips fuller, my eyes smaller. All of Mom's extremes taken down to a less frenzied level.

"Funny," she says, and goes to rumple my hair, which she did when I was a kid, but stops. She doesn't like the feel of hair product on her hands, so she hasn't done that since I started using it, which was when I hit puberty and realized my hair could easily become the mess of curls hers is. She sits down on the sofa next to me and looks at the TV. "*SVU* rerun? Can't we watch something funny?"

"There's nothing funny on," I say. She takes the remote, still shoveling the food into her mouth, and turns to a sitcom. The audience laughs. There's a gay joke. The audience laughs again. Mom switches the channel to another sitcom, an angsty one on a premium channel.

I came out to Mom when I was thirteen. She didn't look up from her computer as I stood in the doorway of her bedroom. She held her laptop over the covers, her knees drawn up like a mountain. "That's great, honey," she said. "I'll write a check to PFLAG." That was it. It was kind of awesome, maybe? But...I don't know. We didn't talk about it much after that. I mean, she asks about boys, sure, but...I'm not complaining. It could be so much worse. She didn't kick me out or send me to a camp to pray it away, or even tell me it was just a phase. It was great. Just great.

We watch the ironically funny show for ten minutes in silence before the jokes that earn no more than a smirk from either of us get to me, and I stand up to head to bed.

"Already?" Mom asks. The Tupperware is empty on the coffee table, the fork resting in it. I pick them up and take them over to the dishwasher and put them away. "I thought we could talk," she calls to me.

"About what?" I ask, crossing to my bedroom.

She shrugs, takes a throw, and bundles it up around herself. "I don't know. Just seems like what we're supposed to do, right?"

"How was work?" I ask her.

"Fine," she says. "How was school?"

"Fine," I say. No way I'm telling her about the notes. "See? We talked."

"Okay." She smiles her doctor smile, which could be sad or it could just be fine, then shrugs again. "Good night, kid."

"Good night, Mom."

I go back to my room, which has nothing aeronautical about it—it's kind of dull, really, aside from a big Tom of Finland poster (only PG-13 rated, Mom put her foot down about that). I have gray walls, black sheets, and bulletin boards covered in stuff I've torn from magazines. Oh, and a vanity, which is always a mess of eye shadow and hair gel. As I'm taking off my makeup and getting ready for bed, Ben texts me a few photos of costumes he's making for the school play. He can sew, and he loves historical clothes, so when he found out they were doing *Les Miz*, he couldn't volunteer fast enough. I flip through the photos of French Revolutionary wear—sashes and frock coats and hooded dresses that should look more miserable, but Ben can't make anything miserable.

These are really great

Thanks. I think so, too!

I hope Ms. B likes them

She will

I wrote my column for Jenna. She said it sounded like my first time getting fucked was kind of rapey

Send it

I send it and wait for him to text back as I strip down and get into bed. His "..." shows up and hovers there for long enough it starts to stress me out.

It's not. It just seems that way because Keith was being an asshole

That's what I said

I mean, you wanted to sleep with him, right?

I purse my lips and stare up at the phone that I hold over my face, the light from it the only light in the room.

> Everyone has to get fucked sometime, right?

> Well yeah. But you can choose when and with whom

I consider that for a moment. Ben hasn't even kissed a boy. Says he's waiting for the right moment. And sometimes I'm jealous of that, of knowing that his first times are all going to be right, and romantic, and perfect. But then I think about not having sex for the past three years, of not kissing cute boys, and of masturbating alone in my room every night. That sounds more miserable than I can put words to.

> I did choose. It was the right choice for me

> That's all that matters. Are you sure you want the world to see all this, though?

I smirk in the dark.

> Why not? People are just going to make shit up about me anyway. Let's see what they do with this

4

THERE ARE NO NOTES THE NEXT DAY AT SCHOOL. OR THE day after that. By Thursday morning I decide they were some joke that someone got bored with, until another one falls out of my locker after third period. It's folded like a swan, but flat. A pink silhouette. I stare at it on the gray tile floor, then look around. A few people are hanging out by their lockers, but no one is looking at me. I pick it up and unfold it.

Thinking of you. Wish we were together right now. Can't wait to have you naked in my arms. I can't wait to feel your mouth on my mouth.

My lip curls into a sneer and I begin tearing the note up. I tear and stack the pieces on top of each other and tear again and again until they're confetti, and then I drop them all on the floor, right under my locker. It looks like an explosion. I feel much better.

Of course, Principal Pattyn walks through the hall at that moment and stops when he sees the pink fireworks under my open locker.

"What's this?" he asks me without actually looking at me.

"Someone glitter-bombed my locker or something," I lie. "It fell out when I opened it."

He sighs and walks away without saying anything. I close my locker and leave the shredded paper, hoping it will send whoever is leaving those notes a message: Stop. I manage to get through English without worrying about it too much, but in art, the thoughts bubble up again.

The art teacher, Nance, is amazing. She's just shy of fifty, has dark umber skin and a white buzz cut, wears suits over old band T-shirts, and tells us to call her Nance, not Ms. . . . whatever her last name is. Today we're supposed to be using clay and found objects to create a sculpture that "fights against modern forms of oppression." To my left, London Williams is creating a life-sized clay fist rising into the air. To my right, Gerard Stein is rolling joints out of toilet paper. I stare at the lump of clay in front of me and the handful of buttons I grabbed from the supply closet, but nothing comes to mind.

"What's up, Jack?" Nance asks me. I turn around. She's leaning on the table behind me, clay and glue getting all over her white suit.

"Not sure what to fight," I tell her. Which is true, but that's because I'm not thinking of it—I'm thinking of the pink confetti on the floor around my locker. What if it gets cleaned up before the note-writer sees?

"What makes you angry?" Nance asks. "Right now? What are you thinking about? You look angry."

"I..." I almost tell her about the notes, but stop. Oh, boo-hoo, I have a secret admirer who creeps me out. It's not like I'm being gay-bashed as passersby watch. "I feel like everyone wants something from me," I say finally. "Like they feel like they deserve some part of me—or all of me—because of...I don't know. What they've heard, or who I am, or they are."

Nance nods. She's got a great nod, almost like an approving drill sergeant—chin out front, but she also bites the inside of her cheek, like she's really considering what I said, and narrows her eyes.

"That's something to rebel against," she says. "Today, with social media and all that, people can communicate faster and across huge distances, but it also means that sometimes people feel like because they follow you on Instagram or whatever that you're in some sort of relationship with them. And maybe you are. But you both get to choose that. They don't get to decide for you."

"Yeah." I nod, even though I'm not sure that's what I meant.

Nance puts her hand on my shoulder and gives it a squeeze. "Just punch the clay. That always makes me feel better."

I take her advice and punch the clay for a while. Nance walks around the room, talking to each student about their stuff, and I just keep punching. It feels good. The clay is hard, but I can still make a dent—feel strong. After ten minutes, though, my arms get tired and I start sculpting.

"Nice," Nance says toward the end of class. I've created a sculpture. It's a hand giving the middle finger, but at the bottom the base of the palm turns into two testicles, and the top of the middle finger isn't a finger. "Probably can't show it at the student art fair, though."

"I can break it down," I tell her.

"Nah, we can fire it when it's done. I just won't put it on display where Pattyn can see it."

I take a piece of wire and give it a Prince Albert piercing before covering it in a cloth so it doesn't dry out. Mom probably won't like it, either. I'll have to hide it in my room. Or maybe give it to Jenna. She'll love it, and her parents don't go in her room much. Her mom isn't even in the country much.

I wash my hands and head to lunch. The cafeteria buzzes with conversation and smells like broccoli left in the microwave too long. Jenna and Ben are already there, flipping through a fashion magazine.

"No," Jenna says to a brightly colored paisley dress. "I like the shape, not the fabric."

"I love the fabric," Ben says. "If that were a button-down shirt, I would wear it in a heartbeat."

"That would be cute," Jenna says, sipping her Diet Coke through a straw. "But not this."

"Agreed," I say, sitting down. Jenna flips the page. A perfume ad. She flips again. A woman in a low-neckline bright red dress with loose long sleeves and a flowing skirt. A gold scarf is wrapped around her waist, and she's wearing a huge-brimmed red hat.

"Lose the scarf, change the hat to black, and I'm in," Jenna says.

"I'll take the scarf," Ben says. "Wear it as an actual scarf, too. I bet I could make you a hat like that."

"You're making hats now?" Jenna asks, looking up.

"I'm trying. It's a new skill, and my parents like me making hats more than women's clothes." Ben is out to his parents, but they still call it a phase when they think he can't hear them. His dad is a record producer. "My dad really likes the hats, actually. Says they're on-brand."

"You have a brand?" Jenna asks, impressed.

"I think he means his brand."

"Oh." Jenna sticks her tongue out. "You deserve your own brand."

"You totally do," I say.

"Ben Parrish," Ben says. "Hatter. Milliner?"

"Just Ben Parrish," I say. "Leave yourself open to expand into other accessories and fashion."

"Agreed," Jenna says. "But start by making me this hat in black." She tears the magazine page out and hands it to Ben, who takes it and carefully folds it. "I'll pay, of course."

"It'll take a while," Ben warns.

"No worries," Jenna says, waving him off. "It's getting too cold for it, anyway. More of a spring hat."

Ben nods. "I'll bring my tape measure tomorrow to get your head size."

"It's huge," Jenna assures him with a wink.

"You know what they say about girls with big heads," I say. She turns to me and raises an eyebrow. I pause.

"That they only start jokes they have punch lines for?" she asks.

I laugh. "Something like that."

"I have a final edited version of your column, by the way. Just a few grammar tweaks, periods, commas, no substance. You want to go over it?"

I swallow. My column. That people will be reading soon. "Before Monday? I have an essay due tomorrow and then the PSATs on Saturday. I'm sure your changes are great."

"They are, but I'm sending it to you anyway. Just to go over it."

"We're going shopping after the PSATs, right?" Ben asks.

"Oh yes," Jenna says. "Retail therapy. Then party therapy. Want to start at Bloomie's? Then we can hit men's, too."

"Promise?" Ben asks.

"For sure," I say.

"Good, 'cause I've been thinking about it, and I want a new three-piece suit for the winter," he says. "I'm thinking houndstooth?"

"We'll see," Jenna says, sucking the final drops of Diet Coke out of the can. "I like you more in plaids."

"Plaid isn't great on my figure, girl."

Jenna waves him off. "We'll find you something cute." She

stands up. "Anyway, later, fellas. I have an algebra test I desperately need to study for. See you tomorrow, or I'll text you Saturday after the big test." She winks and saunters away. I turn back to Ben, who grins.

"Anything new from your secret admirer?" he asks.

"No." I shake my head to cover my annoyance and the lie. "I don't want any more, anyway. They were creeping me out."

Ben nods, but looks sad for a moment. "It must be nice, though," he says. "To have someone so interested."

And then I immediately feel bad. I shouldn't complain at Ben, who is amazing and sweet, but too shy to talk to boys he likes. To him, a secret admirer would be a gift. Romantic, but safe behind anonymous notes. I look up at Ben, wondering if I should apologize or if that will make it worse, but he's smiling again, flipping through the fashion magazine Jenna left behind.

"Like this!" he says, turning to a page with a woman in a chunky black-and-white houndstooth suit. "But, for a man. I mean, if I could fit in women's sizes..." He stares at the photo for a while, smiling to himself, imagining his suit. I smile, too, trying not to worry about the PSATs, or stupid pink notes, or the fact that next week I have a sex column going up where I talk about getting fucked in the ass. Way more fun to focus on clothes.

5

THE PSATs ARE WEIRD. THERE'S NO OTHER WORD FOR IT.
I mean, I've studied, done more practice tests than I can count,
met with tutors, et cetera, et cetera. But there's something about
being in a classroom in your school, but with a mix of kids you
know and don't—and with a teacher you've never seen before
reading a car magazine, feet up on Ms. Hendrick's desk, occa-
sionally glancing at his watch—that makes the whole experience
much more real, and much more surreal. It's like being in a bad
play. Or a bad movie with cheap effects, like the ticking of the
clock on the wall growing super loud. Even when it's over and
we all file out into the halls, no one talks, like we're all in shock.
Or maybe just tired.

I want to go home and crash. Or maybe drink. But my phone
vibrates with a text from Jenna to Ben and me.

I'm done. Be at Bloomies soon. Will meet you in women's shoes

Jenna took the test downtown, closer to where she lives, so she could get up later. But Ben and I were at good ol' Parkhurst, just not in the same classroom. I look for him outside and spot him as he walks out, looking as dazed as I feel.

"How was it?" I ask as he sees me.

"I mean, okay? I think? Did we have the same test, do you know? Did you say that fluid is to liquid as solid is to hard or like gaseous is to oxygen?"

"I don't even remember," I say.

"Okay," he says, looking right through me and back to the test in his mind.

"Come on." I pat him on the back. "Let's get some coffee and buy some clothes and forget about everything."

"Right," he says, his eyes coming into focus. "Yeah. Coffee would be good."

We get coffee at a Starbucks on the corner and take the train down to Bloomingdale's, where we meet up with Jenna, and then we shop. Every floor. We spend hours. Jenna finds a long flowing black dress with a deep V neckline down to her belly button, plus some cute skirts, sweaters, and a top. She goes pretty crazy. Ben doesn't find his houndstooth quite like he wanted—the men's department doesn't have anything that loud in their suiting. But he does find a gray flannel suit with pink pin-stripes and more of the neon polos he loves to wear, plus a pair of purple suede leather shoes. But I totally win the day with my new jacket. I spot it on a mannequin in the women's department right by the escalators. I immediately flag down a salesperson to see if they have it in a large or extra large, and they do. A black leather bomber jacket with cutouts all over in the shape of skulls and trimmed in dark red fox fur at the collar. I know, I know, fur is bad, but the animal is dead already, and I wear leather shoes. Foxes are cuter than cows, sure, but once you're wearing dead things, you're wearing dead things.

I zip the jacket up and it fits like a dream—fashion's preference for flat-chested women often tends to work out in my favor. I walk up and down the store in front of a wall of mirrors in the new jacket. It's fantastic. Even the salesperson applauds. I make sure to find her manager after and say how great she was, because I've had salespeople tell me I should shop in the men's department. Like they didn't want my money.

Anyway, I get new jeans and a bright red tank top to wear under the jacket tonight and a few pairs of new briefs in fun colors and patterns. I look at some new combat boots, but I have three pairs already, so I decide it's a bit excessive. I may have a credit card that my mom pays for, but the jacket alone is already pushing how much she says I can spend a month—by like three months. Then we head down to the makeup department, where we loudly critique a lot of the perfume samples, and Jenna gets a lipstick and I pick out a new indigo eyeliner.

To be clear, I'm not, like, a drag queen. I'm not trans. I just like how I look with my eyes outlined in dark colors, or sometimes some color on my eyelids or lips. Call me femme if you want, or a queen, but whatever it is, it's just me. And after sitting in a room with a dozen other kids and knowing thousands of other kids are also sitting in rooms, taking the same test, making us all anonymous little filled-in dots on answer sheets, I desperately want to feel like me again. I deserve to. So I buy me, or at least the things that make me feel like me. Capitalism must be so proud of what it's made me into.

I wear the jacket as we leave. The fur tickles my neck.

"You going to wear the jacket on Monday?" Jenna asks as I catwalk out of the store.

"What? No. To the party tonight. Why Monday?"

"I just thought you'd want something fancy to wear in the halls on the day of your big premiere."

I tilt my head back and groan. "Can we not talk about the column? I'm nervous about it enough as is without worrying about how to dress for it."

"Writers always look good in white," Ben says.

"No," I say, "if people throw things at me, it'll stain. And we're not talking about this." I can feel my heart rate—slowed by shopping since the PSAT—start rising again.

"Okay, okay," Jenna says. "Party talk only—Brandon Summers's place is closest to me—pregame at my place? Like, eight?"

"Sure," I say, rolling my shoulders so the fur caresses my chin.

A passerby stares at me and I stick out my tongue at him when he can't see me.

"Think I can fit my suit by then?" Ben asks, looking at his bag. He does measurements and alterations on all his own clothing, and sometimes ours, but he knows we have no idea how long it'll take him.

I look at my watch. "It's three."

"Maybe just the jacket," Ben says.

"Whatever you do, it's going to look fabulous. We're all going to look fabulous," Jenna says. "See you at eight."

I wiggle my eyebrows at her and she winks back. I am so looking forward to this party. I deserve this party. I'm going to make sure it's fucking amazing.

At home, Mom is working on her laptop on the sofa, some mindless sitcom on low volume in front of her.

"So, how was it?" she asks without looking up.

"It was...weird," I say, plopping down next to her. "I think I did okay."

"Where'd you go after?"

"Retail therapy with Ben and Jenna." I shake the bag in front of her. She looks up and takes in my new jacket and smiles her weird, unreadable doctor smile.

"How much did that cost?"

"Wouldn't it be more fun for you to worry about how much it cost for a while and then, when the bill comes and it's less than your most expensive guess, be relieved?"

"I could go online and check right now."

"You could."

Mom smirks and goes back to her computer. "Well, let's call it a PSAT prize. Assuming you did as okay as you think you did."

"We'll find out in a few weeks," I say, standing and walking to my room. "There's a party tonight, so I'm going to crash for a little while before heading over to Jenna's."

"All right," Mom says, eyes on the computer. "I have to get back to the hospital anyway. Have a good time."

"Thanks."

I shut the door and take off my new jacket, hanging it carefully in my closet. Then I throw the new jeans in the wash, just to loosen them up a little, and lie down for a nap. I'm out in seven seconds.

I wake up a few hours later, feeling groggy, so I shower, throw the jeans in the dryer, and make myself a sandwich. Mom is gone. There's a note saying she loves me on the counter. After I'm done eating, I start getting ready—hair gel and blow-dryer to keep it from curling but with the right amount of volume. A little wax for shine. Then I put on my new eyeliner—a perfect cat eye. Next, a pair of new briefs—black and covered in gold-foil crowns—the new jeans and tank top, and then I survey my shoes: I have a few pairs of high-heeled boots, but I don't want the extra height tonight, and so go with my dark oxblood combat boots. They should match the fur on my new jacket. I pause to admire myself in the mirror. The new jeans are tight and make my ass look really hot, and the tank top hangs just right and is very slightly sheer. I throw my jacket on, and you can see the red tank top peeking through the cutouts. I look amazing. I'm ready to party. I head out the door and grab a cab to Jenna's.

We have a very specific pregame ritual: cucumber sandwiches. It's not because we're fancy—although we absolutely are—but it's more thought out than that. Cucumbers are extra hydrating, which is good for the skin, and also good to ward off hangovers. The bread absorbs alcohol to keep you from getting drunk too quickly, and the cream cheese helps you feel full. Jenna has a plate of them and a bottle of champagne waiting when I get there. She opens the door and grins at me. Her fake eyelashes are drag-queen long.

"Hey, boo," she says, air-kissing me on the cheek. "Come on in, goodies are waiting."

Ben is there already—he's wearing the pants from his new suit, which fit him perfectly, and a pink cardigan that matches the pink of the pinstripes. Under that is one of his paisley shirts, and he's traded out his usual red-framed glasses for clear plastic. Jenna is dressed in the low-V black number she picked out today, and her hair is up, coiled high on her head into one of those buns that's so intricately woven it looks like a basket. Because her summer bleached-hair experiment is half grown out, the bun is blond, but the hair pulled back tight from her face is black, so the bun looks more like a hat. She's also wearing huge gold-and-emerald earrings that dangle from her lobes like Gucci satellites. We look fucking fantastic. We're going to light up this party.

We eat cucumber sandwiches and drink champagne for a while before Jenna takes out a joint and lights it up. "My folks are out of the country," she says. "Eastern Europe. Dad is visiting Mom." She inhales and holds the smoke, then blows it out in a fine ribbon. "Nowhere dangerous, though." I nod and take the joint from her. This is why I never complain if my mom isn't home much. At least I know she's somewhere safe, and not reporting on missiles or uprisings.

We sit on the yellow semicircle of sofas in the living room, champagne and sandwiches on the table in front of us. I've already had three, and they're finger-sized, so I think that's enough. Plus two glasses of champagne.

"So, any plans for the evening?" I ask, exhaling and passing the joint to Ben. "I mean, any specific in-party plans?" I can feel Jenna wanting to talk about the column again, so I try to direct the conversation elsewhere.

"I just want to get drunk and judge what people are wearing," Jenna says. "Unless a college boy shows up, then I might reconsider. But honestly, probably not. Not feeling it tonight."

"I wonder if your secret admirer will be there," Ben says, passing the joint back to Jenna. "Maybe he'll make his move."

"Let's not talk about that," I say, watching Jenna inhale and wishing she would do it quicker. I haven't told them about the notes beyond the first one. I take a long drink of champagne instead, emptying my glass. No one says anything, and I wonder if my tone was too harsh. Jenna passes me the joint and I take a long drag off it. I like pot. I mean, not, like, as a daily thing, but just to relax with. It makes things seem easier. Smoother. It makes little pink notes fade into little pink memories.

"Well," Ben says. "If Bobby is there, I might make my move."

Jenna laughs. "No you won't."

Bobby is Ben's big crush. Senior. Football player. Big, hairy, looks thirty. Definitely straight.

Ben laughs. "No, I won't. But if there's a gay version of him at the party tonight, I will totally stare at him long enough to make him uncomfortable."

"We should put you on Grindr," I say, passing Ben the joint.

Ben shakes his head. "Fat and black? I don't need that many people telling me I've been disqualified from fucking them before we've even met. Besides, I want a date, not a screw."

"There are assholes on there," I say, "sure. And lots of photos of assholes, too. But we're queer! Gay men can and do fetishize everything. You are someone's type. I promise. More than one. And some of those might be your type."

Ben grins, exhaling and passing the joint to Jenna. "Maybe when I turn eighteen," he says. "I don't like lying online."

Jenna snorts a laugh, causing smoke to come out of her nose. "Right, 'cause you never look at porn," she says.

Ben blushes. "Shut up," he says. "We should get going. The party started half an hour ago."

"Yeah, yeah," Jenna says, looking at the nearly finished joint. "Anyone want to try for the last bits?" We shake our heads and stand up, and after checking ourselves in the mirror and spraying the pot stink away with some of Jenna's perfume, we head out.

Brandon Summers's place is a brownstone in the Village, a few blocks from Jenna's. We walk, Jenna holding the bottom of her skirt looped around her wrist so it doesn't drag on the sidewalk. When we get there, the door is unlocked and pop is playing loudly. Inside, we're almost immediately separated. We only meant to be fashionably late, but it feels like we're the last ones here. People are everywhere. The prewar brownstone has been redone in an aggressively minimalist style, aside from the antique chandeliers in every room. But you can't see the various shades of off-white on the walls for all the people. They dance and crowd and make out in the corners.

"I guess people wanted to take the post-PSAT edge off as badly as we did," Jenna says loudly, appearing at my side. "I'm getting a drink!"

She vanishes into the crowd and I try to follow, but don't see her. A few minutes later, I catch sight of Ben, talking to some of his theater friends. I find my way to the keg, but I don't want that swill, so I head downstairs to the basement. It's quieter and less crowded down here, and there's a big bottle of gin and one of tonic water laid out on a table next to red plastic cups, just calling my name. I mix myself a G&T and then start dancing to the pop music. There are a few other people dancing, some I know, some I don't, but I'm not dancing with them, really. I'm just moving, showing off a bit, feeling the booze and pot burn the stress out of my body. No more standardized tests, no more little pink notes. It feels good.

I'm refilling my drink when Ava, Emily, and Kaitlyn, the bathroom gossips, come downstairs. They're all decked out in shades of blue, like they planned it. When they see me, Kaitlyn waves shyly, and I wave back. No point being a bitch just because they gossip about me.

"Hey, Jack," Ava says as they approach the drink table. They never even make eye contact with me at school, but I guess at parties it's okay to chat up the slut.

"Hi," I say. "Cool gloves, Kaitlyn, and that dress is great, Ava." I sound sincere, even. I nod and make to leave, but Ava keeps talking.

"Thanks," she says. "I love your makeup. It's so unfair that you're so good at that."

"Um, thanks," I say, waving at someone I don't know across the room.

"What are you drinking?" Kaitlyn asks as I step toward the dance floor.

"Gin and tonic," I say.

"Oh, will you make me one?"

"What?"

Kaitlyn smiles and shrugs. "I'm so bad at mixing drinks."

"Okay...um, here. It's a fresh cup. I can make myself another." I hold out my drink for her and she plucks it from my hand, smiling like I won her a giant stuffed pony at a carnival. I turn back to the bar to make myself another, stronger drink.

"Oh, make me one, too?" Ava asks.

"And me!" Emily says. They come up close around me, surrounding me, their bodies pressing in, breathing quick, giggling breaths. I take out three cups and splash some gin and tonic in each of them, pouring without stopping as I switch from cup to cup so the liquid splashes on the table. I hand each of them their cocktail, such as it is, and Ava and Emily say thank you and laugh as they drink.

"So strong," Emily says.

"I love it," Ava says.

Kaitlyn says nothing, just grins at me, trying to look shy, like she wasn't the one who asked for my drink first.

"Glad you like them," I say, drinking about half of mine in one swig. "Later." I throw myself back into dancing, but I can feel their eyes on me for, like, twenty minutes before they go back upstairs.

At some point, Jenna shows up and we dance for a bit, and then Brian Kennedy tries grinding on me, but he was a lousy lay, so I back away from him and go back to the table to get another G&T.

There's a guy standing there I don't recognize, nodding to the music. He's cute. Broad shoulders, nice jawline, kind of wavy dark blond hair. Really great body—husky, like someone who used to play football, but he's just wearing a flannel shirt and jeans. Probably straight, but that doesn't mean I can't stare.

But then he catches me staring. I smile, awkwardly, and go back to mixing myself a drink.

"That guy was really all over you," he says, nodding at Brian.

"Oh, yeah," I say. "We fucked once, I think he wants a repeat."

"But not you?"

"No," I say, taking a sip of my drink.

"You gay guys have it really easy, though, I bet."

"Why's that?"

"Well, with guys, it's, like, I want sex, let's have sex, right? I mean, that's how I'd be. With girls...I don't know. Maybe it's me. But I feel like I have to be careful. Like I can't be blunt and just say, 'Hey, let's fuck tonight and maybe never talk again.'"

"It's just you," I say. "Or the girls you talk to."

"Yeah?"

"Yeah."

"Well, then I'll try to be more blunt with the ladies."

"Just remember that if they say no, be a gentleman and walk away. Though it's hard to imagine anyone saying no to you," I say, letting my eyes linger on him. I never said I was shy.

He laughs. "Thanks."

"I'm Jack, by the way," I say, extending my hand. He shakes it.

"Jack Rothman?"

"Yeah."

"Wow, dude, you're legendary. My sister Ava talks about you a lot. You get a lot of action. Way more than I do. And in way more varied places and...numbers."

I laugh. "I don't know what you've heard, but it's not all true."

"No?"

"You're Ava Richard-Rose's brother?"

He nods. "Sorry. I'm Caleb." He reaches out to shake my

55

hand, then realizes we've done that already and instead lets it drop down to his pocket.

"I thought you were in college?"

"Yeah, freshman. But I'm home on break."

"And you came to a high school party?"

"Dude, a party is a party. Booze is booze." He shrugs.

"And getting laid is getting laid?" I ask.

"That obvious that's what I'm here for?" He looks down at his drink, but I can see him grinning.

"The jealousy in your voice at my having an easy time of it tipped me off."

"Yeah, well. Freshman year is not the wild orgy they'd have you believe. At least not for me. But you're probably over orgies."

"So last year." I shake my head. "One-on-one is back in style."

"Yeah?"

"Meet me out front in ten minutes and I'll show you."

His eyes widen slightly and he downs the rest of his drink in one gulp, then looks up at me, a faint grin on his face. It's hard to read straight guys. I've slept with two before. I'm not one of those guys who does it for the challenge or the toaster or whatever. I just like men, and I like sex, and I don't mind offering sex to men, even when there's a good chance they'll say no. I'm only worried if that "no" comes with a punch in the face, but Caleb doesn't strike me as a gay-basher.

I put my hand on my hip and wink at him.

"You know what?" he says. "All right."

6

LIKE I SAID, I'VE SLEPT WITH TWO GUYS WHO CALLED themselves straight. The first came out of the closet the moment he saw my dick. He went to town on me and, when he came up for air, said, "Yeah, I'm gay," and that was that, until we were done and he said I was a good boyfriend. I took off pretty quickly. The other guy, when we were done, immediately went into the shower and cried, loudly. I took off from there pretty quickly, too.

So I'm a little worried when Caleb and I are done. His place was nearby and no one was home, so I'm lying in a bed with gray sheets and staring at shelves covered in sports trophies. I pull off my condom and tie it off, then sit up. Caleb is breathing heavily next me.

"That was fun," he says, sitting up. I stand and look for a trash can, and find one under the desk. I toss the condom in there. He can deal with it later.

"Yeah," I say, sitting back down on the bed. It's damp with sweat. "You were good for a first-timer."

"Good teacher," he says, and winks at me. "You want a water or anything?" He opens a mini-fridge next to his bed and takes out a bottle of water and hands it to me, then grabs one for himself. We drink in silence. I can still feel my heart beating. I stare at him. He's watching me drink. I like the trickle of sweat between his pecs.

"You want me to go?" I ask.

"What? Nah. I mean—if you want to, that's cool. But I'm not kicking you out or anything."

"Okay," I say, lying back on the bed a little more, settling in.

"I always figured guys would be better at blowjobs," he says after a moment. "But I didn't realize how much better."

"Yeah." I nod, laughing a little. "You were pretty good, too."

"Thanks," he says. "It was fun. I mean, I don't think I'm going to do it again—no offense—but I was always a little curious. And now I know. Sex with a dude is, in fact, awesome."

"But you don't want to do it again?" I ask, trying to sound more curious than disappointed.

"I...sorry, man. I mean, it's like eating kangaroo or something. It could be delicious, but are you going to do it regularly?"

"I'm a kangaroo?"

"Your cock is," he says, laughing. "No, I just mean...I love breasts. I love vag. I love sex. This sex was awesome, but it didn't have breasts or vag. And while I liked this, I did miss them a little."

I nod. He's very laid-back about it. "So you don't want to do it again next time you're in town?"

He tilts his head back and forth. "Probably not," he says carefully. "I mean...if I'm really horny and can't get a chick, maybe...but only if it were like tonight where you were hitting on me, making me feel hot."

"Too bad," I say. "I was going to put you in my rotation."

He laughs. "I want a rotation. Man. Think it can be this easy with girls, too? Just talk to them, tell them you want to fuck, laugh about it afterward, go on your way. Like...like it's for fun, and not for anything else?"

I scrunch my eyebrows together in confusion, then pity as I look at him. "Sex is for fun," I say. "The anything else comes later, or gets mixed in there somewhere. But it's still for fun. I mean, having a boyfriend doesn't mean you start having sex out of obligation." I say it, and then immediately realize I've never had a real boyfriend, and so might not know what the fuck I'm talking about.

"Yeah," he says. "I guess it's just me, and what I think girls want."

"Well, get over it," I say, smacking him lightly on the stomach. He flinches, bringing his legs up for a moment, spilling a little water on himself, then starts laughing. I start laughing, too.

"You sure you don't want me to leave you my number?" I ask. "It was a lot of fun."

"Sorry, dude...I mean, you can leave me your number, but I think this was a one-time performance."

I nod. "Oh well."

"Hey, at least you fucked a straight guy in the ass until he came. That's gotta be an accomplishment, right?"

"Yeah." I grin. He holds up his hand for a high five, and laughing, I slap it. "Give me your phone anyway," I tell him, holding out my hand. "You can text me if you're having trouble with the ladies. What to say to them so they know it's just for fun. And, you know, send me any dick pics before you send them out so I can give you honest and critical feedback."

He laughs, but hands me his phone. "You just want to jerk off to my cock, don't you?"

"Maybe," I say, putting my phone number in.

"That's hot. Tell you what...I got one more round in me, if you're up for it."

"Yeah," I say, grinning over his phone. "I think I could manage that."

7

Dear Jack of Hearts,

I think my boyfriend just broke up with me because he didn't like the blowjob I gave him. We've been going out for a while, like three weeks, and I really like him. Liked him. No, I still like him. Anyway, we were going slow—my request. I'm a virgin. But I was feeling like I was ready, and so, the other night, since his parents weren't home, and it was after our sixth date, I thought I could move things forward a little. I didn't want him to think I was a prude, and I know guys need sex. So, we were making out on the sofa, and I could feel his erection, and I said, "Pull it out," and he smiled at me, and he did, and I sucked *it. I mean, I'd never done it before—which he knew! I think I did okay. I got it all in my mouth. I sucked and licked and stuff. But he didn't come, and after a while he started to go soft, and so I sucked more, but he told me to stop. Then he zipped up, and we watched a movie. When it was over, he kissed me good night. And since then, he hasn't responded to my texts or emails. Did he really break up with me because I don't give good head? How can I convince him I'll do better next time? And…how **do** I do better next time?*

—Bad BJ Breakup

I wake up Sunday afternoon in my own bed, makeup still smeared across my face, but feeling wonderful and relaxed. No hangover—the cucumbers worked. I grab my phone and see I have a text from an unknown number, but it's a photo of a familiar cock, sent this morning, so I know whose it is. I find myself smiling at it, then shake my head. I'm not going to be one of those gay guys who gets a crush on a straight boy.

I stretch out in bed and eventually manage to get up, take a nice bubble bath, and then eat something. Mom is at the hospital again. I spend my day doing my homework and texting back and forth with Jenna and Ben about the party. They assume I got laid, want to know with whom.

I believe Caleb when he says he's straight and it was a

one-night thing. Guys are . . . horny. I know, it's a generalization, and it's not always true—there are asexual guys, and guys who want to be in love, and all that. But guys like Caleb and me, we're just horny guys. And we like sex. And, because we like sex, we want to try it different ways. I tried it with a girl once at summer camp before sophomore year. It did not go well. But just because it went well—very well—with Caleb doesn't make him magically queer. I think it's probably like sleeping with a guy you're not attracted to—which I've done. You're horny, he's available, so you fuck him, and maybe the sex is great, but it doesn't mean you want to do it again. You're not into him. You're into sex.

Though I am sad he didn't want a repeat performance. I wouldn't mind being his one boy toy on the side for when he can't get any twat. Maybe I can still take that role, but it would probably require a lot of work, and then it's like a relationship, and he definitely doesn't want that. And neither do I.

So I text Jenna and Ben that I'm a gentleman who never tells, and they let it slide, assuming I'm embarrassed. They probably think it was Brian again. I do some more homework for a while, make myself dinner. I'm working on an essay for English about how Romeo and Juliet were killed by ideas of romantic love when my phone buzzes.

Column going up tomorrow. Any last minute changes?

Nope

> Awesome. This is going to be great.

> I hope so

> No need to hope. I know it will be

I grin at her confidence, but feel suddenly very nervous. My sex life has always been out there, talked about, but now I'm talking about it, too. I don't know if it's going to just make the rumors and stories worse. I want to douse the fire, not throw gasoline on it. And I genuinely don't know which this is. But it would be nice to go into the bathroom on Monday and hear the girls talking about someone else.

> Yeah

I stay up until midnight and keep hitting refresh on Jenna's page, waiting for it to show up. I finally realize it won't be until dawn, and get to bed by one.

8

IT'S UP. I FEEL LIKE A BAD ACTOR WALKING THROUGH THE
halls, the ones who don't even move right. I'm too aware of the
swing of my hips, the ways my arms move. Maybe this was a terrible idea. It's just sex, I remind myself. It's just stories and advice.
You'd have no problem telling that story to a room full of drunk
friends, so why be worried it's on the internet?

I can't tell if I get the usual amount of stares or not, but no one
comes up to me. No one says anything. By the time I get to my
locker, I feel a bit better. But when I open it, a little pink shark falls
out. I frown. The torn note wasn't enough. I pick it up, but before
I can unfold it, Greta Churchill-Jones is next to me. She's my year,
but we've never talked much. Kind of nerdy and shy, does theater tech stuff. I go through the reasons we might be talking, but
can't think of any—we have no classes together. Ben is our only

mutual friend. I'm not opposed to making new friends, but if this is because of the column, I need to find a way to tell her off—politely. And then never write another. I don't want new friends who think I'm going to improve their sex lives. Or something.

"Hey," she says, after staring at me for almost a whole minute. I close my locker.

"Hi," I say. She looks down, then up again nervously.

"You wrote the column, right? The Jack of Hearts?" Her voice is soft.

"That's the rumor."

"Well...if it is you, then thank you," she whispers.

I tilt my head. This is His Anaconda Want? I try not to widen my eyes. "You wrote that letter?" I ask in a whisper.

She nods. "I feel so much better now. I'm going to try it. When everything is right. But if I don't like it, I can tell him to stop."

"Yeah." I nod. "And if he doesn't, push him off you and scream."

"Oh, no, he's not like that." She shakes her head. "I just...I wanted to know I wasn't a freak for thinking about it."

"Oh." I inhale on the word. "Honey, no. It's your body. You get to do whatever you want with it—try whatever you want."

She sniffs a little and looks up at me through giant round glasses. "I know. I mean, I know now. Or, I did know, but now I believe it." She looks down again. "Anywaythanks," she says as one word, then darts off. I watch her practically run down the hallway and turn a corner.

Okay, so even if the column does make things worse, even if

66

being a professional slut is a bad career move, at least there's that. That was a good moment.

I turn back to the locker and take out some books, remembering the shark in my hand as I reach up. I unfold it and read the note.

I wish I had been your first.
I would have treated you right.
So I don't know why you don't
treat these notes right. Did you tear
it up on purpose? Maybe you wanted
to keep it a secret with you.
That's ok. I wish you had gone home
with me from the party. I saw
you with that college boy. He
can't treat you right. I
would, though.

They were at the party. They saw me. They were watching me. Again. I crush the note in my hand and slam my locker. When I turn around, Jenna is there, eyebrow raised.

"Something the matter?" she asks, looking at my fist, where a little piece of pink paper sticks out.

"It's nothing," I say, cramming the note into my pocket. I don't want to deal with this now. I want this to go away.

"The column is super popular. Lots of hits."

"Great." I smile. "I need to go get something from the art room. See you at lunch?"

"Sure," she says, though she narrows her eyes, knows I'm hiding something. I walk off to the art room, even though I have math. I'll be late, I don't care. Nance stares at me when I walk in.

"Wrong class, Jack," she says.

"My locker needs a little redecorating," I say. "Can I take some supplies?"

I don't know if it's the expression I can feel on my face—one I don't think I've seen in the mirror but that feels angry, scrunched, or if it's just Nance being Nance, but she nods.

"Sure, just don't make a mess."

"Thanks." I grab some tape, cardboard, and scissors and head back to my locker. The hall is empty, class has started. I open my locker. It has vents, that's how the pink notes keep getting in. Why do lockers have vents? Maybe to keep air circulating, make sure they don't get stuffy and smelly? Well, I don't mind smelly textbooks. I take the tape and cover the vents on the inside, sealing them. Then I cut strips of cardboard to match them and tape those over the tape, so the secret admirer can't just shove his notes through. And then, as an extra measure, I take a piece of cardboard the size of the inside of the locker door and I tape that over everything. Then I slam the door shut. I try shoving some paper in through the vents. The layers of tape and cardboard won't budge. I'm safe.

I take the supplies back to the art room, thank Nance, and am only twenty minutes late to math. Ms. Moreno frowns at me but doesn't give me detention. I would have happily taken it, though.

After math is my free period. My smoke break. When I hear about what I did over the weekend. Let's see what they make of the column. I head to the bathroom and sit next to the sink. I take out my Monday cigarette and light it. I don't know why. It's like the inhale and the nicotine and the gossip all help me relax and prepare for the week. The girls arrive a few minutes after me. I hear the door open and close. They're already talking.

"I'm so excited he's writing that column."

"I know. I want to write in, but I don't have any questions."

"We should come up with one."

"Did you think his story was kind of sad, though?"

"No. It made me happy that his first time was sort of weird, too."

"Plus, gay guys are all about meaningless sex, so it's probably normal that they're so cold to each other. I mean, I doubt they like to snuggle. Men don't like to snuggle."

"Jason liked to snuggle."

"Maybe he was gay."

"That doesn't make sense."

"I mean gay like acts gay, not like really gay."

Long pause.

"He was grinding pretty hard with Brian Kennedy at the post-PSAT. Think they fucked?"

"Probably!"

Laughter.

"Okay, but then which one tops? They're both obviously bottoms. They act and dress like bottoms... so who bottoms when it's two bottoms?"

"You're saying bottom a lot."

"Bottom, bottom, bottom."

More laughter.

"Why don't we ask him that?"

"What?"

"Who bottoms when it's two bottoms?"

"That's a great idea! We're totally doing that. Get out your phone, we can do it now."

"Okay, okay..."

"I think my brother got lucky this weekend, too."

"Someone from school?"

"I don't know, he wouldn't say."

"Okay, here's where we write the Dear Jack email. What should we say?"

I stub out the cigarette and toss it out the window, then hop down and leave. I'll see the email when it comes in. Probably won't answer it. It would be too long, and way too complicated, and probably wouldn't make a bit of difference. They've decided who I am and what I do in bed already. I doubt the truth will change their minds.

I spend the rest of my free period doing homework, then history and Latin. Ms. Costas is wearing neon pink stilettos with leopard-print racing stripes and black soles. They are fucking awesome, and between that and a slide of a nicely cut carving of Zeus, I'm pretty into class. Halfway through, though, the seldom-used loudspeaker system kicks on with a high-pitched shriek. Everyone goes silent, staring at the ceiling, looking for the actual speaker in the room, somewhere to direct their focus. Even Ms. Costas looks around for it before spotting it directly above her.

"Jenna Rodriguez and Jack Rothman, please report to the principal's office," says Principal Pattyn. "Principal's office"— not "my office." As though we wouldn't recognize his voice.

Everyone turns to look at me. I shrug, then roll my eyes, gather up my stuff, and leave in silence. I head upstairs—the principal's office is on the top floor, on a corner of the fort that looks at the river. There's a waiting room outside it, with cream-colored suede sofas from the '80s and a vase with fake flowers in it. Jenna isn't there yet, and the secretary doesn't even look up at me, so I plop down and wait.

What have Jenna and I done recently? The column is the first thing that comes to mind, but that's not school related. There's really nothing. I mean, I bend the dress code so hard I'm astounded I haven't been here before, and Jenna got in way more trouble when she was on the paper, but generally, we're good. We don't start fights, don't vandalize . . . we shouldn't be here.

"What the fuck?" Jenna asks, appearing next to me. She

walks around and sits down, then leans her head on my shoulder. "This is so about the column," she says.

"That has nothing to do with school."

"Which is what I'll say. Let me do the talking."

"Okay…" I frown. I didn't think the column would get me in trouble at school. I hope they don't tell my mom. I really hope Mom doesn't read it. She wouldn't, I tell myself. She wouldn't.

Principal Pattyn steps out of his office and points at both of us, then waves us in. He goes back into the office so by the time we get there, he's already sitting at his desk. Diplomas are on the wall behind him. A window to the left looks out on the river. His desk lamp is on, but not the overhead light, so it's sort of dim. Grayed out. There are two chairs opposite his desk and we sit down. Principal Pattyn looks us over as if we're misbehaving children. Which, I suppose, we are. He folds his hands over his stomach and does this obviously fake, disappointed sigh.

"So," he says. "You know why you're here?"

I open my mouth but Jenna puts her hand on my leg. She wasn't kidding when she said she should do the talking.

"Why don't you tell us?" Jenna says.

"You run a website, Jenna—" he starts.

"Because you kicked me off the paper."

He clears his throat. "You run a website, Jenna. And Jack, you seem to now be writing a column for it. A sex column. That's unacceptable. I need you to take it down."

"Or what?" Jenna asks.

"Excuse me?" Principal Pattyn's disappointed-but-calm demeanor cracks slightly, revealing an angry glare underneath.

"Or what?" Jenna repeats, slower.

"Jenna, it's one thing to report on teacher gossip, but when one of our students starts telling other students about anal sex, you've crossed a line. And I think you both know that. And I think you both knew it when you started writing the column. You've had your fun, but now you need to take it down."

"The school's name isn't anywhere in the column," Jenna says. She sounds like a lawyer—like her dad. "In fact, Jack's name isn't anywhere in the column. It's not even attributed to him. It's written by Jack of Hearts. The website isn't affiliated with the school, and neither is the column."

"The website is maintained by a student," Principal Pattyn says, his voice rising. "You. And everyone knows you and Jack are close friends. That, combined with Jack's...lifestyle, and it's not hard to deduce the author."

I feel my face getting hot.

"Oh, so this is because Jack's gay?" Jenna asks, folding her arms. She's still pissed about the time he made me change into my gym shirt and take off my MAKE HETERO ILLEGAL tee because "people" were offended. I never could understand how a hippy-dippy school like Parkhurst could have a tight-ass like Pattyn as a principal.

"Of course not. Parkhurst prizes the diversity of its student body and welcomes everyone. The lifestyle I was referring to was his...reputation. As the sort of person who could write a column like this."

I look down. My face is on fire now. Principal Pattyn thinks I'm a slut. Awesome. The idea that Pattyn, with his perpetual frown and wrinkled little nose, thinks that he knows anything about my sex life makes me feel gross. The fact that some of what he thinks he knows could be lies...I can't tell if that makes it better or worse.

"His reputation, which is just a fancy way of saying rumor and gossip, wouldn't hold up in a court of law. At least, not as evidence that he's the author of the column."

There's a long pause. "Who said anything about a court of law?" Principal Pattyn asks.

"Well, you're attempting to violate our First Amendment rights. It would be one thing if we were linking the column to Parkhurst, or to Parkhurst students, but we work hard to keep everything anonymous to protect people—and institutions. I've done my due diligence. The author of the column is anonymous, the people who write in are anonymous. The only name on the website is mine. And while I may be a Parkhurst student, I don't think the school can tell me what to do outside of school grounds. And I'm sure my father would agree."

Principal Pattyn frowns and puts his hands on the desk, tapping his thumb. "If I find you working on this in school, I'll suspend you," he says. "And if there's ever any mention of... goings-on on school property, and it's in any way identifiable at Parkhurst, I'll expel both of you."

"You'd have to bring us in front of the discipline board first."

"No." Pattyn smiles. "I wouldn't. This isn't suspicion of academic fraud or cutting class. This is about the school's reputation with the outside world. That's the one thing solely under my purview."

"Fine," Jenna says, standing. "But if you call us in here again, I'm talking to my dad. We have a right to say whatever we want."

"As long as it doesn't harm the school's reputation," Principal Pattyn says. Then he turns to me and does his disappointed sigh again. "And, Jack, I'd reconsider this. If I knew it was you, I assume many others will as well. Maybe even college admissions officers. It's one thing to have a reputation in school, but you aren't helping yourself with this, you know. It might seem funny, but it's just going to make people think less of you."

"Come on, Jack," Jenna says, pulling me up out of the chair. She links her arm through mine and walks me out of the office and down the hall. She pushes me into the girls' bathroom and locks the door behind us, then runs the sink.

"Splash some water on your face," she says. "You look like you're about to cry."

I run some water over my face and take a deep breath. "Maybe he's right," I say.

"No," she says.

"If even the principal thinks I'm some big whore...I thought the column would kill my reputation. I think it's just making it worse."

"You can't kill a reputation. All you can do is live your life."

"I could live it more...covertly." Knowing my classmates gossip about my sex life is annoying. Knowing the teachers might is just so icky. I've always wanted to live my life openly... but maybe there's such a thing as too openly.

"What? Go back in the closet? Take a vow of chastity? Because other people talk about you? You'd be that miserable just so people don't call you a slut behind your back?"

"Or to my face."

Jenna sighs and leans against the wall next to me. "If you don't want to do another, of course I won't make you. But Pattyn was trying to scare you. It's not going to affect your college chances—everyone might assume it's you, but no one can act on that assumption. You think college admissions people care about high school gossip? Your name isn't on it. All anyone can do is talk. And they're going to do that anyway. And I think this column can help people, too."

"Yeah," I say, thinking of Greta and her big glasses. Afraid of her own body, unsure where her desires and her boyfriend's meet, and how to negotiate that.

I turn off the sink and stand up straight, looking at my reflection. I look tired. My eyeliner is a little smudged. Jenna walks up behind me and hugs me around the shoulders.

"You're amazing," she says softly. "Don't let anyone tell you otherwise. Don't let them tell you what to do, or how to act. Just do what you want. I'll support you."

I hold her hands where they clasp at the front of my chest. "Thanks."

"Anyway," she says, letting go. "Lunch. I need my Diet Coke or I'm going to fall asleep in statistics."

"Go on ahead, I want to redo my eyeliner," I say.

She grins and leaves me alone. I take out my eyeliner and reapply, trying to work the smudge into an artsier line. My phone vibrates with a text.

> Hey man, is it true you have a blog or something?

It's from Caleb. Comes in right under his dick pic.

> Sort of

> You're not going to talk about me, right? I mean, if people find out you gave me a bj it's not a big deal, but the other stuff...

> Don't worry

> I just don't need that kind of reputation, you know?

> I'm not like sorry about it

> I get it

> I just don't want people talking about me

> I won't write about you. I promise

There's a long pause, and I go back to fixing my makeup. I'm glaring at my reflection, so I make the lines angrier, too. Batman villainess eyeliner.

> Thanks

I put my eyeliner away. Straight-boy crush is over. Now I'm just annoyed. Annoyed by shame and straight people. Annoyed at Principal Pattyn. Annoyed at the girls who gossip in the bathroom. I take a deep breath. It could be worse, I remind myself.

I could be just like them.

I sit down at the lunch table where Jenna and Ben are flipping through another fashion magazine.

"So," I say. "When did you want the next column by?"

9

Dear Bad BJ Breakup,

You gave him a blowjob on the couch, he got soft, and now he's not speaking to you. There's a lot going on here, so this might be a long one. Yeah, I can give you some great blowjob tips, but let's talk about everything else first.

So point one: Guys don't "need sex." Yeah, a lot of guys like and enjoy sex. I do. But some guys aren't into it the way I am, and some are shy and inexperienced and unsure what to do. You don't mention if your BF is also a virgin, but that may have been his first blowjob. That's a lot of pressure for him, too. Is he supposed to hold your head or not touch you? Talk, or not talk? What if he doesn't like it? Does that make him less of a "man"? That's not to say that all your anxieties aren't at the same level (or above). I'm just saying he could have been anxious as well, and that could be why he lost the erection.

He could also have been nervous about doing it in the living room, where his parents could come home, or maybe his position hurt and he wanted to move but was afraid if he moved, you'd stop. Or, possibly, he didn't like it.

None of that is your fault, though—not even the part where he didn't like it. What you need to be doing during sex to make sex good is communicate. Any kind of sex—handjob, blowjob, full-on penetration, dry humping, whatever. This runs from the most basic, "Can I suck your cock?" to the way less basic, "What do you want me to do?" But the best question to ask, especially when you're both trying something new, or at least new for you, is "Do you like that?" And if you don't like something, you should say, "Oh, maybe not that" or something. It won't ruin the mood, I promise.

I remember I once gave a blowjob to this guy who had a bunk bed. Not with a bed underneath, just a loft bed, with his computer underneath, but for some reason, we were up there, and it really wasn't enough room. So he's kind of sitting up, but the ceiling is low, so he's also curved over, and I have my face in his lap, but the bed is against a wall, too, so I have to bend my knees, but I'm a little too tall so my knees are pushing into the wall, my feet are on the ceiling, his head keeps banging the ceiling, and I'm trying to bob my head up and down . . . it was like a Cirque du Soleil torture chamber.

So after a few minutes of this, and him banging his head as he tries to enjoy himself, I stop and I say, "Is this working for you?" And he says, "You are, but this position is all wrong," and we laugh and we figure out how to fix it. We ended up throwing a blanket on the floor and 69ing, which worked so much better and we were able to enjoy ourselves. But I'm sure if I hadn't asked that, he would have lost his erection, I would have lost mine, and no one would have been happy.

So always ask. And it's okay to ask "What do you like?" too. That's my favorite question—but not everyone is good at answering it. Some are very specific—"I love having my neck licked while you take me from behind"—but some are much more vague, like, "I like you." Everybody is different. Figure out what someone likes by trying things. Sex isn't something where you just fall into it and it's amazing and easy. It takes practice. If you're both having fun practicing, though, it should be okay.

Now, as to why that guy hasn't called you back— he's probably embarrassed. It's hard for a guy to lose an erection. It makes you feel less manly, like there's something wrong with you, or you messed up somehow. But it happens—more often than you'd think. Don't tell him, "It's okay," or, "It happens," like they do in the movies. They're already telling themselves that and not believing it. Instead, turn the focus on you. Tell them what you want them to do to you that doesn't involve their hard cock. Once they get their heads off their flagging hard-ons, they usually return, in my experience. When I lose my erection—and it's happened to even me—I just focus on pleasuring the other guy. It usually comes back after a bit.

And now, since you've made it through talking and erections, finally, some blowjob tips: (1) Use your lungs to suck, not your lips to pull. You're not trying

*to yank the dick off with your mouth, you're trying
to make it feel good. (2) Use your tongue. Lots of
different ways. Ask him what works as you're trying
them. (3) Use your hands—stroke the shaft if it's too
big to swallow, or grip his balls, or touch his taint,
or finger his ass. Don't forget you have hands. (4)
Each dick is different, and sometimes the same dick
is different day to day. So always try new things—
suck the head, lick the shaft, or vice versa. Listen for
his moans and breathing, juggle what parts of your
mouth you're using and what parts of him you're
using them on. If he's read this column, and he should,
he'll tell you what he wants you to do. Oh, and use a
condom—flavored are fun. I know most people don't
think you need them for blowjobs, but you can get
STIs from precum or cum in small cuts on your gums
left by brushing your teeth. So…yeah, use a condom.*

*As for the guy not calling you—here's what I'd
do—send him a link to this column, and if you want
to try again, include the note, "Want to try again?"
And this time, talk while you're doing it.*

—*Jack of Hearts*

When I get home, Mom isn't there. The annoyance I had with
the world is still there, though, but as the day went on, the idea

of Principal Pattyn telling my mom about the column rose up to compete with it. Not that Mom would react that badly, I think. I mean, she's big on safe sex. She bought me my first box of condoms when I was fourteen. She's cool. I think she'd be cool with the idea of my giving sex advice. . . . It's just I don't think she'd want to read about the sex I'm having. Which isn't embarrassment. I like sex. I don't want to be embarrassed about that. Even if people say I like it too much or something. But it's different with parents.

But she's not there, so I don't know yet what she knows. I start my homework, which isn't too bad for a Monday. I finish it pretty quickly, then begin looking through the Jack of Hearts emails for another question. I already picked the one for Thursday and wrote a draft on the way home, but the next Monday isn't too far after that. There are a lot more now than there were yesterday—and far fewer ones just calling me a fag. More blowjobs, handjobs, guys wondering about penis length—and yes, the one from Ava, Emily, and Kaitlyn asking how two bottoms have sex. I flag that one to deal with later. There are a few other interesting ones, and a lot of boring ones I delete. When I'm done and turning on the TV, my phone vibrates.

It's Charlie White. He lives a few blocks away. Goes to the High School of the City, one of those way-out-there private schools where they use experimental teaching techniques. Every day is a field trip for them, I think. He's a power forward or something on the basketball team, and we've hooked up a few times at parties. But we never really hang out. I don't think we even really like each other with our clothes on. I text back just to be polite.

> Hi

So that's you, doing the Jack of Hearts thing?

Ah, another asking me not to mention him in the column. Well, too late. Charlie's bunk bed situation was hilarious. I didn't describe him. Plenty of people have loft beds. And it's not like he's in the closet.

> That's what they tell me

That's pretty hot 😊

Okay. So maybe he's not texting to make sure he's not mentioned.

> Thanks?

You going to mention me?

> Would it be a problem if I did?

No. I think that would be kind of hot 2

I grin. Maybe this being-famous thing has other perks.

Well, the more stories I have to tell about you, the higher the chance one of them shows up in print

What are you doing?

Nothing, really. Watching TV

Can I come over?

Let me see when my mom is going to be home

K

Charlie has this really sexy thing he does when he's turned on where he licks his upper teeth. I know that sounds gross, but he has great teeth, and they're really white next to his onyx skin, so when he does this half smile and runs his tongue against his teeth—it's just hot. And I know that's what he's doing now.

When will you be home?

Probably not until 10. Sorry.

That's ok

That's perfect. I text Charlie.

Come on over

10

CHARLIE PEELS HIS CONDOM OFF AND TOSSES IT IN THE
trash—perfect shot. He's tall, really tall, so when he lies down
next to me on the mattress, even though we're eye-to-eye, his
feet hang off the bed. He kisses me once—one of those full-
mouth, postcoital, lazy-tongued kisses that taste like sweat.

"Enough to write about?" he asks.

"I guess it depends on the kind of questions I get," I say, scoot-
ing up on the bed and leaning against the headboard so he can
do the same and his feet won't dangle. But he doesn't move, so I
stare down at him and his half smile. "You really want to be in
the column that bad?"

"I mean...not by name. Not full name. Not, like, Google
results. But, it's hot. It's hot to read about the things you do...."

he says, turning slightly and letting his hand walk over my stomach. "Hot to think about you doing them."

"Well, I just wrote a draft of a column with the bunk bed."

Charlie laughs. "Nah, not that, come on," he says.

"You won't be named."

"Aw, man. I wanted to be some sexy pseudo-celebrity, and you're making me the guy with the kid's bed."

"I don't know how you even fit in that thing."

"I sleep curled up." He shrugs.

"That's a funny image."

He lifts himself up and stands, and I watch him as he bends over and grabs the end of my sheets to wipe himself off before dressing.

"I have to get home," he says. "Practice early tomorrow."

"Ah, sports-ball," I say sagely. "With the sexy uniforms."

He frowns, unamused. "It's important to me. I like things other than fucking, you know."

"Yeah," I say apologetically. This is why we don't talk much.

"But I promise to wear my uniform next time. If you think it would be good for the column."

I laugh. "Only one way to find out," I say.

"Cool." He smiles and licks his teeth, and I grin. He winks before walking out the door. Being a sexlebrity has its advantages, I guess. Wouldn't mind seeing Charlie in a jockstrap. And that's the first time we've hooked up without booze. I guess fame is its own social lubricant.

After he's gone, I shower off and make myself dinner and eat while watching a science-fiction show where the women get naked a lot, but the men never do. Mom still isn't home. I'm debating waiting up or going to sleep, and decide to go through the Jack of Hearts emails again. With the amount that came in today, I imagine it's going to get difficult to keep up with all of them.

I scroll through the letters on my phone, deleting the boring ones, marking the interesting ones. Second from the bottom, though, isn't a question. Not a sex and relationships one, anyway.

Subject: Why did you block your locker?

I swallow as I open the email. The text is all pink.

Jack-

I tried giving you another of my little love letters today, but your locker was blocked off somehow. I couldn't get my note into it. Why would you do that? Are you trying to hurt me? Like how you fucked that basketball player. He doesn't even really like you. He's just using you. That's all those other guys want from you. I would never use you like that. I care about you. I'd make you SO happy. And yet, you block off my notes. My special notes. I don't like that, Jack. That's not how you should treat me. And I'm going to show you what happens when you do.

11

I STARE AT THE PINK FONT ON MY PHONE SCREEN FOR A while, then go to my bedroom window. The blinds are closed. I peek out of them, but the city is dark. No one is lurking in a pool of streetlamp light. There's one old man in his gym clothes walking a dog, a few businesspeople coming home late from the office, ties askew. No one my age. No one watching me.

My heart is racing. I think of calling down to the doorman, asking if he saw anyone, especially when Charlie came in, but then he might tell my mom I was asking, and I don't want her to know. She'll worry too much. She'll lock me in my room, make me a nun until she knows I'm safe. But I know I need to tell someone now. I can't just shove this in my pocket and hope it goes away. I need someone who can help me. I call Jenna.

"I haven't heard my phone ring in forever," she says, after

picking up on the seventh ring. "I'd forgotten my ringtone. I thought I was just hearing Paloma Faith, like in my head, like a stroke or something."

I don't say anything. I don't say texting would have been too hard because my hands are shaking.

"Can you see the Jack of Hearts emails?" I ask.

"Yeah, I can log in."

"Do it."

"Okay . . ." I hear her typing on her phone.

"Second to last."

"Your locker?" She goes quiet as she reads. "What the fuck, Jack?"

I tell her everything. About all the notes, and what I did to my locker to stop them. About how Charlie was just here.

"I thought that would end it," I tell her. "I really did. I figured if I made it even a little harder, they'd stop trolling me."

"This is stalking, not trolling."

"Yeah, I guess." I'm starting to wonder if telling Jenna was a bad idea. She sounds angry. Really angry. I just want this to go away quietly. She doesn't seem quiet.

"You guess? Jack, the dude saw someone come and go from your apartment. They're watching you. Maybe through your computer or maybe with binoculars. You put your shades down, tape over the camera on your computer?"

"I . . . the shades," I say.

"Tape the lens. Now."

I get some black electrical tape and put it over the camera on my computer.

"Can you track the email, though? Then we can just talk to them. Tell them this isn't funny anymore."

"I don't think it's supposed to be funny. And no. I told you, it's an anonymizing email client. It's third party. I can't, like, enter a password and get their information. I can hack a little, but I can't do that. It's a good client. There probably aren't that many people who could crack it."

"You can't email the people who made it and explain?"

"It doesn't work like that. But... I'm going to talk to my dad, okay?"

"No," I say quickly.

"Jack, this is important. I'm going to talk to my dad."

"He'll tell my mom."

"I'll tell him not to. Not yet. We know that this pink-obsessed stalker—Pinky, we'll call him—has to be a student to have been able to leave those notes in your locker. So we'll talk to the principal. Maybe get some security measures. And my dad will talk to the police, show them the email, make sure there's an open file."

"That sounds like a lot of work."

"Don't worry about it."

"Principal Pattyn won't help us. He hates us right now."

"This is about student security. I'll make him help us. No matter what he thinks of us, we're still students, and this is serious. My dad will help."

"No," I say, then swallow. "We can go to the principal, but don't tell anyone else, okay? Not your dad or the cops. I still think it's just some idiot fucking with me."

"Even if it is, Jack, this is over the line. Get to school early tomorrow. I'll meet you outside the principal's office."

"Okay. Thanks."

"Yeah."

I hang up and stare at the phone for a while before putting it down. I go brush my teeth and wash my face. Mom gets home just as I'm done.

"Hi, honey," she calls. I walk out of the bathroom. Her hair is even crazier than usual, the circles under her eyes dark, but she's put on her doctor face, so I can't tell if she's stressed or just didn't sleep well. "How was your day?" she asks.

"Fine," I say. She's tired. This will be fixed soon, so no point telling her. She'll freak out. And I don't want that. She has enough to worry about, and our relationship is weird enough without making her worry even more. After all, it could be so much worse. I'm healthy, alive, rich, and generally happy. An excited fan isn't that big a deal, even if Jenna thinks it is. Even if that fan scares me. "How about you?"

"Long day," she says. "I ate at the office. Going right to bed, I think. You?"

"Yeah, was just heading there."

"Okay, honey. Sweet dreams."

"You too. Love you, Mom."

She stares at me for a minute after I say that, and I wonder if I've said it funny, or I don't say it enough or something, but she smiles—not the doctor smile, but a big, gentle smile, like when I was little.

"Love you, too."

12

JENNA IS IN THE WAITING ROOM OUTSIDE PATTYN'S OFFICE
when I get there, and she's ditched her usual boho/goth look for
a navy blazer over a white blouse and black tuxedo pants with a
purple stripe. Her hair is back in a ponytail. Her shoes are bright
red. I feel underdressed in just black jeans and a black-and-blue
striped tank top under a gray cardigan. When Principal Pattyn
walks in, he does a double take, glancing at both of us.

"Why are you here?" he asks, unlocking his office.

"Jack is being stalked," Jenna says, her voice all authority—
maybe too much authority.

Principal Pattyn sighs and goes into his office, turning on the
lights. Jenna follows him, sitting down in one of the chairs opposite his desk before he even gets settled. She motions for me to
sit next to her, so I do. Principal Pattyn takes his time, sipping

some coffee and booting up his computer before looking back at us. Jenna shoves her phone in his face. The pink email is open on the screen.

Principal Pattyn reads the email, then frowns slightly. "This isn't a school email."

"No, it's the Jack of Hearts email, where people write in with questions."

Principal Pattyn leans back in his chair and clasps his hands over his stomach. "I can't do anything about something happening off school property. I think you made that quite clear yesterday. Besides, this email could be from halfway around the world. It could be a prank—probably is."

"Except he's gotten notes, too. In his locker. Pink construction paper."

Principal Pattyn purses his lips and nods. "All right. Let me see."

Jenna turns to me and bites her lower lip. I shrug.

"Well?" Principal Pattyn asks.

"I threw them out," I admit.

Principal Pattyn stands up. "I don't know if this is a test, or a publicity stunt for your column, but either way, I don't appreciate it. Please leave."

"But it's real," I say softly.

"Perhaps, Jack, if you attracted less attention, you wouldn't be getting emails like this. If this is real, I'd suggest stopping the column, and trying to keep a low profile."

"That's it?" Jenna practically screams. "He's being stalked, and threatened."

"I see no evidence of that. Jack of Hearts is being threatened, perhaps, but as you said yesterday, there's no proof that that's Mr. Rothman here. None of this has anything to do with the school. I'll let our security know about the email, but I don't know what else you want me to do, Jenna. Publicly condemn the email, perhaps? That would look lovely on your blog, wouldn't it?"

"This isn't for publicity," Jenna says. "You need to fucking do something."

"Leave now, Miss Rodriguez, and I'll forget that little outburst. Otherwise, I'll start handing out detentions."

"Jenna, come on," I say. "He's right. We have no proof." I take her arm, and after a long moment of her glaring at Principal Pattyn, she finally turns and walks out with me.

"Fucking asshole," she whispers.

"Could be worse," I say. "At least we didn't get detention or anything."

"What's the rule?" Jenna asks. I realize I've slipped up.

"I'm not allowed to say 'could be worse.'" It's a rule she came up with toward the end of freshman year. She says I say it too much. I use it to minimize when people do bad things to me. She came up with the rule when Tom Krall blocked me from going into the boys' bathroom and called me a faggot. I just used another bathroom one floor down. Jenna wanted to know why I didn't push through, why I didn't seem angry like she was. I told her because it could be worse. And she said, "That might be true, but that doesn't mean it's not bad. That doesn't mean you don't

97

try to stop it from being bad." Since then, I'm not supposed to say it. Out loud, anyway.

"And honestly, Jack, I'm not sure how it could be worse. This stalker could be planning to hurt you. What's worse than that?"

I shrug. We walk in silence through the halls of the administrative part of the building, which are tiled in beige instead of gray, for some reason.

"If Pattyn won't help, we'll figure this out ourselves. When do you have art?"

"Third period today," I say, pulling open the door to the stairs and heading down to where the classrooms and our lockers are.

"Great. I'm going to visit. We need to find out who's been taking a lot of pink construction paper."

"You can get pink construction paper anywhere."

"Maybe. But it's a start. It's something. We have to do something, don't we?"

"Or maybe Pattyn is right, and I just...ignore it. Keep a low profile."

"You invited a guy over for a quickie yesterday. That's not a high profile. Unless you plan on locking yourself in your room and not doing anything ever again?"

"No." I sigh.

"Do you want to stop the column?"

"No," I say a little louder.

"Great. See you third period."

She kisses me on the cheek and takes off. I follow.

For the next two periods, I constantly look around at the

other students, just to see if any of them are looking back at me. No one really stares at me. I catch Jeremy Diaz, the GSA president, looking at me once, but when we meet eyes, he just glares. I already ruled him out after the first note—Jeremy thinks I'm a whore who gives the Queer Community a bad name, so I doubt he'd have a crush on me. But seeing as the notes have gone from crush to creep, maybe it's like...some weird psychological disorder. Can't eliminate anybody. That's what Jenna would say. Except...not Jeremy. It can't be him.

By the time third period comes around, I've learned nothing from any of my classes except that a lot of my fellow students are really good at looking like they're paying attention while actually half asleep. I hope nothing that was taught today will be on any tests.

The art room smells like clay. We're still doing sculpture. There are glazes set up today, for the sculptures we were working on last time. A few other students are there before me, already working. I look around for Jenna, but she's not here yet, so I grab my middle-finger sculpture and bring it over to the table. Jenna arrives before I take the cloth off.

"You're not in this class, Jenna," Nance says, tilting her head as Jenna comes in. Jenna looks over at me.

"We have a question for you," I say. "Jenna and I. But...in private."

"Okay," Nance says, raising an eyebrow. She walks over to the far corner of the room where she has a desk. We follow. "What's up?" she asks in a low voice.

"Has anyone been taking a lot of pink construction paper?" Jenna asks.

"No." Nance shakes her head. "What is this about?" Jenna looks at me and I stare back. I don't want to tell anyone else. I don't want to make a big deal out of it, like Jenna will if I don't stop her. I just want it to go away.

"It's just a silly thing," I say.

"It's not silly," Jenna says before I even finish. "It's for an article . . . for my website—you know it?"

"Yeah. What story has pink construction paper—something happening with Mr. Block?"

Jenna licks her lips. "Did Mr. Block take a lot of pink construction paper?"

"For the set, for *Les Miz*," Nance says. "Apparently the paper, when painted first with a watered-down gray acrylic and then with a solid black, looks like dirty bricks under the right lighting. But, that's all I know. If you're doing something on the show . . . or on the cost of supplies, you should talk to him. But we all share supplies. That's normal. It's not evidence that the theater department is underfunded or anything."

"Okay." Jenna nods. "Thank you. That's all I needed to know. I better get to my real class now." Jenna squeezes my shoulders affectionately before rushing out.

"What is she doing a story on?" Nance asks. "What do you have to do with it? I can tell when people lie to me, Jack."

"It's nothing," I say. "Really."

Nance gives me a long look. So long I can't keep eye contact and look down at my shoes. "Okay," she says finally. "Back to work. You should do something with the ring you stuck in it last time—it should pop."

"Good idea," I say, turning away. "Thanks."

Back at my seat, I can still feel Nance's eyes on me as she walks around to the rest of the students, so I try to focus on my sculpture. I take off the cloth that's been keeping it damp, but underneath, where once there was a ridiculous sculpture with a simple copper wire for a Prince Albert, now the copper has beads on it. Pink beads, with letters and hearts, like a bracelet you make at summer camp.

♥ I ♥ L U V ♥ U ♥ J A C K ♥

"Oh," Nance says, coming up behind me. "Guess you already did something."

"Yeah," I say, pulling the wire out. The beads fall to the table, hitting it as loud as hail in my ears. My heart is pounding. I swallow. "I don't like it, though. I'm going to do something else."

Before she can say anything, I punch the sculpture down, and I keep hitting it until it's just a lump of clay again.

13

Dear Jack of Hearts,

So, what do you do when there are two bottoms—
gay guys—who want to have sex? Do you take
turns? Like, during that night, or maybe you just
switch every time you hook up?

—*Bottom Curious*

"Everyone has access to the art room." Jenna sighs at lunch, after I've told her about my sculpture.

"Yeah. It might not even be related. Just a stupid prank."

"Sure," Jenna says, her tone making it clear she doesn't believe that in the least. "But the pink paper was a good lead—we have to tell Ben, though." I look over at Ben, still in line, taking an iced tea and putting it on his tray.

"He'll freak out more than you are," I say.

"Freaking out is good. Someone needs to. You can't just ignore this and hope it goes away."

"It might. Maybe he'll get bored."

"Who'll get bored?" Ben asks, sitting down.

"Jack's stalker," Jenna says, opening her Diet Coke.

I sigh. I can feel Ben turn to me, nervous. I don't say anything.

"The pink notes," Jenna says, sipping her soda. "He got more of them, they got creepy. Creepy enough that he blocked his locker up. Now he's getting emails." Jenna pulls out her phone and shows the email to Ben while I study the cafeteria table. It's plastic, and someone has drawn a dick on it in Sharpie.

"O. M. G.," Ben says. "This is not cute. Sorry I ever said it was cute."

"You didn't know," I say. "And besides, it's not that bad. It could be"— I stop myself as Jenna glares at me— "a harmless prank," I finish.

"But we've started doing a little digging," Jenna says. "And we need your help."

"Me?" Ben asks.

"The notes were all written on pink construction paper— Nance says the theater kids are using pink construction paper for the *Les Miz* set?"

"Yeah." Ben nods. "There's a big stack of it backstage. But everyone has access to it."

"And you can buy construction paper anywhere," I point out, for what seems like the hundredth time. Jenna ignores me, focused on questioning Ben.

"Who's everyone? How many people?"

"I don't know.... Actors, backstage people ... Forty? Fifty?"

"Well, that's less than everyone in school, at least," Jenna says, frowning. She takes a long sip of her Diet Coke. "We have to make them show their hand. We have to ... like, plant a camera watching the paper. And then make Pinky act."

"Plant a camera?" I ask as deadpan as possible. "We're the CIA now?"

"I have one," Jenna says.

"And if we get caught? What? Suspension? Expulsion? I'm pretty sure the school guidelines have rules against filming students without their knowledge."

"It's not like my name is on the camera or anything."

"Serial numbers are," I counter. I watch a lot of cop shows. "Besides, if we're going to film something, why not my locker?"

"I thought about that, but it won't work. There's nowhere to put the camera in the hallway it won't be spotted. It's small, but not, like, hidden. It's my mom's. For reporting, not spying. But backstage, there's a mess—props, costumes, the rafters—we can hide a camera pretty easily there."

"Except, Pinky isn't even using paper anymore," I say, crossing my arms. "He's gone digital, remember?"

"So unblock your locker."

"And how will Pinky know I unblocked my locker?"

Jenna pauses. Ben, who has been eating potato chips and watching us, takes a very loud sip of his iced tea.

"We tell him," Jenna says finally.

"What?"

"We email him back—something kind of flirty, like, 'I liked it better when you slipped notes in my locker. I liked to keep them in my underwear.'"

"Gross," Ben says.

"Yeah, that's not flirty, that's disgusting. And I don't want to be flirty with this guy. I don't want to encourage him. I want him to go away."

"What even started this?" Ben asks. "If you figure that out, you can figure out who he is."

"I don't know." I look down at my unopened yogurt and peel the foil back. "People talk about me. I don't know why. Because I have sex and they don't?"

"Yeah," Ben says, "but you've been having sex for a while. What happened last week to make this guy go nuts and start writing you notes? Did someone ask you out and you said no? Did you hit on someone, then walk away?"

I take a spoonful of yogurt and try to think back on last week. The weekend before was the party at Hannah Ling's, but that was it. Mom was actually home all of Sunday so we watched old movies and ate popcorn. No one tried to hit me up for a date or sex, either. There was one guy on Grindr who tried chatting me up, but I didn't respond, and he didn't seem to care. Plus, his photos put him as way too old for high school.

"I didn't do anything," I say after a moment. "I mean, there was the party at Hannah Ling's, but all I did was make out with a few boys." I sigh. "I guess the fourgy rumor could have started it?"

"I know what it was," Jenna says quietly. I turn to look at her. She's staring at her hands, spread out on the table, nails painted a dark purple and gleaming. "I told people you'd be writing a sex column for my website."

I don't say anything.

"That could be it," Ben says. "You weren't just being talked about. . . . You were talking about sex. Or were going to be."

"I didn't know that, though."

"But they did," Jenna says. "I used the rumor mill. Everyone knew. I told Emily on Friday morning. The whole school probably knew by that night, plus a few other schools. I'm so sorry."

"That's okay," I say, "you didn't know." She looks up, but I keep staring at her nails. I can feel her eyes trying to meet mine, seeking some forgiveness. But my head just feels too heavy.

"So now you go from being talked about, to talking," Ben says. "And that's enough to get them to write you those notes. The idea of people sending you letters, asking questions. Maybe they were jealous of everyone else. Plus, now you're, like, famous, like—"

"A sexlebrity," I say. "At least, that how I've been thinking of it."

Ben giggles, then immediately stops. "Sorry. It's funny. I mean, it's not, but it's a funny term."

"So, your sexlebrity status makes people want you," Jenna says.

"That's why Charlie called."

"And it makes Pinky want you but not in a normal way," Ben says.

"Creepy," I say.

"Creeper," Jenna says. Her purple-nailed hands crawl across the table and grab one of mine. "I'm really sorry."

I look up finally, take a deep breath, meet her eyes. "It's okay," I say again. She really didn't know. There's no point in being angry with her. She was being Jenna. The anger I feel will be gone by tomorrow. Better to act like it's not there until then.

"Okay," she says. She holds my eyes for a while, then frowns, but immediately forces herself to smile. "So how do we catch this guy? I still think cameras are the way to go. Unless one of you has a better idea?"

I don't say anything. Ben shrugs.

"Great," she says. "I'll bring the camera tomorrow."

"We still need to make him write me again."

"Well," Ben says, "if it's the column that started this, probably just writing more will make him act up more, right?"

"More?" I ask.

"And raunchier," Jenna adds.

I cock an eyebrow at her. "You're not Pinky, are you? Doing all this to make me write more, get your hits up?"

"I would never," Jenna says with more sincerity than I've ever seen from her. It almost scares me, because that's how serious this is to her. "You know that, right?"

"I was just kidding," I say quickly. "Okay, more columns. I can do that. I'll just send them to you as I write them."

"I'll put them up after the camera is in place. And then you message the guy back saying your locker is open. And then we catch him!" Jenna sips from her Diet Coke, looking satisfied.

"That's the plan?" I ask. "Bait a crazy man into sending me more notes."

"Pretty much," Ben says. "Don't worry, though. He's not violent. Just a creeper."

"At least, not yet," Jenna says.

"Why did you have to say that?" Ben asks. "We all knew it. Don't say it out loud. Now he's going to be even more freaked out."

"No," I say. "I'm fine. I'm going to be fine. A creeper isn't bad. And we have a plan to catch him. At least I'm not being stalked in the South by some hillbilly homophobes who want to skin me, right? This is manageable. Could be so much..." Jenna glares at me as she sucks soda through her straw. "More dangerous."

"Right," Ben says. I nod, but I feel like I'm lying. Sure, it could be worse, but it could be much, much better, too. I just want it to go away. But if ignoring it won't do that, then I guess this plan is the next best thing. Besides, there's a Jack of Hearts email I'm dying to answer.

14

Dear Bottom Curious,

First, for our readers who don't know: "Bottom" is when you receive anal sex, and "top" is when you give it—penetrate. For some it's an identity, for some a verb. But now, on to you, Bottom Curious: I think what's telling about this letter is your use of the word "you" and the way you needed to clarify that "you" meant "gay guys." Specifically, you wrote: "What do you do when there are two bottoms—gay guys—who want to have sex?" Not "What do we do?" Not even "I'm a total bottom but so is this boy I really like, any sex tips?"—which leads me to believe that you're not a queer dude. I'm *guessing you're probably not even a guy. You're a straight girl and you're fetishizing gay men. So let me explain a few things to you: First, not all gay men have anal sex. A lot of them try it now and then, but it's with about the same frequency as straight couples. There are plenty of other things two (or more) guys can do without putting the P in the B. And many of them are very satisfying. So don't assume all gay guys you see are just having nonstop anal sex. Some are, sure. But not all.*

Secondly, not all gay guys are strictly tops or bottoms. Again, some are, but those who really identify as a capital T Top or B Bottom tend to view that as a huge part of their identity, and would make sure not to go home with someone of the same identity, because of sexual incompatibility. Also, personally, I think those guys are missing out. Sure, a preference is fine, but versatility is fun, not just because you get to experience both sides, so to speak, but because when you're in the mood to top or bottom, you can just say you're in the mood.

I'm going to get lecture-y for a second and add that I think the entire idea of Tops and Bottoms—especially when coming from straight people who fetishize gay people—is an attempt to place some sort of hetero world over gay people. "Oh, you bottom, so you're the woman." Gay guys who are strictly Tops or Bottoms tend to embrace this idea, too. Being a Top Only means you're manly or whatever. Because not being manly is considered bad by, like, adults and TV and stuff. Gay guys can buy into that crap just as easy as straight people. Whenever you see "Masc4Masc" on Grindr or whatever, what you're seeing is someone saying, "I don't want people to think I'm like a woman, and I don't want people to think you're like a woman, because then people will think less of us." Sure, people have preferences, but these ideas of "masculine" and "feminine" are kind of meaningless. I wear makeup. I think I'm pretty manly. We're all told this crap all the time, but you can reject it. Instead, you're enforcing the idea that there is masculine, and there is feminine, and that masculine is, for some unexplained reason, better.

Finally, and this should probably be clear after the last bit, but you can't tell a top or a bottom or what a person's preferences are just by looking at him. Big hairy muscled men love taking it up the ass—trust me, I know. And slim, makeup-wearing types? We love to fuck (and, in my case, get fucked, too—like I said, versatility is the best). So, in summary: It's wrong to assume all gay guys are having anal sex all the time, and it's ridiculous and offensive and

stereotyping and hurtful to think that those who are
penetrated are "girly" and those who penetrate are
"manly"—something you've been doing.

So here's my question for you, Bottom Curious.
Assuming you are a straight girl, why have you been
thinking about gay men like this? And why the fuck
do you care so much about gay sex anyway? I mean,
curiosity is fine, if a little creepy. Maybe you just
get off on two dudes going at it, which is cool, too,
but that doesn't mean we're here to perform for you.
I keep looking at your letter—"What do you do?"
you asked. If it was a fantasy, it'd be whatever you
wanted. And if it was just curiosity, then honestly,
it's none of your business, and anyone who thought
of gay people as people, and not hilarious sitcom
characters, would know that. But you wrote to me.

"What do you do?" You assume I'm a bottom,
that gay men are specific types—based on what?
Makeup? Clothing? Your email is more like a mean
joke you tell your friends, and I think that's because,
secretly, you hate the way you're always being told
what a girl should be like, and when you see a gay
guy blurring the gender lines a little (like me), you're
jealous of him. You want to put him in his place. You
want to say he's not a man. Because if you can't blur

*those gender lines without being told you're gross
or wrong, then you want to make sure that anyone
who does cross those gender lines gets punished. The
way you would. But you shouldn't be punishing gay
guys. You should be breaking down the barriers that
keep you from being who you want to be. I feel sorry
for you that you don't see that. Instead, you giggle
about gay sex and declare guys to be "total bottoms"
based on their look, without having ever spoken to
them. Gay people are just jokes to you. So until you
realize we're actual people, don't write me again.*

*Oh, but if, on the off-chance, a gay boy is reading
this and wants a real answer—if you and the guy
you want to get naked with are both really craving
some cock in your ass, either take turns or grab a
double-headed dildo. Or even just one dildo if you
can take a position where the one getting fucked can
reach around and really push and pull that dildo out
of the "top's" ass. Hope that helps.*

—Jack of Hearts

Mom is already home when I get there. She's making dinner, too,
so I freeze up. That usually means she has something bad to tell me.

"Everything okay?" I ask.

She's at the counter, a huge array of vegetables laid out in front of her. It's only five o'clock, so we won't eat for a while, but if she plans on chopping all these, we won't eat until midnight.

"Fine," Mom says, breaking apart a head of garlic with a loud crack. "Fine."

"You're a really bad liar," I say, setting my bag down.

"It's something at work." Mom shakes her head. "No big deal. It'll work itself out. A surgeon left a sponge in a patient. The patient is fine now, but that's a big mistake. We have to go through a whole review, and hopefully I won't have to fire him. But it's fine. It could be worse."

"Right," I say. I'm well aware where I get it from. "I'm going to do some homework."

"Sure, honey." I walk to my room. "Oh," Mom calls after me, "and I think your column is great. Just don't mention the school name, or your name, please. Principal Pattyn was very insistent on the first one, and I hear colleges Google potential students now, so the second is just in case."

I froze the moment she said "column," but now I turn around, slowly. She's moved on from separating the garlic to putting it in one of those rubber tubes and rolling it around, grinding it into the counter.

"You know about my column?" I ask. My voice comes out hoarse.

"Calm down," she says, looking up with a grin. "I just skimmed it. I don't want to know the details of your sex life any more than you want me to know them. I skip over those parts. But you give good advice."

I can feel my face is hot—it must be scarlet. "Mom," I say, and then stop. What else do I say? Can anxiety actually build up so much that it leaks out of you? How about embarrassment? I feel like I'm drooling, and wipe my mouth, but it's dry.

"Jack, relax. Safe sex is good, sex is good, telling people how to have fun sex is good. You think just because I had you via sperm donor that I'm a virgin? I've had plenty of sex, Jack. Plenty of men, and more than a few women. Once both at the same time."

"MOM!"

Mom starts laughing, like this is the funniest thing in the world. She stops rolling garlic and keeps laughing and laughing, until I feel my body relax a bit, and I laugh, too.

"That's for not telling me you were going to be writing that column," she says, wiping away tears.

"You're just messing with me?"

"I can be messing with you and telling the truth. But seriously, I'm proud of you. It's a good thing you're doing. I promise not to read them anymore if you don't want me to, though."

"If you do, just don't tell me."

"Deal." Mom snorts a little laugh, then goes back to rolling the garlic. "Now do your homework."

I pause in the doorway. I really am so lucky. So many things could be so much worse.

I think about telling her about Pinky, the notes, the email... but no. Ben and Jenna's plan will work fine tomorrow, and then it'll be over, and I won't need to say anything. Everything will be fine.

15

Dear Jack of Hearts,

*I think I'm finally ready to come out. I've known I'm
into guys for a while now, but I just haven't wanted
to deal with it. It seems like it has to be such an
event—an announcement on Instagram or Snapchat
that everyone likes and comments how proud of you
they are, or, like, a party where you tell everyone.
I don't want it to be a big deal. I don't want people
to think I'm different. I just want to start asking
boys out. And . . . I don't know how to do that, either.
Do I just go up to a guy and say, "Hey, want to
grab coffee?" What if he's straight? Will he get it?
What if I think we're dating and he thinks we're just*

*friends and then on date three I try to kiss him and
it all goes horribly wrong? And what if I don't want
to date? What if I just want to get laid? Do I ask
someone if they want to have sex? That seems ...
very forward. Are there signals I can give that I just
want to have casual, no-strings sex? Everything
seems so much more complicated when you're gay.
How do I do this?*

*—Almost Out but
Logistically Terrified*

Jenna's camera isn't that small. I can see why she didn't think she could hide it in the hallway. It's about the size of my closed fist. But backstage is crowded and lit only by one light bulb on a tall, shadeless lamp and our phones. We get there before school starts, and Ben lets us in. Sometimes he stays late to work on costume fittings and stuff like that, so he has a key. The problem is finding a spot to put the camera where it can see the stack of pink paper and where it won't get jostled.

"The thing is," Ben says, "it's, like, total chaos back here when we're all here. Costume changes, set changes ... eaves that go up and down." He's trying to sound worried, but there's also this tone under his voice, like he's talking about one of his favorite things but is embarrassed by it and trying to make it sound like he hates it.

Jenna walks over to the paper, which is in a stack against the wall, next to some folded canvas and a table covered in small props and outlines in masking tape where props should be.

"We don't do dress rehearsals too much, but the schedule is always changing, so we change the sets," Ben says.

Jenna surveys backstage from right in front of the paper stack. "What about there?" she asks, pointing straight up.

For some reason, my heart begins to pound. Like what we're doing—planting a camera, being backstage when we shouldn't, looking for a creeper sending me notes—suddenly all rushes into my chest at once.

"I don't go up on the catwalk," Ben says, shaking his head. "That thing is wobbly, and I don't have the slim girlish figure of my youth, y'know?"

"I'm sure it's fine," Jenna says.

"I heard a kid at Highbrook fell off one, broke his arm and his leg," Ben says. "I don't do heights."

"Fine," Jenna says. "Jack and I will do it. Stay by the paper."

"Good," Ben says, glancing at the door to the hallway and then at the curtain, which is down. "But be quick. I don't want to get in trouble."

Jenna rolls her eyes and waves me over to the ladder at the side of the stage. She shines the flashlight of her phone on the ladder and motions me to go up first. I take a deep breath. I climb up without saying anything, and Jenna climbs behind me, our hands making hollow ringing notes on the metal ladder. My hands feel shaky—or maybe it's the ladder, not totally attached right. I don't know why I'm so scared right now, but climbing a ladder to a catwalk in the dark isn't helping.

I reach the top of the ladder and step out onto the swaying catwalk. I can see why Ben didn't want to come up here. It's black metal but a grate, and I can see the stage below me—farther than I thought. I would not look good as a splatter on the floor. It's not my ideal body type.

I grab the handrails as the catwalk rocks slightly and stride over to where Ben is. Jenna is right behind me, walking with much more confidence—and in higher heels—and gets down on her knees to look at the paper stack.

"Do people come up here a lot?" Jenna calls down.

"Shhhh," Ben says, in a stage whisper. "And yes. They have to do lights and stuff."

"Fuck," Jenna says. She stands and looks around some more. "Think you can reach that?" She points at a wooden beam suspended from the ceiling, even higher than us. It's not part of the stage stuff—no lights are hanging from it or anything. It's a real support beam. And it's about three feet away, just out of reach.

"I mean..." I stare at her. "If I really stretch or something. And don't fall."

"You'll be fine," Jenna says.

"What are you guys doing?" Ben whisper-shouts from below.

"Planting the camera," Jenna whisper-shouts back, then turns to me, shaking her head. "What else would we be doing?"

"I don't know if I can put it up there," I say, looking at the rafter.

Jenna takes my hand and puts the camera in it. It's weirdly smooth, not just like plastic, but like old, worn-out plastic. I wonder how long her mom has had it for. I wonder what horrible things it's recorded.

"Just try," Jenna says.

"Okay, but hold my legs."

"What?"

"Hold my legs, so I don't tip over the edge."

Jenna rolls her eyes but kneels down and grabs my shins, placing her phone on the catwalk with its light shining up, creating dramatic, horror-movie shadows. I lean forward on the handrail, and the catwalk tilts, extending my reach. Jenna's hands go tighter on my shins. I stretch my arm out and place the camera.

"Don't forget to angle the lens," Jenna says.

"We couldn't do that before?" I ask, now trying to carefully adjust the lens of the camera so it points at the paper without knocking it off the rafter.

"We didn't know the angle."

To angle the lens exactly right, I have to look down. Not great. It's not that we're super high up, but it's high enough and I'm pretty much already falling, and I'm not sure what's keeping me from toppling off, aside from Jenna's hands, a flimsy guardrail, and force of will. I imagine myself splattering on the stage below, the pink construction paper flying out from the force of my fall and covering me. That would be appropriate.

I look back up. My hands are sweating now, but I manage to

nudge the lens in what I think is the right direction. But now I realize that the catwalk is almost horizontal.

"Pull me back, pull me back," I say.

Jenna tugs on my legs and then on my shirt until the catwalk and I curve back into place. I sit on the catwalk. It sways, but at least it's something between me and a fall.

"Is it in the right place?" Jenna asks.

I nod and point. I'm breathing too heavily to answer.

Jenna looks over. "Okay, yeah. That should be good."

"Good," I say. "Because I'm not doing that again."

"Well, we'll have to get it back," Jenna says, walking to the ladder. I crawl behind her. "But that should be easier. We can just knock it with a stick and Ben can catch it or something."

"You want me to catch something?" Ben says. We're climbing down the ladder now and he's looking up at us. "I have butterfingers. You know that."

"Okay, okay," Jenna says. "I'll catch it. Or Jack will. Whatever."

My feet touch the stage as I disembark the ladder. The floor is gloriously solid. No sway at all.

"I am so not a theater fag," I say, leaning against a wall.

"It wasn't that bad," Jenna says. "We got the camera in place."

"It looked pretty bad from beneath. I moved so Jack wouldn't fall on me."

"Thanks," I say.

"We need to get out of here before someone catches us, though," Ben says. He glances at the exit. I take one more breath and we head for the side door, but just as we're getting to it, it swings open, and in walks Holden Chaffe, star of the musical—and every musical for the past three years.

"Hey, guys," he says, narrowing his eyes and elongating the *s* in "guys" when he sees us. He's tall, fit, with pale skin and black hair, and as always, he is perfectly put together. Pink button-down, wavy hair that doesn't frizz, skintight black jeans, black vest, and a tie with a Mondrian-style pattern on it that shouldn't match the shirt but magically does. He runs his hand through his hair, which is the sort of move that would be sexy on other guys, but feels so practiced with him it turns me off. "What are you up to?"

"Hey, Holden," Ben says, the lightness in his voice a little forced. "What are you doing back here?"

"Mmm-mm," Holden says, waggling a finger. "I asked first."

"I was checking something for a story," Jenna says, stepping forward. "Ben let us in. Jack was taking some pictures for me. Please don't tell, though—I don't have all my facts verified yet, so it could just be a rumor."

"Hmmm…" Holden smirks. "What's the rumor? I love gossip."

"The school could be taking funds from the theater department for athletics," Jenna says. She's good at lying—she knows her audience.

"Oh my god, right? Of course they are," Holden says, shaking his head. "All right. Well, you keep up the good work."

"What are you doing here, though?" Jenna asks.

"Oh, I get here early to practice," Holden says with a shrug. He walks to the side of the stage and pulls a switch. The curtain begins to open, and he walks toward the front, staring out at the empty seats. "I know there's no audience, but something about singing in the theater just invigorates me. You can stay if you want. I'm just going to do some warm-ups first. Meee-meee-meee." He starts to sing.

"Oh, no," Jenna says.

"We have to get to class," I say.

"Sounds fun, though," Ben adds. "Maybe another time."

Holden stops singing and smiles at us. "Any time. And don't worry. I won't tell the teachers. Fight the power, right, sister?" He holds up a fist. Jenna nods and mirrors him.

"Later!" Ben says. Holden goes back to singing to the empty theater, and we exit, quietly.

Out in the hall, Ben lets out a long sigh.

"What are you sighing for?" Jenna asks. "You weren't on the catwalk."

"I let you in—it was my ass on the line, too. Good thing you had that story for Holden."

"Yeah," Jenna says as we walk. She goes silent for a moment, in the way that Ben and I know means she's thinking. Then she stops walking. "What if it's him?" she asks.

"What?" I say. "What's who?"

"What if Pinky is Holden?"

"Oooooh," Ben says, nodding. "Yeah, that makes some sense—access to the paper. Super gay closet case."

I shake my head. "Nah. I don't think he's a closet case."

"Girl," Ben says, "you saw that perfect outfit same as I did,

123

and you heard him singing, not to mention the way he walks, how his wrists move, and the swish in his step. He's as straight as I am."

Jenna nods. "He's, like, the biggest closet case in school. It would make sense if he had a crush on you but was, like, too nervous to come out so he wrote these notes—they're so dramatic, too, and the boy loves drama."

"He loves drama *class*," I say. "And I don't buy Holden as a closet case, sorry. Sure, he can put together a fierce look, and he's a theater nerd, but those are just stereotypes. He's had every opportunity to come out. Everyone thinks he's queer already. Maybe he just wants to do it in his own time, but he's said he's straight. Like, a lot. I have no reason to think he's lying aside from stupid ones planted in my head by society about how gay and straight people are supposed to act."

"You act that way," Jenna says. "I mean, not all of it, but people are going to assume just as much about you as they do about him, and they'd be right about you."

"So?" I shrug and start walking again. People are starting to show up and the halls are less empty. "So they'll be right about me. I live the stereotype. I don't mind. That's me. Doesn't mean it's everybody. Plenty of guys I've fucked pass for stereotypically straight, but no one goes around saying they're in the straight closet or whatever. And most of them suck cock just as good as the flaming faggots. Stereotypes exist because some people conform to them, but the moment you start assuming that everyone conforms to them, you're a homophobe, or racist, or whatever."

I take a breath, feeling a little empowered by my rant. "And I know you guys aren't that."

"Wow, you really sound like Jack of Hearts," Jenna says. We've reached my locker and I start opening it, but pause to look over at her, confused. Her eyes are wide, like she's a little surprised.

"I am Jack of Hearts. Did you have a stroke?"

"Yeah, I know, but I mean you sounded like him just then. Like . . . that was an impressive response."

"Yeah," Ben adds.

I shrug and turn back to my locker, but I can feel myself blushing. "Whatever."

"Still, we shouldn't eliminate him as a possibility. You could be wrong."

"Maybe you're just jealous he dresses better than you," Ben says.

"Bitch, you take that back." I mock-glare at Ben, who grins.

"It was a great outfit," Jenna says. "But stereotype or no, he has access to the theater. He's on the suspect list."

"I don't think it's him," I say. "But you're right, I can't prove it. Still, he shouldn't be more than a weak 'maybe.'"

"I'll keep my eye on him," Ben says. "Let you know if he does anything weird. Takes a lot of paper."

"Good," Jenna says. "I guess now you have to send Pinky an email back saying you want the paper notes again, then we wait until you get one, and then we check the camera."

"Ew," I say, the thought of it making me shiver. "Do I have to email him?"

125

"You want me to do it?" Jenna asks.

I take a textbook out of my locker and put it in my bag, then take out my phone. I load up the Jack of Hearts inbox and click on Pinky's email. The shade of pink of the text makes the letters seem to swim. Like the email is supposed to make me dizzy.

"What are you going to say?" Ben asks.

"Just say 'I liked it better when you sent me notes. I'll unblock my locker,'" Jenna says, hand out for the phone.

"No," I say. "That's not . . . I don't know what this guy wants, but that's not a good reason."

I catch my reflection in the screen for a moment, and I don't love it—bewildered, nervous. That's not who I want to be. I make myself glare at the screen. I lift my chin. I cock an eyebrow. So, some creeper wants to creep on me? Fine. It won't be the last time, most likely. But he's going to do it on my terms.

I don't know why you keep this up, I type. *But this is my place of work. I'll unblock my locker, but only if you never email me here again. I take this column seriously. If you really want to impress me, you'll do the same. Paper only from now on.*

"That's a bit confrontational," Ben says, looking over my shoulder.

"Yeah, wouldn't something flirtier work better?" Jenna asks.

I hit send. "I have to write it the way I would really write it, right? I mean, Pinky is into me for some reason. If I want him to do what I say, I have to tell him to do it as me."

"Well, it's done now," Jenna says. "I guess all we do is wait."

126

16

I SPEND THE REST OF THE DAY FEELING LIKE SOME REALLY amazing music is playing in my head. Like some serious dance mix. I'm electric. I'm waiting for the beat to drop—or, in this case, for an awful pink note to show up in my locker so we can check the video and figure out who's writing them. But nothing shows up that day. Or the next. Or the next.

"Maybe your email scared him off," Jenna says, pointing a carrot stick at me during lunch. "I told you to be flirtier."

"Hey, if he's done because I sent him a mean email, I'm fine with that." I take a long drink of my Coke. "More than fine. Thrilled. I stood up to him, and he backed down. That's the way it should be. I just... didn't have the nerve to stand up to him before."

"Awww," Ben says, nudging Jenna. "He means before we

started helping. We gave him the power to stand up to his stalker-bully."

"We're not My Little Ponies," Jenna says, biting her carrot stick with a loud snap. "And I don't like this silence. I don't think it would end that easily, and I don't know how long the video camera can record for before we have to take it and erase the footage to make more room."

"I really think it's over," I say. Which is more like when New Age people try to will things to be true by saying them over and over. But maybe it is? I'm sort of exhausted from waiting for a note for the past two days. It's like knowing someone is about to kick or slap you, and so you close your eyes and you wait, and wait, and nothing comes. But it would be awesome if the slap just isn't coming. Thing is, if you open your eyes, you know that's the exact moment it'll happen.

"Let's hope," Ben says, taking a bite of his sandwich.

"But we should still check the camera," Jenna says. "In case it isn't over." She sighs and spreads her hands out and lays her forehead in them. Her sunglasses slide slightly from her nose. "I should have checked how long the camera can film for before we hid it. I just thought it was such a good idea, and I could help. . . . I rushed into it. I'm sorry."

"We can probably just check online," I say with a shrug.

"Yeah," she says. "But I have to stop doing this. Rushing into ideas without thinking them through, without planning, without realizing there could be consequences." She pauses, but doesn't lift her head. "That's the whole reason you're in this mess."

Ben stops eating and raises an eyebrow at me. I shrug. I have no idea what she means, either.

"Sweetie," Ben says. "What do you mean?"

"The column," Jenna says. Her voice is softer now, weaker. "If I hadn't decided Jack was going to do the column before I even asked him, spread the rumor...then he wouldn't have a stalker. He would have just said no, and that would've been the end of it."

"Jenna..." I say. I wait for her to look up at me. She does, but she keeps her sunglasses on, and I stare at my reflection in them. "It's not your fault." And I mean it. Any anger I had the other day is gone. "It's his. It's whoever is writing these notes. We don't know the column made him do it. Maybe he's been crazy for a while. Maybe I slept with his ex without realizing it. I don't know. But you didn't make him do this. You asked me to do something, and I did it. And he responded like this. Like a fucking crazy person. That's not your fault."

Jenna takes a deep breath and reaches out and squeezes my hand. I squeeze back.

"Plus," I say, "I kind of like doing the column. I'm, like, expressing what I've always thought but never put words to before."

"You're confronting people," Jenna says. "Nonconfrontational, 'it could be worse' Jack is finally calling people out on their weird little lowercase *h* homophobic assumptions."

"I'm not calling people out," I say. "Except maybe that last one, but that's 'cause I know who wrote it."

"Who?" Jenna asks.

"Ava, Emily, and Kaitlyn."

"Of course."

"But even before that," Ben says, "with, like, the blowjob one—way helpful by the way, thanks—but, you were calling out people who don't talk about sex, you were calling out anyone who thinks there's a right way to have sex."

"Yeah," Jenna says, "you were calling out anyone who thinks sex is, like, bad."

"Okay, so like a general callout," I say. "But I'm not shaming people by name or anything."

"No." Jenna nods. "You're talking about stuff in general."

"Okay," I say. "I like that."

"Well, good. Because you need to keep them coming if we're going to get Pinky to send you another note so we can catch him."

"I picked out my next one," I say.

"Thanks," Jenna says, and squeezes my hand again. I know she doesn't mean for writing the column. Then she pulls her hand back and takes her phone out and types a few things into it. "Okay . . . so the camera can record for, like, four hours to three days depending on the memory card in it."

"What size card is in it?" Ben asks.

"I don't know," Jenna says. "Fuck. I should have bought a new one. One of the ones that's always streaming, and then we could have hooked it up to my computer and had it record forever."

"Wouldn't that take up a lot of space on your computer?" I say.

"Yeah," Jenna says. "But we wouldn't have had to go get the camera back to check it."

"And we have to do that now, I guess," Ben says. "We can't leave it up all weekend."

"After school?" I ask.

"Rehearsal," Ben says. "But...I have an idea for that. Just meet me in the hallway outside backstage."

I look at Jenna, who shrugs and then takes a sip of Diet Coke. "Works for me."

"Oh," Ben says, "I almost forgot." He takes out a tape measure and dangles it in front of Jenna. "Time to measure your head."

"For my hat?" Jenna asks, excited. "Awesome." She lowers her head, like Ben is about to knight her. He slips the tape around her head and pulls it snug, then takes out a pen and writes the number in a notebook.

"So am I large-headed?" Jenna asks, looking up. "Don't tell me I'm small-headed. I don't think I could handle that."

"Seven and a half," Ben says. "A little above average."

"Only a little?" Jenna frowns. "Boo."

"You're next," Ben says to me, holding out the tape measure.

"What?" I raise my eyebrows. "I don't want a hat. I don't look good in hats."

"Please." Ben rolls his eyes. "You're a skinny white boy. Everything is made with you in mind so of course you look good in everything. Now let me measure your head so I can make you a hat so I get better at making hats."

I roll my eyes. "Fine. But only to help you." I get up and kneel on the bench and lean over.

"Are we going to the party at Karen Cohen-Eng's this weekend?" Jenna asks. "It's kind of far uptown, but she always has good booze."

"I want to," Ben says. He's across from me so he stands and wraps the tape measure around my head. I feel it go tight as I'm forced to stare at the table, Ben's half-eaten sandwich, and the cafeteria floor to the right of me. There's a weird black splotch under the bench. I wonder if it's mold.

And then a familiar pair of black loafers stops right in front of us, and one foot starts tapping. I used to think that was cute.

"What the hell are you doing?"

I trace the loafers up the skinny-jeaned legs. Jeremy Diaz is there, arms crossed over his perfectly pressed white polo shirt.

"Hi, Jeremy," I say. "Ben is measuring my head."

"Not that, I don't care about that. I mean the column."

The arms-crossed thing is something he does when he wants to talk. Not talk with, talk at. Lecture. Jeremy is president of the Gay-Straight Alliance, vice president of the Multicultural Student Union, a shoo-in for Harvard or Yale, and sure to win first place in any competition for being condescending. He's also, if you want to use the term loosely, my ex.

"What do you mean?" I ask.

"I mean you're giving us a bad name. Playing into stereotypes. Furthering the idea that all gay men do is fuck and dance in glitter."

I roll my eyes. I'd be pissed if we hadn't had this argument a hundred times before.

"Well, I'm sorry, Jeremy, but I was all out of glitter."

"We need to combat stereotypes, Jack. And you—" He looks at Jenna, who puts her hand on her chin, bored behind her sunglasses. "También debes saberlo mejor, hermana. This is like if you wrote a weekly column on amazing bean recipes."

Jenna stares at him and takes a long drink of her Diet Coke. He taps his foot.

"I don't cook," she says finally.

"Seriously? Do you not see what this is going to do, Jack?"

"Oh, we're back on me," I say to Jenna.

"Stop that," Jeremy says. He lets his arms fall to his sides. The foot stops tapping. He's moving on from angry lecture to emotional appeal—almost done. "Stop acting like this is funny. We're minorities in a world that sees us as jokes and caricatures. And them seeing us like that—it's what lets them create laws to make it okay to fire us for being gay, or deport us for being brown. They don't see us as real people. And you're making it easier for them. Please, Jack."

I'm already kneeling on the bench, so I stand up, close to him. I'm a little taller and he has to look up. "How about you be the kind of faggot you want to be, and I'll be the kind of faggot I want to be, and we let all the straight people just figure it out? How about that, Jeremy?"

He hates the word "faggot." He starts turning pink the moment I say it.

"Go to hell, Jack," he says, and turns, marching away. I watch him go. He has a nice ass. Then I sit back down. Ben stares at me silently, while Jenna drinks more soda.

"Why did you ever go out with him?" Jenna asks.

"Things happen," I say.

"He's the worst," Jenna says.

"Does he think I shouldn't be sewing?" Ben asks. "Designing, or working in theater? Because that makes me a stereotype?"

"Don't take it personally," I tell Ben. "He just really wants to be president one day, and lives in perpetual fear that the voters will look at him and see someone like me, because they think all gay people are the same. And maybe he's right. But even if I stopped talking about cock forever and started wearing white polos, that's not going to change. Straight people are the worst. He just hasn't figured that out yet."

"I…" Ben looks at me, confused. "Do you really believe that about straight people?"

I shrug. "Kinda."

"Then how did you two end up dating in the first place?"

"Oy," I say. "That's…"

"I think we deserve a smoke break," Jenna says, standing suddenly. "You can give him the long version outside."

17

THE LONG VERSION ISN'T REALLY THAT LONG. IT WAS freshman year. I was freshly out, and virginal, if you can imagine it. I can't, thank god. I decided I wanted to get laid, or at least make out with tongue. We were in a new building, new students had come in, and we could finally join clubs. I, of course, wanted to join the Gay-Straight Alliance—I figured it would be a good place to meet the boys to make out with. That's how I met Jeremy. I got the room number the GSA was meeting in wrong, so I was running and I reached out to grab the door handle not even seeing him, and my hand and his hand landed on the doorknob at the same time. Total meet-cute, right? So I said sorry, and he said it was okay, and I asked if this was the GSA, and he nodded and said he was a new student, named Jeremy. And I said my name was Jack and we shook hands for maybe longer than we needed to, staring at each other—and he was cute. Still is. Black hair, great jawline, eyes like dark leather. And then, after we looked each other over, and smiled, we walked into the GSA meeting, practically already a couple.

For two weeks, we were pretty much inseparable. Even Jenna got annoyed with me. And Ben, who was also a new student and also in that GSA meeting—I didn't even realize he existed. Jeremy and I went everywhere we could together, held hands, heads in each other's laps, all that. He told me about his huge Cuban family and how he wanted to go into politics, and I told him about my mom and unknown donor-dad and how I had no clue what I wanted to do. By the end of the first week, we were making out. By the end of the second week, I felt ready to unzip his pants. So I did. He . . . wasn't so into that. Said he wasn't ready. I said that was fine, cool, kept on making out. But things changed after that. He started talking about how we needed to combat the stereotypes of gay men in the media. We needed to be an "ideal couple"—the only other queer couple in the school was a pair of lesbian seniors, and he said different stereotypes applied to them. We had a duty, he said, to be respectable—not slutty, all over each other, or overly . . . whatever. He frowned the first time he saw me in eyeliner. It didn't take too long for the whole thing to fall apart. And I never even got to fuck him.

I fix my makeup in my compact as we smoke in the park, telling all this to Ben (which, I know, I'm breaking my one cigarette rule, but I'm reliving something emotional, so I deserve it), who only knows the part where we cuddled in the halls all the time.

Ben and I didn't get close until we had history class together second semester of freshman year and I brought up Germany's pre–World War II queer scene in class and we started talking. Mr. Harris assigned us a project together and even an awful hag like me couldn't help but like Ben. He's the definition of likeable.

"You must have been really thirsty," Ben said.

"Parched," I say, redoing my cat eye. "Always."

Ben laughs and Jenna blows rose-scented steam through the chain of the swing she's sitting on.

"I should ask him to write his complaints in to the column," Jenna says. "Let you guys hash it out for hits."

"Good luck," I say. "He's not going to be talking to me for a month, at least." I snap my compact closed and move from a park bench to the swings where Ben and Jenna are. I kick myself off and fly forward, legs out.

"Do you think it could be him?" Jenna asks. She puts her e-cig away in her purse.

"Who?" I ask. "Pinky? You think Jeremy is Pinky?"

"I mean, if he still has feelings for you, is obsessing over you, super jealous that you're fucking all these guys who aren't him…"

"No," I say, "Pink paper? That's playing into stereotypes way too much for Jeremy. He'd rather claw his own eyes out than even wear pink."

"But that could be what he wants you to think," Ben says, pushing himself forward and swinging much farther out than me.

"I just don't think it's him," I say.

"It fits, though," Jenna says, giving in and pushing her swing as well. "He hears you're writing a sex column. He thinks that's bad for, like, queer representation or whatever, and he has these weird love-hate feelings for you, so he tells himself he's going to send you these notes to scare you out of writing the column, but he gets wrapped up in it, takes it too far. Now he has to just keep going. Plus, you haven't stopped writing them."

"You sound like the narrator on some late-night true-crime show," I say.

"Ooooh, think they'll make one of those for you?" Ben asks. "Who should play me?"

"Pink Notes and Pink Holes," Jenna says. "The Jack Rothman Story."

"No," I say, leaping off my swing. "That would absolutely not be the title, that sounds like a porno, and not even a high-quality one. And there's not going to be a movie because no one is going to find out about this because then my mom would know and she'd freak out. Okay?"

I've turned on them and they've stopped swinging and are looking at me silently, maybe because my voice has gotten a little high and loud. But Mom does not need to know. Especially not when she's starting to really treat me like an adult.

"Just kidding around," Jenna says.

"I'm just waiting for an opportunity to say, 'You in danger, girl,'" Ben says. "Don't need a movie if I get to do that."

I laugh at that one. "In a wig, and the earrings Whoopi wears in that meme?" I ask.

"Totally," Ben says.

I sigh and sit down on the seesaw. The other end of it goes up. "I just hope it's done. I hope I don't get any more notes. I just want this to be over."

Jenna gets off her swing and takes the other side of the seesaw, pushing me up into the air.

"It will be soon," she says. "One way or another—Jeremy is going down."

"It's not Jeremy," I say. "Besides, I don't think he even knows origami."

Jenna's legs go limp and I fall slowly back to the ground. Ben stops swinging.

"Origami?" Jenna asks.

"Yeah," I said. "The notes are folded into little shapes—a crane, a shark."

"You never told us that," Jenna says.

"I showed you the first note."

"That was all crushed up," Ben says.

"What does it matter?" I ask, pushing myself off the ground so Jenna is down again. "So they're origami. Does that really make a difference?"

"I guess not," Jenna says with a shrug. She pushes off and now we're actually seesawing, like children. "But it's a clue."

"We'll know more when we get the camera," Ben says. "But for now, I don't know about you, but I have class."

"Ugh, right," Jenna says. She dismounts the seesaw and I follow them back to school.

The rest of the day goes by slowly. The music in my blood goes from dance to techno, and every sound is louder than it should be. Is this over? Are we going to see anything on the video? I don't even notice Ms. Costas's neon green shoes until the end of class. I just want it to be over, but I can't stop thinking about it. It's like that feeling of a zit forming on your face—where the skin starts getting tighter, and you know you shouldn't touch it, but you keep rubbing at it, wondering if the zit is there yet and you need concealer.

When I get to the hallway outside backstage, Ben is already waiting, camera in hand.

"How did you get it?" I ask. "Getting it up there was like a circus act."

"I piled up a lot of fabric underneath it, and then I pointed it out to Greta, who was up there already. She pushed it off with a broom, and I caught it in the mountain of fabric. She owes me for altering a dress for her, so she didn't ask any questions."

"Smart," I say.

"What's smart?" Jenna asks, coming around the corner.

"How Ben got the camera down," I say.

"That's 'cause he's a smart guy," Jenna says, holding out her hand for the camera. "Did you look at the footage yet?"

"No," Ben says, handing it to her.

Jenna presses a few buttons and looks at the screen on the back. I step behind her to watch, and I realize I'm breathing heavier than I need to be. I shake my shoulders out. This isn't something to worry about. I haven't gotten a note in days. It's over. I think. I hope. I guess I still want to know who it was, though. But all the screen shows is black.

"Let's take it back to my place," Jenna says. "I can plug it into my mom's computer."

"What's wrong with it?" I ask. My confidence of a few seconds is gone. Suddenly I know it isn't over.

"I don't know," she says, tapping a few buttons. "It's like it's not getting any light. . . ." She hits rewind and it starts running backward, showing black for hours and hours.

"Maybe it's a small memory card," Ben says.

Jenna doesn't say anything. She knows that's not it. So do I.

"Let's just go back to my place," Jenna says, turning the camera off.

We take the train downtown in mostly silence. Jenna keeps rotating the camera in her hands, turning it over and over as though that's going to fix it. But we all know the camera is working fine. It wouldn't have hours of footage, otherwise. Ben tries to make conversation by talking about Karen Cohen-Eng's party—he's excited for the "yacht party" theme, even though it won't be on a yacht, or even near the water, since Karen lives off Central Park. But he has a seersucker suit he says he never gets to wear. Jenna and I smile and nod, and appreciate what he's doing, but can't bring ourselves to participate.

At Jenna's place, we go right to her mom's office and Jenna plugs the camera in. A program comes up and she clicks a button and the entire recording—three days' worth—appears on-screen in the form of thousands of still images. All of them are black.

"Fuck," she says. She scrolls through them, going back to the opening hours of the video. The blackness vanishes. "Okay, good."

There are shots of backstage, of the pile of pink paper, of us walking to the door, of Holden coming in, and of students pouring in and working after we were gone. It records for several hours before turning black. Nothing unusual in the video as Jenna skims through it—but no one going after the paper, either. Jenna focuses in on the moments before the camera goes black. The lights seem to be out.

"After school," Ben says. "Late, if no one is there."

"But it's not totally black," Jenna says.

"Well, yeah, there's light from the stage light—the light bulb you leave on all the time."

"But there isn't later," Jenna says.

"Just watch," I say, leaning in. The faint bluish lines and shadows ripple as the side door opens, and a figure walks in. It's impossible to see much of them besides a shadow. Bulky. Wearing a baseball cap. Maybe a sweatshirt? I can't tell. He keeps his head down and walks under the camera. Nothing happens for a moment. Then, suddenly, the camera jerks, and turns.

"Someone is making it face the ceiling," Jenna says.

It's mostly black now, just a faint light. But then something dark flutters and lands over the lens.

"It...there was some black fabric under it when Greta knocked it into my pile of fabric," Ben says. "But I thought I was imagining it—it was just in the pile before. Sorry."

"It's not your fault," I say, backing away from the screen. "Someone saw it and covered it. Someone didn't want to be filmed."

"Yeah," Jenna says, now scrolling through the black fabric. "Pinky."

"Maybe," I say. "A lot of people don't like being filmed without their consent, though."

"How would Pinky even know?" Ben asks.

"If it's Holden, he could have been suspicious when he found us in there," Jenna says. "He could have searched."

"Or someone could have seen you and me coming out from backstage and thought it was weird."

"It could have been someone working on the lights, too," Ben says. "The camera could be seen up there."

"So . . . we got nothing," Jenna says.

"I don't think so," I say. "It might have been Pinky, yeah, and he might have hidden himself—but he also hasn't sent me any more notes or emails. Maybe he saw the camera and moved it as, like, a sign of a truce. He didn't smash it, right?"

"Maybe," Jenna says. She loads the video from before the camera is rotated onto a flash drive, then deletes everything from the computer. "We need to start keeping track of this, though. So we have something to give to the police—in case it's not over."

"I don't want to involve the police," I say.

Jenna stands and walks out of the office. I look at Ben, who

143

shrugs, and we follow her to her room. She's done the place in monochrome—gray walls, silver furniture, black sheets. She sits at the silver desk, and Ben and I plop down behind her on the bed. She opens a drawer and takes out a pink notebook and shows me the first page. It's a list. Holden is on it. She writes Jeremy's name at the bottom of it. I start to feel my pulse speed up. She has that face she has when she's figuring out a big story.

"Suspects," she says.

I take the notebook from her and look over the list. Each name has a bunch of notes written around it in her shorthand, which I can only half read. In addition to Holden and Jeremy, she has Brian Kennedy written down . . . and Principal Pattyn.

"Pattyn?" I say. "Ew."

"Not, like, 'cause he wants you—but to shut you up. To scare you into stopping the column."

I shake my head. "That's ridiculous. And how would Brian Kennedy get on campus? He goes to Melton."

"He's got friends," Jenna says. "Maybe they just think they're delivering cute love notes."

"He is pretty obsessed with you," Ben says. "He was all over you at the last party."

"He was such a bad lay," I say, leaning back. "Wasn't that punishment enough?"

Jenna takes the notebook and writes something next to Brian's name.

"Why are you taking all these notes anyway?" I ask Jenna.

"You're not going to write about this, right? 'Parkhurst Won't Protect Its Gay Students'—nothing like that?"

"No," Jenna says. "I promise. I just... yeah, I'm approaching it like a story, because it's how I think. I want to figure this out. And we have some good suspects. Now we have to add origami to the list, and access to the backstage."

I take the notebook and slap it closed. "No," I say. "No more. Because it's done. So the camera was turned around—so what? Why turn it if they weren't going to take more pink paper? And they didn't take more pink paper, because there have been no notes in my locker."

I realize my voice is a little louder than I want it to be. I've been doing that a lot today. Typical hysterical queen.

"Jack," Jenna says. "You can't just wish this away."

"I can if it's over," I say. "These notes, these theories. You're the one wishing it wouldn't go away. It's like you like me being stalked."

Jenna's face closes up and I feel a stab of regret, but then a flash of anger to go with it. I know I hurt her, but I'm not wrong, either.

"I'm just trying to protect you," Jenna says. Her chin is up, her voice is cold. "So fuck you."

"I think," Ben says quickly, "that Jack is just saying that he feels like it's over, and doesn't want to move forward without more evidence because it's upsetting for him. And Jack, Jenna is just saying she wants to get to the bottom of this because she's worried if we don't—and soon—it'll get worse for you. And she loves you."

He stands up, casting a shadow on us and the bed. But Jenna and I aren't looking. We're just staring each other down. We don't fight much. Sophomore year she accused me of stealing her lipstick (I didn't, turned out it was her mom—I had just bought the same color on my own). We didn't talk for a week, but we did stare at each other in the hall. We're both excellent starers. I like to think I can really convey how little I think of a person, but Jenna has this thing where you can feel yourself diminishing in her eyes. Like you're actually growing smaller and smaller until you're just a speck and she can step over you.

Ben sits down between us, breaking the stare. "Stop it," he says. "Seriously. What the fuck? This is the dumbest thing you could fight over." I glance up at Ben, who is alternating looking at both of us, rolling his eyes.

"I'm going home," I say, standing. "I'll see you at the party tomorrow."

"Okay," Ben says, "maybe we just need some cool-down time. We can pregame at my place tomorrow. My parents are in Atlanta this weekend."

I walk toward the door and turn back. Jenna is still staring me down. "I think I'll just meet you at the party," I say. And I leave.

18

Dear Almost Out,

First, congrats! Seriously. It's great that you feel comfortable with your sexuality. That can be a hard thing to get to. And maybe you're not totally comfortable with it—few are—but you're comfortable enough to make that next step and act on it. I personally have mixed feelings about the whole "coming out" concept. On the one hand, coming out is important to show solidarity, encourage folks to come out, and so forth. On the other hand, the entire concept is essentially playing into straight society's game that anything but strict heterosexuality is something that needs to be *announced, warned about. The closet exists because straight people shoved us in it, and because if we try to leave it, they're often angry and/or violent.*

But that being said, it's a big step, a brave step, and you should feel good. I started coming out in eighth grade (it never really ends) but I knew two years before that, and those two years were the worst: always wondering if people knew, wondering if it was something I could change, thinking every little thing I did somehow gave me away—did I not agree strongly enough that Becky is pretty, or not laugh hard enough when they called Billy a fag? It's the worst. That's too light a term. It's like being in a horror movie—the part where you know the killer is around and could jump out and kill you at any moment. It's like that, but all the time. For years. And you are leaving that. That is worthy of celebration.

But you don't have to make it a big event. Just start telling people. Hell, you can just start by telling your friend you think Bobby has a hot ass or something. That's pretty much what I did. Eighth grade, my best friend asked me who I thought got hot over the summer, and I told her . . . well, I won't name names (spoiler: I fucked him last year). She just squeezed my arm—which was weird, she's not big on physical affection. And later, she texted me, "I'm so happy for you." That was it. It was perfect. Not a big deal, but she acknowledged how big it was for me. That's the ideal. But you get to decide how to come out, and how big a deal it should be. If Instagram confession is your brand, go for it. If just not hiding your lust for guys is your style, then that's all you need to do.

But also, be prepared: Not everyone is going to be thrilled. Because straight people assume other people's sexualities based on stereotypes and bullshit like that, people might be shocked—"But you like sports" (or whatever). They might not believe you. They might think you're confused. Or, on the flip side, they might laugh and tell you they already knew that, and not be as excited for you as you want them to be.

So the first thing you have to do is prepare yourself for the sad truth that not everyone is going to react how you want them to. If they're homophobic or act like you having the bravery to be who you are in a world that tells you you shouldn't be isn't a Big Deal, then call them out. A "That's not cool" or "I'm glad you thought you knew, but this is a big deal for

me, so maybe treat it like that." Nothing friendship
ending. Just be honest. Even real friends might
take a little while to adjust, but will be supportive
the whole time. Straight guys may think you're
into them when you SO aren't. People might start
thinking of you as deceptive, or a liar, because they'll
think you've been lying to them this whole time,
pretending to be straight. It can be pretty bad. But
it can be pretty good, too. Because even if no one
responds how you want them to (and that's really
a worst-case scenario), at least you get to respond
how you want to from now on. No more worrying if
people know, if you're not acting straight enough, if
everyone suspects and is testing you and if you fail
they'll beat you.

That's how I always felt. Like everyone was
watching me, waiting for that one slip, so they could
attack me, call me names I had to deny, tell me
my rights were going away, that my opinions now
counted for less. That's what being in the closet is.
Perpetual paranoia. And you're shrugging that off.

I should also mention—and I know I come from a
place of privilege being some rich kid in liberal New
York City—but make sure you have a safe place to go
before coming out to your parents. If there's even a

*chance they'll kick you out, or get violent, you want
to make sure you have a space you can retreat to.*

*Now, as for the rest of it—asking people out, wanting
to fuck, all the fun parts—just be clear about what
you want: "Hey, I'm into you, want to go out for
coffee?" or "Hey, I'm into you, want to come back
to my place and gag me with your cock?" (That one
is only appropriate if you really know the person
would like it or you're at a leather bar, though.) Yeah,
if you try it on a straight guy, and he's the wrong
kind of straight guy, he might throw a punch. But
I'm assuming you're in NYC, where it's not too bad.
It did happen to me once at a party. A guy swung at
me. It was around a lot of people, and I just vanished
into the crowd and iced the bruise. And that's just
once. I've propositioned a lot of men. And usually it
works out well for me. So the odds are in your favor.
In NYC anyway. In the right group. If you're not
somewhere like that—if you're somewhere where
there is no crowd to protect you, try to find queer-
only spaces. Clubs or online. Places where violent
straight people can't get to you. And I'm sorry you're
there. I hope you get somewhere better.*

*If you are somewhere better, just ask when there
are a lot of people around—your friends, if you can*

handle them possibly witnessing your rejection.
And yeah, telling a guy you want to fuck is forward.
Just inviting them back to your place to "hang out"
is pretty good code, though. And some might say
they'd prefer to get to know you first—which is
sweet, and not a rejection, but if it's not what you
want, then move on. Know what you want. Ask for
it. Be prepared for people to say no. That's the best
any of us can do. Oh, and I hope this goes without
saying, but use condoms, get tested regularly, and
ask your doctor about PrEP. Welcome to the club.
It's going to be super fun.

—Jack of Hearts

I'm trying not to be mad at Jenna. Ben had a point. Maybe she was just trying to help me. But the notebook, the shorthand, the way she was SO into figuring it out, even when I wasn't . . . I mean, it's my drama, right? She shouldn't make it hers. And when I say it's over—which hopefully it is—then she should respect that, and drop it. Not start putting together an article about it—even if she wasn't going to publish it.

I'll be nice to her at the party. Like, not super nice, and I'm for sure not apologizing, but, like, I'll say hey, and she'll say hey, and then it'll be over. Neither of us likes fighting with the other.

I make dinner and watch TV, and Mom comes home and reheats dinner and watches TV.

"Can I say I liked your column today?" she asks.

"Yeah. Today wasn't too intimate."

"Who punched you?"

"Some guy from St. Jude's. He was drunk. It wasn't a hard punch."

She frowns. "Maybe you shouldn't go to so many of these parties. Drinking, punching."

"One punch, once," I tell her. "Don't go crazy-mom on me, or you're not allowed to read the column."

"I don't mind you having sex," Mom says. "Safely, of course. But drinking, drugs, fighting...I'm allowed to worry about that, Jack."

"I promise, you have nothing to worry about. You didn't even notice the bruise, that's how light the punch was."

Mom turns back to the TV. It's a period drama. Women are riding horses. "Mmm," she says after a moment. "What was his name?"

"Not telling," I said. "He's at college now, anyway. Doesn't matter." I don't like the idea of Mom worrying about me. Not because of all the typical teen I'm-my-own-person stuff, though that's part of it, but because it sometimes feels like Mom and I are yelling at each other across a football field, like we have to strain to get each other, and when she worries, we get further apart. And lately, we've been getting closer, I think.

"Fine...just, next time you get punched, tell me. It could seem like it's minor, but be a broken rib or something."

"I promise," I say, rolling my eyes. "But I don't plan on getting hit again."

"I just don't know what I'd do if something happened to you," Mom says, putting her arm around my shoulders. I lay my head on her and she squeezes. "I know, it's a stupid, cliché mom thing to say. Just be careful, okay?"

"Okay," I say. "You're not going to lecture me on drinking?"

Mom smirks. "I was sneaking into Studio 54 when I was your age. Drinking is going to happen. Just don't overdo it, or I'll bring home photos of diseased livers."

"Right. I'm going to go to bed now."

"Anything fun this weekend?"

"Party. Yacht themed, but not on a yacht."

"For the best. You don't want to party on a boat, trust me—rocking, salt water, diseases . . . it's gross."

"Good night, Mom."

"Good night."

I get into bed and close my eyes. I didn't lie to my mom because there's nothing to lie about anymore. That's what Jenna needs to see, too. It's over: We scared Pinky away with a video camera, or by telling Pattyn about it, and now he's gone. Keeping it alive—stressing about it, trying to figure it out—is just going to make me crazy. So Jenna can't do it anymore. None of us can. We're all just going to go to this party and have fun and everything will be like it used to be.

19

I KNOW MY NEW JACKET ISN'T EXACTLY YACHT THEMED, BUT I wear it anyway. I put on some ocean-blue eye shadow and wear a navy polo with white booty shorts and a white scarf like a cravat, which I think is pretty yacht-y. If I had a sailor hat, I would totally wear that, too, but since I don't, and there's no time to get one, I think I'm just going to go up to random hot guys and say, "Hey there, sailor," to make up for it.

When I go outside I immediately realize the shorts weren't the best idea—it's cold. But I tell myself that I look hot, and so I should be hot, and that kind of thinking takes me far enough I stop shivering. I do sort of regret telling Ben we wouldn't pregame, though. That was stupid. Now I'm hungry and not as relaxed as I usually am when I get to the party.

It's not super crowded yet. I can still see the walls. I don't know if the apartment—a duplex in pale blues with tan leather furniture—is normally decorated like this or if Karen Cohen-Eng just really got into the yacht party idea, but there are nautical pieces everywhere. An old-looking ship's steering wheel on one wall, paintings of boats everywhere. If she didn't decorate this way, one of her parents is really into boats.

I find Ben in the kitchen, talking to a big white guy with five-o'clock shadow and an open flannel shirt showing off some chest hair, but a baby face that tells me he's probably still in high school. His one concession to the theme is boat shoes. Ben, on the other hand, has on his seersucker over a neon blue button-down dotted with a pattern of white sailboats. Ben waves when he sees me mixing myself a rum and Coke and walks over after a minute.

"Hey," he says.

"Hi," I say, looking over at the burly guy, who's staring at us. "Having fun?"

"I don't know," Ben says, his eyes all worry. "Do you think he's gay?" Ben glances over at his conversation partner, as though I couldn't guess who he meant.

The burly man waves awkwardly at Ben.

"Oh yeah," I say. "And he's totally into you."

"What?" Ben asks, and slaps my wrist. "No."

"Go get it. He's your type, right? And he's...I mean, he's a high schooler, right? He's not, like, Karen's dad."

"Don't be a bitch," Ben says. "He goes to Sadler, the small school downtown."

156

"Then go get it," I repeat, sipping my drink. I glance over at the man in question—he's staring sadly at his own drink, which I think could be seltzer. Like, plain seltzer.

"Are you sure?" Ben asks. "I don't want you to be alone, especially with you and Jenna—"

"I'm not going to be alone for long," I promise him. "I got plans. Go talk to the boy who thinks you're cute."

"Okay." Ben smiles and turns to go, then turns back. "Wait," he says in a whisper. "What do I say?"

"What?"

"I mean...to let him know I think he's cute. That I'm interested."

"Ask him if you can give him a blowjob in the laundry room."

"Shut up!" Ben says. "No, I mean...like, to date."

"Ask for his phone number. He'll figure it out."

Ben's eyes go wide. "Right, should have figured that one out by myself. This is why you have the column."

"It really isn't."

Ben laughs and walks back to his new crush, and I take my rum and Coke and explore the house some more. There's a pile of coats in one of the bedrooms, and I sadly add mine to the pile, because as fabulous as the jacket is, it's not on theme and why wear booty shorts and cover them up, right? As I'm leaving the bedroom, though, I'm blocked by Ava, Emily, and Kaitlyn, who have all come in giggling but stop short when they see me. Their faces go hard as they try to put on haughty looks. It's funny, I've never really looked that closely at them before. Ava, the alpha, is blond but strawberry tinted, with long hair parted on one side. She's wearing a little white dress with a blue handkerchief at her neck to try to make it look like a sailor's costume. Emily, her chief yes-woman, has dark skin, and hair that falls in perfect, super-high-maintenance-looking ringlets. She's wearing a blue button-down open low enough to show a white bra, and a tan pencil skirt. Her earrings are large anchors, which is a cute touch. And then Kaitlyn, the quiet one. Her hair is bleached white and pulled up in a bun tonight, and she's wearing a double-breasted navy jacket with gold buttons, and nothing underneath, like a dress.

"Hi, Jack," Ava says, but it sounds like she's telling me to do something.

"Ava, Emily, Kaitlyn—love the outfits."

"Thanks," Kaitlyn says softly. Ava glares at her and she immediately looks down at her feet.

I make as if I want to go past them, but they don't move.

"What's up with your column?" Ava asks.

"What do you mean?" I ask. I think I'm doing a good job of keeping my expression neutral—I don't want a big confrontation about this. I said everything I needed to say in my column. I don't need this drama.

"Do you have a problem with straight girls?" Ava asks.

"What?" I ask.

"It's a problem in the gay community," Emily says. "Misogyny. Touching girls' bodies without their consent. Saying vaginas are gross."

"Well, I haven't said anything like that, or touched a woman without her consent." If I did, I could push past them right now. "I just don't want to have sex with them."

"I just thought your column was kind of mean," Ava says. "Telling someone you thought was a straight girl she couldn't have questions about what it's like to be gay."

"I don't ask what you like to do in bed," I say, feeling a little annoyed at this point.

"I don't write a sex column," Ava says. Which is fair.

"I just think that when straight people ask about gay sex, it's to laugh at it, or fetishize it. Straight girls can be just as bad about gay men as straight men are about lesbians. And that's fine, get off on whatever—but only as long as everyone is consenting. Gay people aren't there to turn you on or entertain you with their sex lives." Ava folds her arms across her chest. "No matter how much you like to gossip about them," I add.

Ava opens her mouth and leans slightly so her weight is on one hip, but before she can say anything, a voice comes from behind her.

"You're blocking the door."

The girls turn and frown, making room for Jenna, who walks in looking like a mermaid—hair down, dress with flowing layers of ombré blues and greens, and matching glittery makeup. She even has some small fake gems glued to her face.

She sees me and raises a single blue-painted eyebrow. "Making friends?" she asks, before throwing her coat on the bed and turning to go. I quickly follow her.

"They cornered me. They were asking about the column," I

say in the hall, walking next to her. She looks at me from the side of her eye and then grins a little.

"Price of your sexlebrity status," she says, and I know we're cool.

"I love your outfit," I tell her. "I did not think outside the box at all for this one."

"You just wanted to wear short shorts."

"Can you blame me? My ass looks amazing. I am so getting laid tonight."

"Did you see Ben?" she asks, stopping and giving me a grin. "He has a boy."

"I know!" I grab her hand in excitement. "I hope this goes well. Not many guys his type in high school, much less gay ones. If they don't end up married, I'm going to die. I'm so invested in this relationship and I don't even know his name."

Jenna frowns. "It's Ben."

"The guy Ben likes is Ben?"

"Yeah."

"Oh," I say, dropping her hand. "Less invested now." I shake my head, rallying my enthusiasm. "But no. I will remain excited. We just have to come up with a cute nickname for one of them and use it until they don't go by anything else."

"Should we go interrogate him to figure out what his nickname should be?" Jenna asks as we move to the living room, where people are starting to dance.

"Nah, let's let them actually, like...what's that thing?"

"Get to know each other?"

"Yeah," I say. "That."

We take a corner and watch as people file into the party. It's nice knowing things are normal now. At least, I think they are. I know she's not going to write a story on my stalker, but I also know she may not think it's over. But at least she won't talk about it around me now. And then, when nothing else happens, she'll stop worrying about it and the whole thing will become a distant memory.

I sip my drink, which is hitting me a little hard without the cucumber sandwiches to absorb the booze, and watch the dancing. It's the usual people, the usual scene. Ava, Emily, and Kaitlyn file in at one point, but purposefully ignore me, for which I'm grateful. Holden shows up, too, wearing a white captain's hat, white suit, and a blue-and-white striped tank top underneath. He grins at us as he walks by and looks Jenna up and down.

"Love," he says, framing her with one hand and drinking from a red plastic cup with the other. "The glitter, the siren thing. Totally hot. You're going to win tonight."

"Thanks, Holden," Jenna says, giving me a look that conveys she thinks this proves he's gay. "I like your outfit, too."

"Do you want to dance?" he asks.

Jenna looks at me and I shrug.

"Sure. Come on, Jack, we can all dance together."

"I'm not drunk enough yet," I say, eyeing the still half-empty dance floor. "I'm going to refill. You get the party warmed up."

Jenna smiles and goes out on the dance floor with Holden, who I have to admit is wearing a better outfit and might be a better dancer than me. Clearly I need more liquor. I go back to the kitchen, which is now pretty full. Ben is still in the corner talking to Other Ben, but when he sees me he waves me over.

"This is Jack," Ben says to Other Ben.

"Hi," I say. "You're Ben, too, right?"

"Yeah," he says in a surprisingly high voice. "Ben Hazan."

"Hazan is a good name. You ever think about going by just Hazan?"

"What?"

"Ben goes to Sadler," Ben says quickly, shooting me a glare.

I grin back and then turn to Other Ben. "Oh yeah. Is it as wacky there as I hear? Poetry slams in the middle of lunch period?"

"Just once," Other Ben says. I wish I could call him Hazan in my head, at least, but it's not sticking.

"He's going to Sarah Lawrence next year, though," Ben says.

"So you'll be close," I say. "Good." I take a step back, trying to still engage them while mixing myself a new drink, but the moment I'm out of direct view they swivel back to each other. They're smiling as they talk. It's painfully cute. I wonder if Jeremy and I were like that. I finish making my drink and tell them I'm going to hit the dance floor, but they barely hear me, just nod and wave.

I get back to the living room and almost bump into Brian Kennedy. He's wearing a white button-down shirt—totally open—and a blue speedo. Maybe he's at a yacht party off the coast of Fire Island.

"Hey, Jack," he says, grinning widely. "I was hoping you'd be here."

In fairness, Brian is cute. Tall, thin, a little muscle, blond hair, high cheekbones, and a great smirk—cocky, but, like, the kind of cocky that makes you hate him and get hard at the same time. It's why I fucked him the first time. But he was really into being slapped—not my thing, no judgments—and does this thing when he's getting fucked where he's more into giving you a lap dance than actually taking it up the ass, and it ends up being like trying to fuck a trampoline. And he won't top. So, as nicely as he fills out the speedo, I'm not really looking for a repeat performance.

"Hi, Brian," I say, trying to scoot past him. "Good seeing you."

But he blocks me. Does the thing where he puts his hand up against the doorframe like a bully in a teen movie, then looks me up and down and licks his lips, giving me that damn smirk.

"Maybe you want to just get out of here now?"

I'm not good at telling guys I'm not interested. I don't think I'd be good at it in any case, but with my reputation, it makes it seem like they're the one guy I won't fuck, and Brian, like most Melton kids, is pretty sensitive under all the ego, so I just smile in a way I hope is coy and hold my drink up to hide the lower half of my face.

"I just got here," I say. "And besides, I'm not that kind of boy."

"No?" He reaches around and grabs my ass. I should tell him no right there, but...

"Don't do that." Sometimes I surprise myself. I can feel my eyes go wide and I hold my breath, waiting for him to be offended, make a scene.

"I thought you liked that," Brian says. He's still smiling, but he pulls his hand away.

"I'm not big on PDA," I say.

"As long as there's some D in my A," Brian says, moving closer and rubbing his crotch against mine, "I don't mind a lack of P."

"That's . . . quite a line," I say.

"Thanks. I use it whenever anyone says PDA."

Of course he does. "Well, I promised Jenna I'd join her on the dance floor, so I'm going to go do that. Maybe I'll see you later?"

"You'll see me right now. You know how I love to dance."

I smile as uninvitingly as I can and walk into the living room, down what's in my cup in one long drink, and then hit the dance floor. Jenna and Holden are dancing adorably—almost chastely—and Jenna is talking to him, which she usually doesn't do while dancing.

"So you didn't tell anyone you saw us backstage?" she's asking him. I frown. She looks over at me and gives me an expression daring me to stop her. I don't say anything.

"I mean, a few people, sure. I told them you might be around—as cover for your story."

"So people could have heard," Jenna says.

"I guess. . . . Is that bad?"

"No, no," Jenna says. "Just need my story to be a surprise, you know. Can't have any of the teachers finding out."

"Fuck," Holden says. "I'm sorry. I mentioned it to Emily, so a lot of people probably know by now. I didn't mean to mess up your investigation. I think it's so cool what you do."

I start dancing, trying not to listen to them, and I soon have my hands—or at least my lap—full as Brian tries to grind on me and I have to constantly turn away from him. It's during one of these turns that I see Jeremy in a corner, sipping his drink and staring at me. I roll my eyes and look away, only to find Brian grinding on my crotch again. Definitely time to leave the dance floor. I walk off toward the kitchen for another drink. Brian runs to catch up with me, grabbing me by the wrist and trying to pull me back.

"Done so soon?" he says. "Come on, I haven't even showed you how low I can drop."

"I'm just getting another drink," I say. "I'll be right back. You keep dancing."

He winks at me and grins. "Okay, but you better be back soon."

"Sure," I say.

He dances his way back to the floor, and I leave as quickly as possible.

In the kitchen, the Bens are still chatting away, but their bodies are closer now, and Other Ben is stroking Ben's forearm with one finger. It's so cute. I make myself a drink with lots of ice, because it's getting really warm now—the shorts were a good idea after all. As I'm drinking, Ben comes up to me.

"Hey," he says. "Having fun?"

"Brian Kennedy is sexually harassing me on the dance floor and Jenna is interviewing Holden about who saw us backstage," I say, and take a long swallow of my drink.

"Oh," Ben says. "I...I should stay then. I don't want you two fighting again. And I can play interference for Brian."

"Were you going?" I ask. I can feel sweat pouring down the back of my shirt now. Gross.

"Well, Ben and I were thinking of leaving."

"Did he invite you back to his place?" I ask, grinning.

"No." Ben smiles. "Just out somewhere quieter, get some coffee, talk."

"And then back to his place?"

"I'm not that kind of girl and you know it," Ben says, slapping my wrist, but biting his lower lip, suppressing a giggle. "But I like him. He doesn't sew, like me, but he's an artist. He sculpts."

"Good with his hands then," I say, wiggling my eyebrows.

"Can you stop with that?" he says, his expression happy but his voice serious. "I like him."

"Sorry," I say. "And good. You deserve a guy you like who likes you. Go—have coffee, don't go home with him. Be happy."

"Are you sure you and Jenna won't fight?"

"We're fine," I say, waving him off. "She's obsessing over something, I don't want to think about it, but she knows I don't want to think about it, so she won't bring it up with me as long as I don't try to stop her from talking about it with other people."

"Okay," Ben says, nodding. "Good, good."

"You don't have to play referee with us, you know. You're our friend, not our go-between."

"I know—but the drama of you two fighting is more than I can handle. It's for my own sanity."

I laugh. "Sure. You want a drink for courage before you go?"

"I don't need courage," Ben says, looking over at Other Ben, who's talking to a girl I don't recognize. "It's easy. Just talking to him. It's easy."

I smile and give him a hug. This is what he's always wanted—the rom-com, the meet-cute, the deep meaningful relationship that heads toward "I love you" before sex. For a moment, I feel a pang of jealousy, which confuses me—this is not something I've ever wanted. At least, not now, not yet. Love, monogamy...they sound like a lot of work. They sound kind of boring, too. I love chocolate, but if I could only eat chocolate the rest of my life, I think it would get tedious. Same goes for one cock. But this is what Ben has always wanted, and I realize that what I'm jealous of is that he's held out for something. He's dreamed of it from afar, and now, maybe, he's actually getting it. I've never held out for anything. I break our hug, realizing it's gone on a little long.

Ben looks up at me, his eyes searching my face. "You okay?"

"I just...I'm really happy for you."

"It's just coffee," Ben says, putting his hand up palm out. "Let's not go assuming it's something, because as my mother would say, assuming you got what you wanted early in the game is just asking for god to knock it out of your hand."

"I love your mom."

"Me too. I'm going to go have coffee with a handsome man now."

"Have fun," I say. "Text me everything after."

"I don't kiss and tell," Ben says, walking back to Other Ben.

I sip my drink as I watch them walk to the bedroom together and then come out with their coats on and leave. I don't want to go to the living room, where Brian is, but I can't just stand in the kitchen drinking and talking to no one. I mean, I could, but it would be sort of sad. So I wander back toward the dance floor but stand in the doorway, trying to get Jenna's attention. She smiles and waves for me to come over, but I shake my head and nod at Brian, who thankfully hasn't noticed me yet. She shrugs, clearly amused, and keeps dancing with Holden, who has his arms around her, going up and down her back…pretty far down.

"Hey, Jack."

I turn to see Ricky Gavallino. Ricky is our year, but he's a quiet type. Chess club, Model UN, stuff like that. Not a nerd—and easy on the eyes, if you like them wiry and hairy, which… well, I like all types. He's also, in my opinion, a closet case. I've caught him checking out Dylan Vandergraff's ass on more than one occasion in gym (usually I notice him staring because he's blocking my view), his eyes linger on shirtless men, and there's just something about him…my instincts, my gaydar, whatever. I tried to strike up a conversation with him when we had chem together last year, maybe get him in my rotation, but he didn't make eye contact, and when I asked around, everyone thought he was straight, so I dropped it. But now he's talking to me, drink in hand, wearing a white button-down and white pants with little anchors on them.

"Hey, Ricky," I say, sipping from my drink. "Cute pants."

"Thanks," he says, glancing down at his legs, as if he's forgotten what he's wearing.

"I don't usually see you at these sorts of things. Trying to expand your social horizons?"

Ricky nods and sips from his drink, then nervously pushes up his glasses. "Yeah," he says finally. "That's exactly it. In fact, I was hoping you'd be here."

"Me?" I raise an eyebrow.

"Yeah. I was wondering if you wanted to hang out," he says. "Back at my place."

I feel a smile slowly spread over my face. "You're Almost Out?" I ask.

He nods, staring at his drink.

"And you're asking me . . . out?" I say.

He looks up at me and we lock eyes. He's got black curly hair and dark brown eyes. His shirt is unbuttoned low enough that I can see his chest hair. "I'm asking you to fuck me," he says, the words coming out direct, but also an octave lower than his usual voice.

I lean back on the doorframe, still smiling. "I'm not opposed to the idea. I've always thought you were cute. But . . . you're a virgin?" He nods. "And you're asking me to take your virginity?"

"I . . ." He pauses, takes a sip. "I made a list. Of things I wanted once I came out. And . . . I'm out now. Sex is at the top of that list. And . . . I always thought you were cute, too." He grins in this adorable, embarrassed way and takes another long swallow of his drink. I watch his Adam's apple bob. He's sweating. This is scary for him, but I feel a weird sort of pride, too. I told him to just be fearless, and ask for what he wants, and here he is, doing it. He was inspired by something I said. And now he wants to get me naked. It's kind of arousing.

"Okay," I say. "I just want to make sure we're a hundred percent on the same page, so can I ask you some questions first?"

He nods, his eyes wide.

"Do you want to be my boyfriend?"

Ricky shakes his head quickly. "I mean . . . boyfriend is number two on the list. But that's a longer time investment, and I feel like if I'm trying to get a boyfriend, but also still a virgin, that's just more pressure, and I don't need more pressure." He talks quickly, like he's explaining a complex math problem—or explaining his reasoning during a debate. I bet he's gone over this in his head a lot. "I assume you're not looking for a boyfriend, though, so I wouldn't . . . no offense, I mean, I would, but if you're not interested, then I wouldn't waste my time. I'd pursue other options for that."

"Very thoroughly thought out," I say.

"Thanks." He grins and pushes his glasses up.

"What exactly did you want to do with me tonight?" I ask.

He turns bright red and looks back down at the floor, then looks up again and leans forward, his lips by my ear. His breath smells like vodka and Sprite. "Everything," he says.

"And, would you want to repeat the experience?" I ask. "You're not hoping to fuck your way into my heart or anything, right?"

"I mean . . . let's see how tonight goes," he says. "If tonight is going . . . ?"

I look him up and down. "It's going," I say. "Your parents home?"

"They're down in Florida this weekend," he says.

"Let me just grab my jacket, then," I say with a smile.

He grins back and we head to the bedroom. I strut a little as I walk, enjoying his eyes on my ass. There's something great about that feeling before you fuck someone, when you know for sure it's going to happen, and right now he's probably feeling it for the first time. Why not make it special?

In the bedroom, I bend over the bed, not really paying much attention while I shuffle through the coats. I turn back once. Ricky is staring at my ass. I smile at him.

"Did you have a coat?" I ask.

"Oh, yeah." He nods and starts rifling through the jackets. Now it's my turn to watch. He catches me staring, which was the point, and blushes, before picking his coat out and standing up, holding his coat in his hands over his crotch.

I turn back to the coats in earnest now, catch sight of the red fur collar, and carefully pull it out from under the others.

Except something isn't right. The weight of the jacket is wrong. I pull and everything pops out: my jacket, my new amazing jacket, cut down the middle, both sides tied together with a piece of twine, a pair of pink-handled scissors strung between them.

My knees feel wobbly so I sit on the bed.

"Is that your coat?" Ricky asks. "What happened to it?"

The world feels grayer, somehow, like the actual edges of my vision are turning gray, and I keep staring at the two halves of my coat and the scissors, all on this one piece of string, like some freaky kid mobile.

"Um," I say. I turn back to Ricky. He looks worried. And not, like, just worried that his sure-thing virginity-losing is about to go up in smoke, but worried for me, which is sweet. "I think we're going to have to reschedule."

"Oh," he says.

"I want to," I say quickly. My brain is spinning. "But this is...a thing now. And I need to call Jenna." As I say it, I remember I have a phone, and I take it out of my pocket and call her. No answer.

Ricky sits next to me on the bed and puts his hand on my knee. "You okay?"

"Sure, sure," I say. I am not okay. This was supposed to be over. I was really starting to believe it was. And now it's not over. It's very far from it. I start flipping through the jackets, looking for an origami note, some demand I can fulfill so they'll leave me alone. Whatever it takes. Maybe it's Brian, and I just have to fuck him again. Or it's Jeremy, and I have to stop the column. Or maybe it's even Holden, and I just have to give him secret blow-jobs until graduation—fine, fine. Any of those things. As long as this stops.

I try calling Jenna again. She picks up, breathless.

"What? Aren't you here? Why are you calling?"

"Where are you?" I ask.

"Oh...where are you?"

"The bedroom...with the coats." I know my voice sounds funny. Ricky is looking at me weird.

"I'll be there in a second," she says. There's mumbling on her end of the phone and she shushes someone. "Just a second."

I hang up and look at Ricky and try to smile, but I know it's not my usual sexy smile. I feel the furthest thing from sexy. "I... can you not tell anyone about this?"

"What's going on, Jack? Maybe I can help."

"No." I shake my head. "You're sweet to offer. And I am definitely going to fuck you sideways...just not tonight, okay? Here." I hand him my phone. "Put your number in."

"Okay," he says like a question, and takes the phone. "If you don't want to, that's cool. Your column said rejection is something that happens."

"It is, but it's not happening now, I promise." I put my hand on his leg and I feel like I should lean in and kiss him, but my mouth feels dry and sandpapery, and it would be his first kiss, I think, so I don't want to fuck that up for him. I feel bad, like a cock tease, which isn't the guy I want to be, but any chance of my feeling at all sexy is gone. I stare at the scissors. I know they can't be that sharp, but they glint menacingly.

"Okay," he says. He squeezes my leg and then stands, handing me back my phone. "Something is going on, and I don't get it, but you seem upset, so I'm going to go so your friends can help you. Is that okay? Do you want me to stay until Jenna gets here?"

I look up at him. "You're really nice," I say, and I sound surprised, but I don't know why. I don't really know Ricky.

Ricky opens his mouth to say something, but then Jenna comes in, looking a little flustered, the glitter around her eyes smudged.

"Hey," she says to me, then looks at Ricky. "Hi, Ricky."

"Hi, Jenna. I was just going to leave." He looks over at me again, wanting to know if that's okay, and I nod. He leaves and Jenna walks up to me, confused.

Then she spots the scissors. She grabs them, finds the string, and traces it back to the two halves of my jacket.

"Oh, fuck," she says.

I don't say anything and neither does she for a bit. She takes out her phone and sends a text.

"You were right," I say.

"I didn't want to be," she says. "I just…I wanted to know who it was, in case it did happen again. I'm sorry I got so weird about it."

"You weren't weird. You were sensible. I was in denial, clearly." I look over at my beautiful jacket, the snipped leather, the fur jaggedly cut. I know I should be feeling more, but instead it's like I'm filled with a dull emptiness. My emotions—rage, despair, whatever—are buried way beneath the subway system, in some untouched city bedrock. "Why is this happening?"

"Because someone out there is seriously fucked up," Jenna says. Her phone pings and she looks down. "Come on, we're leaving." She gathers the pieces of my jacket in her arms, the scissors hanging off them and dangling at her waist. She reaches out with her free hand. "Come on."

I take her hand and she pulls me up. "Where are we going?"

"Ben's. I texted him. His folks are out of town. You need a safe place right now."

"Okay," I say. "Sure, yeah."

She wraps her blue trench coat around me like a shawl and leads me outside, away from the party, where a Lyft is already waiting for us. I watch the pink-handled scissors swinging like a pendulum from the bundle in Jenna's arm as she shoves us into the car.

"Costume party?" the driver asks, looking us over suspiciously. "You're not hookers, right?"

"We're in high school," Jenna says. The driver turns back to the road and drives without saying anything else. Ben is waiting at the front door when we get to his place. He hurries us into his brownstone, frowning.

"You okay?" he asks me.

"I...I guess," I say.

He makes a face like he doesn't believe me, and then takes the two halves of the jacket from Jenna. "I can fix this," he says. "Really. I mean...it won't be perfect. The fur collar might have a crease at the seam in the back, and the leather is thin, so the stitching might be visible on it...." He stops. He's looking at me. Jenna is, too. I realize I'm crying. Not just crying. Tears are pouring down my face, and my throat is dry but letting out a low moan. I'm sobbing.

Jenna reaches out and hugs me. Ben wraps his arms around both of us.

"We'll get this guy," Jenna promises in a quiet voice. "We have the scissors, we can take those to the police, have them dusted for prints—"

I pull away from them. "No." I sniff, then wipe my nose with the back of my hand like a child.

"What do you mean, no?" Jenna asks, her eyes going wide, then narrow.

"I'm going to the bathroom," I say, and take off down the hall to the closest one. I look in the mirror. My face is rain-streaks of blue, green, and black, like a puddle. I start washing my face.

We can't go to the cops because then I'll have to tell them why I'm being stalked. About the sex column...my reputation. They won't believe me. I've seen that on cop shows plenty of times. They get episode ideas from real cases. I can picture the TV cops talking about me: "He's a real party boy—can we be sure he wasn't encouraging it? Maybe he was hoping for the attention. You've seen his makeup." Just like Pattyn. The episode will have a terrible title, too. "The Prep School Perv." "Private School Slut Stalker." That'll look great on a college application: *Episode 511 was based on me! I'm the private school slut!*

Even if I don't make it onto a network drama, the real cops will interview students at school, who'll tell them those fucking rumors. I picture Ava talking to a detective, twirling a lock of hair around her finger as she says, "Do you want to know about the fourgy in Hannah Ling's hot tub, or the time he fucked the coach at Highbrook?" The cops leer. Maybe reporters get wind of it, ask the same people the same questions and hear the same rumors. Colleges look at my name on their applications, think it's familiar. My mother, watching the news.

No police.

I look up. The heavy streaks of color are gone, but there's still a faint blue-green tinge to my skin, and a little glitter. I don't have any makeup remover with me, but I should be okay to get home without anyone staring too much. I dry my face on a hand towel (sorry, Mrs. Parrish) and walk out. Jenna is waiting for me.

"Ben's already sewing," she says.

"He doesn't have to do that."

"He wants to. To feel useful. To feel like he's fighting this. The same reason I want to call the police. We can talk to one of my dad's contacts."

"No." I shake my head. "They wouldn't believe me. Think it's a prank, or that I deserve it for..."

"For what? The column? Having sex?"

"Something like that."

"And doesn't that make you mad?"

I pause. I've been feeling sorry for myself. Poor little slutty rich boy. But she's right. It makes me angry, too. I can feel my makeup on my face, sticky and drying in a thin crust. I furrow my brows and scrunch my eyes to make it crack.

"Yeah," I say. "I guess it does."

"So let's do something about it. Let's go to the cops."

I shake my head. "I just said I don't want that."

"Okay..." Jenna says. She walks down the hall and I follow her. Ben's parents have done their apartment in dark wood and clay-colored walls, framed platinum records, gold detailing. It's warm, sophisticated. Ben's room, though, is an explosion of neon. He's hunched over his sewing machine, my jacket under his needle, when we arrive, and he barely looks up. Fabric samples are thrown around the room—bright pink, turquoise, yellow. His bedspread is sequined, his walls painted sky blue and covered in posters—Broadway, fashion, big bearded men without shirts.

"He doesn't want to go to the police," Jenna says, sitting on the bed.

Ben looks up. "Why not?"

"They won't believe me, or if they do and the story gets out I'll become a Lifetime movie or something," I say. "I just want to live my life. Unexamined."

"So you're just going to put up with all this?" Jenna asks. She takes out her pink notebook from her purse and folds it open. There are more of her theories. She puts a question mark over Holden.

"What's that for?" I ask.

"He was going down on me when you called—I only answered 'cause I figured if you were calling, it was bad. He could be bi, but he was really enthusiastic, makes me think he's probably not that into you. Said I tasted fabulous. That's the exact word he used."

"Ew," I say.

"Don't *ew* my vagina."

"Sorry. I didn't mean your lady parts. Just that word choice."

"Who else was there?" Jenna asks.

Ben's sewing machine whirs as he runs my jacket through it. "Brian Kennedy," he says as he sews. "He asked me if you were there when I was talking to Ben."

"Yeah," I say. "He wanted to go home with me."

"And Ricky was there," Jenna says, making a note.

"It couldn't be him. We were about to go fuck."

Ben glances up at me, considers, then looks back at his sewing.

"So what?" Jenna asks. "Maybe he lured you in there to see your reaction when you saw the jacket was cut."

"I guess," I say, not quite believing it. But it could be anyone. "Jeremy was there."

Jenna looks up at me with a raised eyebrow, then makes a note in her book.

"Pattyn wasn't," Ben says.

Jenna nods, makes another note, looks over her list. I do, too, suddenly thinking of the last time any of them looked at me, spoke to me—was there a clue? A nasty glare, a snide remark? I mean...probably. With Jeremy, for sure.

Ben stops his sewing machine and holds up my jacket, now stitched up, looking not quite as amazing as before but still pretty cool. The seam isn't even really noticeable unless you know it's there. But even restored, the jacket leaves a bitter taste in my mouth. Looking at it just makes me feel...so many things. Angry. Helpless. Like everyone around me could be the one who cut it up, who might—what? Want to cut me?

"It looks good," I tell Ben, and he smiles.

"So what are you going to do?" Jenna asks. "What's the next plan of action? The camera didn't work."

"I don't know," I say. "I just want to catch him, and end it."

"We'll figure it out," Ben says.

"Yeah," Jenna says.

Ben comes over and sits next to me on the bed and they both wrap their arms around me, one on each side, like a cocoon.

21

Dear Jack of Hearts,

So, I don't know if you help straight guys, or whatever, but I have this...problem. And I thought maybe you could help. The thing is, I want to be the kind of guy that maybe gets made fun of on TV. But, like, that bro-guy, who drinks beer, and has a lot of one-night stands, and knows how to party, and joins a frat. I am that guy, I think. I mean, I drink lots of beer, party, have lots of sex, and I like that. I think that's how high school and college should be. But the problem is...I'm bad at sleeping around. Like, I want to have no-strings sex, but after I fuck a girl, I get weird. I don't want to say fall in love, 'cause that's like (I was going to say gay, but you're gay, and you sleep around). But I get attached. I really care about a girl after we fuck. And I don't want to, because then I spend like a month moping over her and not feeling like myself, or sometimes we end up dating for a bit, but she expects me to change everything else about myself to be her boyfriend or something, and it's just not me. Easy sex with no feeling is me. But I can't seem to do it. How do you do it? How do you fuck someone and not care about them after?

—Fucking in Love

The next day I wake up and from bed stare at my open closet, the jacket hanging there like a body on a meat hook. I can't see Ben's stitches, but I can feel them, like a scar. My wardrobe has war wounds now. I sit up, grab my phone from the floor, and pull up Instagram. I search #origami, then start browsing the suspects.

The first to come up is Ricky. He has a surprisingly active Instagram—photos of all sorts of random stuff, the inside of his locker, the view from a classroom window. No captions, some hashtags, but just really basic ones, #nofilter #Monday—oddly basic for someone I think of as being smart and kind of weird. But he has a whole slew of #origami from several months ago. Shots of little animals standing next to windows, or small folded boxes laid out against a white table.

I pull up his number from last night. He entered his name just as Ricky, which is funny, because I thought he preferred Richard. Though I did call him Ricky last night—maybe that's why he hates me?

If he hates me, I remind myself. It might not be him. Certainly my gut doesn't think so. Thinking of him as Pinky just doesn't fit. But I know now that I have no idea who Pinky could be—could be anyone. That's what is so terrifying. Pinky is paranoia. I scroll through more Instagram #origami, then find people on Tumblr from school who like it. People I've never spoken to. Could it be them? The sophomore Sarah Walters? I have no idea who she is—her photo is utterly unfamiliar. Leo Chu? He's a senior, and I've seen him around. He takes a lot of art classes. Maybe he's offended by my art, but he's never said anything. Never done more than nod at me in the halls. Peter Das, who I don't recognize, though he's my year. Eloise Bachman, who I have Latin with and sometimes lends me notes—she's a lesbian, but maybe she thinks like Jeremy does, that I'm a bad queer and need to be punished. It could be any of them. I put down the phone as a familiar feeling comes over me. It's not one I have a name for. Anxiety, I think. Some kind of anxiety, where breathing becomes harder and it's like insects are crawling on my skin, but I can't see them and I can't wipe them off. I felt this way in sixth and seventh grade, like all the time. But I haven't felt it since then.

I get up and take a cold shower. That always helped then, and it helps again now. My skin stops moving, and my breathing becomes normal. I towel off and put on a nice pair of underwear and some lounge shorts—but the short, sexy ones. There's a note on the table from Mom saying she won't be home until late. Which, actually, is perfect, though I feel bad that she has to work on a Sunday.

> Ricky posted some origami on his instagram. I'm going to invite him over to take his virginity, and look at his phone for clues

Jenna

> Ooo. Spy-slutting. I'm into it

Ben

> Except if he's Pinky, aren't you just giving him what he wants?

I frown, thinking about that. Does Pinky really just want to fuck me? I feel like I'd fuck whoever if it made all this stop. Then I immediately feel gross about thinking that, because I'm not, like, a prostitute. I don't know. I *would* fuck someone to get it to stop, though. To get the weird insect-skin feeling to stop. But as I think about it, the feeling starts up again, on my legs. I hurry to the bathtub and run some cold water over my feet, which stops it.

> I think what Pinky wants is more complicated. And if he is Pinky, and a screw is what he wants, then everything will be over anyway!

And Ricky seems nice, and he wants to lose his virginity—to me. Which is pretty hot. I try imagining what I'll feel like if I fuck Ricky and then find out he's Pinky, and it's not a good feeling. It's a sick vomiting kind of feeling. But there's also this feeling behind it of relief at knowing it's him, and the whole thing being over.

Ben's "..." hovers in the group text for a while.

Jenna

See if you can get his phone without fucking him first

Ben

Yeah

I can tell he had a more complicated, probably eloquent thought.

Ok

I pull up Ricky's number and send him a text.

Hey Ricky. It's Jack. Sorry about last night. What are you up to right now?

I wait for a while, hoping last night's weirdness didn't scare him off. It would suck if not only was my jacket cut in half but also, like, my sex appeal went down because he thought weird shit was happening. Which it was.

> I was just doing homework. Why?

> Want to come over and hang out?

His "…" lingers for a while, too.

> Yes.

I grin and text him my address, then clean up my room a little. When he knocks and I open the door, I'm still just wearing my short lounge shorts.

"Hi," he says, his eyes going wide at my naked chest.

"Hey," I say. "My mom is gone all day."

"That's … good," he says, not making eye contact. He looks around the apartment. "Nice place. Very … aeronautical."

"Thanks," I say. "Not that I had anything to do with the decorating. Want to see my room?"

Without waiting for an answer I head toward it and he follows me. I glance back once. He's looking at my ass, but then he sees me and looks away. He looks good today—a blue Henley, open and showing some chest hair, gray skinny jeans. In my bedroom I sit down on my bed and cross my legs. He sits in the chair at my desk, staring at me.

"You seem nervous," I say.

"I was drinking last night."

"I could open some wine if you want," I tell him.

He blushes at that, and shakes his head. "You're really not going to talk about what happened?"

"I'm sorry about that," I say. It's my turn to look away now. "It was just a stupid thing."

"Someone cut your jacket in half."

I lie back on my bed and stare at the ceiling. "I don't want to talk about it," I say. "Is that okay?"

He's quiet for a moment. Maybe Jenna is right and he planned the whole thing and now these questions are part of the way he gets off, the power trip or whatever.

"That's okay," he says finally.

I don't say anything back, and after a moment he comes over and sits on the bed next to me, staring down at me. "Do you really want to do this?" he asks.

"What?"

"Whatever it is we're going to do...." He looks away, pushes up his glasses.

"Fuck?" He doesn't say anything. "Yes," I say, sitting up. "You're cute, and you said you know you don't want to get into a relationship with me. You had a little checklist. I thought that was cute. And me being on it was sort of hot."

He laughs at that. "Checklists are hot?"

"Knowing what you want is hot. Being wanted is hot." I pause. "Are *you* sure you want to do this? You don't have to, you know. Just being out... that's a lot. You don't have to... what is it they say in the old movies? Punch your v-card?"

He frowns. "Let's not call it that. But yes. I'm sure. I want to...do this. I want to be able to go out there and talk to guys and kiss guys and whatever with guys—"

"Fuck them," I say.

"Yeah. I want to be able to do all that, and I think it'll be so much easier if I've done it already."

I sit up and look at him. "And you think I'm hot?"

He laughs nervously. "Yes."

"You've never kissed a boy?"

He shakes his head, blushing.

I lean over and put my hand behind his head and slowly kiss him. I make it a good one, too, the kind where you sigh a little and then slip your tongue in. Then I pull away.

"Now you have," I say with a grin.

He smiles, takes off his glasses, and wipes them on his shirt.

"Let me see your phone," I say.

"Why?" he asks, his face very confused.

"I want to see what porn you look at so I know how to best do this," I say, putting my hand out, palm up.

He furrows his brow, still confused, but takes his phone out of his back pocket, unlocks it, and puts it in my hand. I snatch it away and start looking through it.

"What are you doing?" he asks. "I don't have any porn on there."

What *am* I doing? I have his phone, but no plan, no idea what I'm looking for. Time to improvise.

"Wait here," I say, and hurry to the bathroom and lock the door behind me. We have a big tub that's proven fun on other occasions, and also takes a while to fill. I turn the faucet on, throw in some bubble bath, and start going through his phone. He's visited the Jack of Hearts website, but that doesn't prove anything—he sent me the Almost Out letter. I flip through his notes, his sent emails, his photos, to see if there are any of me, like, taken from a distance, stalker-style. Nothing. In the notes, I find a draft of his Almost Out letter, but that's it.

He knocks on the bathroom door. "What are you doing?" he asks.

"Just you wait," I say. "This is going to be fun."

"Why do you need my phone?" he asks.

"A girl doesn't reveal all her secrets," I say, now desperately scrolling through everything—contacts, music, search history. There's nothing to indicate he's Pinky, though. There's not even anything about origami aside from the old photos on his Instagram.

It's not him. I'm, like, 90 percent sure now, which is probably as sure as I'm going to get. I slip off my shorts, unlock the door, and hop into the bathtub, arranging the bubbles artfully around my body. Then I snap a quick selfie with his phone.

"Come in," I say, though he hasn't knocked again.

He opens the door slowly, still confused. I smile at him from the tub. "I thought since it's your first time and all, it should be extra fun."

He grins at me, stares at the bubbles, then blushes and looks away. "Why did you need my phone then?"

"So you have a souvenir later," I say.

He furrows his brow, confused, which is cute.

"Come here," I say, and sit up from lying in the bath to kneeling. The water ends just below my hips. He walks over and sits on the edge of the tub. I pull his shirt off over his head. He's thin and furry, as expected, but also surprisingly muscular. I take my wet hands and drip a little water on his collarbone.

"Ready to get wet?" I ask.

He nods.

"So . . ." Ricky asks, panting. "Is that everything?"

I laugh. We're lying on my bed, having moved back here for rounds two and three—virgins may finish quickly, but they're usually ready for another round pretty quick, too. The sheets are wet with water and sweat. I'll definitely have to wash them when he's gone.

"That's all the basics," I say. "I mean, it's not like we did every position in the Kama Sutra. But all the 101 stuff, for sure. You'll be ready for any third dates you go on."

"Third date," he says, nodding, his eyes going a little blank as he makes a mental note. "That's when we have sex?"

I laugh again and roll onto my side, putting my hand on his chest. "Honey, no. That's, like, an expression. You do it when you feel right. Maybe that's the first date, maybe it's the fifth, hell, maybe you wait until marriage—though I don't recommend that. Finding you're sexually incompatible after the vows feels like a bad situation."

"So there's no three-date rule?" He furrows his brow.

"Nope. When you and your partner—or partners—want to. That's the rule. Talk about it beforehand, though. Like how I asked if you wanted to do something just now before we did it."

"Okay." He nods and turns to look at me and smiles. Amazingly, he still blushes as he sees my naked body laid out on the sheets. "Just . . . when we want to. I think next I want to try having a boyfriend. I know you're not into that," he adds quickly.

"Nah, not right now," I say. "But if you ever want to do this again, just text me."

"Yeah?" Ricky asks, surprised. "I thought this was a one-time thing."

I shake my head. "I'm not opposed to repeats. I just don't want . . . the idea of having to worry about someone else before myself. The idea of having to think, 'Wait, is this okay with my boyfriend?' before kissing some cute boy I just met at a party. I'm . . . too selfish right now. And I'm okay with that, because I'm not, like, getting into relationships and then hurting people." I turn so I'm on my back. "I just want to have fun, and not worry about hurting anyone."

"Or anyone hurting you?" Ricky asks.

I shrug. "I guess. Never really thought of that." I stare at the ceiling for a moment. "Hey, can I ask something random?"

"Sure," Ricky says, propping himself up on a shoulder to look at me. His hand absentmindedly traces up my stomach, making me shiver.

"Do you like origami?"

Ricky looks confused. "Is that a sex thing?"

"No." I laugh again. "The paper folding."

"Oh." He shrugs. "I mean, yeah, I guess. I was pretty good at it in that papercraft elective last year."

"Papercraft?"

"Yeah, for art. Nance taught it. Sculpture, but with paper—origami, cast paper, folding, cutting...We did a bunch of stuff. Why do you ask?"

"Oh, it's just for this random thing Jenna is working on," I lie quickly. "She wants to talk to people about origami for some reason. Asked me if I knew anyone, and I just thought about it."

"Well, she can talk to me, if she wants, but I'm no expert. She should talk to Nance."

"Yeah," I say. I want to ask who else was in the class, but I've pumped him for enough information today.

He leans down and gives me a kiss. He's getting good at it. "Well, I'll text you when I'm free for a repeat," he says. "While I'm still single, of course."

"Good," I say. "Maybe I'll text you, too. I like playing teacher."

Ricky stands up from bed and puts on his pants and glasses. "Definitely my favorite class," he says, zipping his fly. He pauses, looking for his shirt. "Besides debate, maybe."

I laugh again. "Your shirt is still in the bathroom. I hope it's not too wet." I get out of bed and we go to the bathroom, where his shirt is dry, having landed on the toilet seat, and not the floor, which is flooded from the waves we made in the tub. I watch him slip it on and then start trying to clean up the bathroom with the towels. He also picks up his phone from the top of the toilet.

"What did you need this for, really?" he asks.

"Check your photos," I tell him.

He looks at his photos and grins.

"Like I said, souvenir," I say.

"Thanks," he says. He's thinking about kissing me again, I can tell. And more. But he sighs, stops himself. "I'd better get going. I do have homework to do. But...I will definitely text you."

"Looking forward to it," I say, standing up. He kisses me again, and then leaves. I throw the towels and my sheets in the wash, then shower off and slip my shorts back on before texting Jenna and Ben.

> Nothing on Ricky's phone to imply he's Pinky

Jenna

> What if he has two phones? A burner. He's brainy

> No. I went through his phone—there's nothing

> No photos of me, no search history of stalking my instagram or tumblr. He follows me on instagram, but that's not so crazy. I'm like 90% sure it's not him

Ben

Ok. So who is it? Brian Kennedy?

Jenna

He'd need to be working with someone. To get the notes into the locker

I think its Jeremy.

Ricky says he took a papercraft class with Nance last year. That's where he learned origami. If we knew who was in that class, that might help narrow down suspects.

Or, if I'm being honest, maybe not. It's like the pink paper. They could have taken the class...but maybe they know origami from somewhere else. It could be anyone. My skin starts to crawl again, this time on my shoulders. I go to the freezer and take out an ice pack and place it briefly on each shoulder, one at a time, until the feeling stops.

Neither Ben nor Jenna have added anything.

It could be someone we don't even know

I take a deep breath, holding the ice pack to my shoulder.

Ben

Someone who's loved you from afar, but who you don't know exists. That's...romantic

I mean, not in a good way, but in a gothic romantic sad sort of way, and you can see them getting all possessive, like in an old book

Jenna

Its passive aggressive

But I agree that we should try to get the list of people who took the papercraft elective. Ricky wouldn't tell you?

I thought asking would be a bit too suspicious. I'd already stolen his phone

Jenna

Ok. So we need the list from the administrative office. I...have an idea for that

Ben

Can we go over it Monday?

I'm sorry. Nevermind. Sorry. Let's go over it now

What's the matter?

Ben

I'm just getting ready to go see Ben

Our first date

But this is more important. I'm sorry, it was selfish of me

Don't be sorry. Your life is important, too. Important to me. We can go over Jenna's plan tomorrow

Jenna

Yeah. It's probably better it not be on our phones anyway. Go have fun

Oooh, but what are you wearing? We must approve your first date outfit

Ben

IDK! I'm kind of freaking out about it

Jenna

We are here to help. Send us pics of the options

Ben sends us a dozen photos of various outfits laid out on his bed, and after some heated discussion we all decide on the pants from his new suit with a cardigan and a polo.

Ben

Ok I better go. Wish me luck!

You will be great. And if he doesn't see that, he sucks

Jenna

On a first date? Ben is moving fast

Ben

I'm turning off my phone now

Jenna texts a row of eggplants and I laugh before putting the phone down. Jenna has a plan. Ricky is out as a suspect, and out as a virgin. I don't feel much better, but at least I got a lot done today. I peek out the window in my bedroom, wondering if anyone is watching me. On the street, people are walking their dogs, staring at their phones. No one looks up at my window.

I try to do my homework, but I have to stop every hour or so to get the ice pack again.

22

MONDAY, THERE'S A NOTE IN MY LOCKER BEFORE CLASSES even start. It's shaped like a coat. My hands itch as I unfold it, looking up and down the hallway to see if anyone is watching me. No one is.

Jack,
 Spying isn't very nice. You CAN see me when I say so. But a camera? Without consent? you should Know better. Perv. That's why I had to cut your coat. It was a nice coat. My scissors went through it real smoothly. I saw you buy it. I saw how you loved it. But you should just love **ME**. So it's gone now. And I'm hurt. I Know you, Jack. I Know you loved THAT jacket. And I know your mom, too. Have you met her new boyfriend? He's cute, but not as cute as you. He's young, too. But, Jack, now that you know I know you, and you hurt my feelings, I think you need to send me a present. I want photos. Photos of you. Nude. Show me what you'll give me as my boyfriend. Show me all of it. Send them to ILUVJACK@anonymousemail.com. That's how I'll know you're sorry about the camera. Otherwise I'll feel hurt, Jack. Hurt like I was when I cut your jacket. And I might cut more than a jacket next time.

The note falls out of my hand, because it's shaking so much. My throat is on fire and I realize I'm not breathing. I take a loud breath and start coughing. I keep coughing as I bend over and pick up the note and cram it in my pocket. I look up and down the hall, but now a lot of people are staring at me. My coughing is loud. Ricky comes up to me and pats me strongly on the back.

"You okay?" he asks.

"Just...swallowed wrong," I say.

"Okay," he says. "Want some water or anything?"

I shake my head. "Thanks."

"Okay...see you later." He walks off. My coughing is dying down now, but my skin is moving on its own, like it's trying to leave my body. I don't blame it.

"What's going on?" Jenna asks, suddenly behind me. Ben is next to her, typing on his phone. I stare at them silently for a moment, realizing I'm going to have to show them the note. But I don't want to. The demands in it, the stuff about my mom... sharing that with anyone makes me feel queasy. Jenna stares at me, her eyes narrowing. She knows something's up. I take the note from my pocket and show it to her.

"It was folded like a coat," I say. Her eyes scan it, her face growing tighter and tighter.

"Pendejo cabron." She squeezes her fist closed around the note, then hands it to Ben, who looked up when she started swearing. He reads over it, his face growing as sad as hers is angry.

"Oh, Jack..." he says, handing the note back to me. I put it back in my pocket. "But," he continues, "isn't that enough? Proof, I mean. To go to Pattyn?"

"No." I shake my head. "He told my mom about my column. He'll definitely tell her about this—and I don't even know if this will be enough proof."

"Plus, we haven't ruled him out as a suspect," Jenna says, leaning against the lockers.

"He wasn't at the party," Ben says.

"Maybe he told a student they could get out of suspension or something if they did what he told them," Jenna says. "I know it's a long shot, but I don't trust him. He doesn't give a fuck about Jack, or else he would have done something when we went to him the first time."

"So what are you going to do?" Ben asks.

"You can't send Pinky any photos," Jenna says. "Then you'll just be giving him more power."

"I..." I start to say, but I don't know how to finish the sentence. I used to feel good all the time, I realize. I took that for granted. I always said it could be worse, but I never really appreciated it. Now I feel like there are spiders crawling up and down my back and everyone is watching me and every single person I know could be doing this to me for their own amusement. Just to watch me suffer because I was enjoying my life too much. Because I was too damn happy and fabulous.

Well, they've shown me. I barely had it in me to put on

eyeliner this morning. I feel like I'm so aware of everything I do being watched and trying to do what it is that'll make Pinky stop, but I don't know what that is. I take a deep breath. My coughing has stopped, but it's hard to breathe.

"Just . . . forget about it," Jenna says. "We're going to get this guy."

The hall is mostly empty now, and I realize everyone has gone to class.

"I'll tell you my plan at lunch," Jenna says. She hugs me.

"Wait," Ben says. "Are you okay? We can cut class, girl. Play hooky and just go drink hot chocolate all day." He squeezes my arm. "Whatever you need from us."

"No." I shake my head. "Let's go to class." Unless cutting is what Pinky wants me to do. Then maybe I should do it? No. I shouldn't do what he wants and I don't know what he wants. I feel anger rising up in me. Fuck Pinky and these mind games. He's probably lying about my mom.

Ben takes my arm and links it through his like we're on the yellow brick road, and Jenna links her arm through my other, and together, they escort me like I'm someone's grandmother, one foot in front of the other, to class.

Muscle memory guides me through first period. Focusing on the teacher's voice helps keep out the thoughts of Pinky, though I also can't really hear what the teacher is saying. It's like listening to whale songs.

I find myself in the bathroom during second period without quite knowing how I got there. But I realize right away how nice a cigarette would be. I light it up and sit on the counter, blowing smoke out the window. The nicotine hits my chest and makes it warm, makes it feel like my heart is beating again, which makes me wonder when it started feeling like it had stopped.

When I hear the door slam in the girls' bathroom, I immediately snub out my cigarette. I can't hear any rumors about me today. I can't hear about how I got gangbanged by every guy at the yacht party, or whatever. But as I get to the door, I realize they're not talking about me. They're gossiping—about Tori Sidana-Lopez's new, much older boyfriend, about the college boy who hit on Kaitlyn and who Kaitlyn turned down—but nothing about me. Not once. They even talk about Jenna's costume—but never me. I lean against the door, and feel... good for the first time today. Maybe that column got to them, or maybe they're just mad at me, but they're not talking about me, and that feels great. They've changed, and maybe it was because of something I did.

The warmth spreads from my chest to my limbs, loosening all my muscles. As the day goes on, I sometimes think about the note in my pocket, sharp edges biting into my skin, but then I just think about the inane gossip of Ava, Emily, and Kaitlyn—did Holden hook up with someone? Did Hannah Ling go home with that guy from Melton? I take each bit of gossip not about me and genuinely consider it, turning it over in my mind to see all its implications—none of which have anything to do with me. I feel gloriously invisible. The note fades under so much gossip, invisible as I am.

At lunch, I almost feel normal again, or at least I've gotten to the point where I can shut out the note every time it tries to force itself into my brain again, every time I start catching people looking in my direction and wonder if it's because they're Pinky.

I sip a chocolate milk, hoping the childhood flavor will make me feel better.

Ben sits down first and gives me these big puppy eyes, but I just smile and ask how his date with Other Ben went.

He looks confused for a minute, but then smiles shyly and says, "Good."

"How good?" I ask, wiggling my eyebrows.

"Not that good," he says, slapping my arm. "You know I don't put out on the first date."

"But..." I say, hoping for something.

"But we did kiss," Ben says, hunching his shoulders and
ing his hands over his mouth.

"Was it a good kiss?" I ask.

He nods. "Really good. He has these big arms
wrapped them around me....Look at me, I'm get the
ered thinking about it." He fans himself with his

"So what's he like, anyway?" I ask. "We ba
party. Is he into fashion, too?"

"Not so much—he says he didn't think there was any point, fashion was for thin guys, but when I told him I altered and made my own stuff for just that problem, he was interested. And he's way into Broadway. He knows more show tunes than I do."

"Did you sing on your date?" I ask, raising an eyebrow.

"Maaaaaybe." He giggles. "I sound so stupid."

"You met a guy you like and want. That's not stupid."

"Yeah, but . . . I mean. With everything going on . . ."

"No," I say, putting my hand on his arm. "No. You don't get to do that. Pinky is trying to ruin my life. He does not get to ruin yours. You be happy. No matter what happens to me."

"Happens to you?" Ben asks, suddenly looking worried.

"Nothing is going to happen," Jenna says, sitting down and ving her bag on the table. "I have a plan."

rn toward her and take a deep breath, preparing for war.

ve need a list of students from the papercraft elective,

ink we should go to the administrative office and tell

d some transcripts for a study abroad program or

inted out on school stationery, because . . . I'll think

the When they print it out for me, I'll say that my

on it. 've isn't on it. Then they'll bring up the roster for

"But I'll ask them to print that out to prove I'm not

asks, point on it, why would they print it out?" Ben

"Then we with a french fry.

there to distrac oto of the screen. So I need both of you

he photo or whatever needs to be done."

I sigh. "I guess it could work," I say. "I just don't know how much it will tell us. So maybe the people on that list know origami, so what? So maybe the pink paper is coming from backstage—but maybe it isn't."

"Well, the note proves it is," Jenna says. "He wouldn't have cared about us watching backstage with a camera if it weren't his paper supply."

"But that doesn't prove that Pinky took papercraft," I say. "And I bet now he has a new source of paper."

Ben's phone beeps and he pulls it out, smiles, and types something, then stops, fingers hovering over the screen, and puts it away. "Sorry," he says, and I feel like he's just dropped all the fabric in his wardrobe on me. I hate that my stupid problem is keeping him from texting his new crush. "Why not just ask Nance?"

"I . . . yeah," I say, nodding my head. "I can do that."

"Think she'll tell you?" Jenna asks.

"I hope," I say.

"Okay, but if she doesn't," Jenna says, "we're doing it m Unless you want to ask Ricky."

"No, he's already way too suspicious."

"Okay, so ask Nance," Ben says.

"I just . . . what's the point?" I ask. "What will this out us? Some people who know origami. That's not . ilk that

"It's not nothing," Jenna says. She frowns k, I know and carefully pries my hands off the bottle of I'm clutching, and holds them in each of

you're feeling powerless right now. We tried to fight back, and it got even worse. But that doesn't mean we stop fighting. We have to get this guy, because otherwise it'll keep getting worse anyway. You send him those photos, he'll know he's winning and push—push you to do more things you don't want to do, push you to be who he wants you to be. So you can't give in, okay? You have to fight with me."

"I...okay," I say. She's right. I can't just wish the problem away like I did before, and her scheme is something.

"We'll catch him," Jenna says. "Try to get the list from Nance, and text us if you do. If not, we'll go to my plan."

"Okay," I say.

"Got it." Ben nods. His phone beeps again.

"...ke it out," I say. "Text him back."

...grins and takes his phone out and goes back to typing ... grin on his face.

...oing well?" Jenna asks.

...en says, looking up. "I might just have to write my ...ack of Hearts soon."

...t ask me, you know," I say, finishing my milk. I ..., but I'm not hungry.

questio...

your ans... ...u don't know it's me. And besides, maybe my

"Okay." ...lots of other little boys and girls have and

"Whatever m... ...hem," he says, fluttering his eyelashes.

...rst time I've laughed today, I realize.

...ppy."

"What'll make me happy is catching Pinky so we can make lunch all about me again," Ben says.

"You wish," I say. "I'm the one who got laid this weekend, don't forget."

"Hey, I got head from Holden," Jenna says, eating her yogurt.

"Yeah, you and your fabulous puss," Ben says, and we all laugh.

"He was pretty good at it, though. Maybe I'll ask him if he wants to do it again sometime." She leans back, takes a fashion magazine out of her bag, and flips through it as she eats her yogurt.

"You want to fuck Holden?" I ask, surprised. "No judgments."

"Judge away," Jenna says. "But no. I just want him to go down on me while I read *Vogue* or whatever."

"That's actually a pretty good fantasy," Ben says.

"Thanks," Jenna says. "Now, how's my hat coming along?"

The rest of the day feels almost normal. My skin doesn't crawl, but I do keep going over the gossip that wasn't about me in my head. And sometimes, when I catch someone looking at me, I feel this shudder through me, like . . . I don't know. Like the opposite of an orgasm, like instead of your body shuddering and being filled with hormones that relax you and make you happy, it's hormones that make you stressed and sad. But when I start thinking of it that way, I immediately try to think of something else, because I don't want to ruin sex by connecting it with whatever that feeling is.

Of course, the more you try to not connect things, the more

they connect. So I try to focus on class instead, and I halfway succeed. At the end of school, I'm exhausted, though, and I realize I can't remember a single thing from class. All day, every bit of energy I've had has gone toward not feeling that feeling. And it hasn't even really worked.

I have one more thing to do before I go home, so I stop by the art room when school is out. Nance is there, carefully washing off some sculpting tools. She's holding some cutting wire in her hands and running it back and forth under the faucet, like she's weaving.

"Nance?" I say, and she looks up and smiles, then nods at me to join her.

"Hand me that rib," she says, nodding at the dirty tools to the side of the sink. I hand it to her. "What's up?" she asks, washing. I watch her hands. There's something soothing about the back and forth of them as she washes.

"I was wondering if you could give me the class roster for the papercraft elective you taught last year," I say as casually as I can, still watching her hands.

"What for?"

"To see who was in the class."

She snorts a laugh. "I figured that. Why do you want to know?"

I take a deep breath, but don't tell her. Nance is great, but I don't want her involved in all this.

"Is this for that article Jenna is writing?" Nance asks. "I don't know how I feel helping you out with that, Jack. I know she's fighting the good fight, in her mind, anyway, but school funding is complicated, and we all know that. If there was real under-funding, it would be one thing, but she's making mountains out of molehills."

"It's not that," I say.

"No?" She looks at me. "What is it then?"

"It's . . ." I should have come up with a lie earlier. For some reason I just thought she'd give me the list. She's cool. "For some-thing else," I say, my voice going up at the end, like it's a question.

Nance raises an eyebrow, then turns back to her tools. She puts the clean rib down and grabs a loop tool from the pile. "Those ros-ters have to be given out through the admin office," she says. "And I don't appreciate you lying to me, Jack. And I especially don't appreciate you not even having a good story ready. I'm not dumb."

"I didn't mean that," I say quickly. "I just can't tell you."

She looks up at me again and narrows her eyes. I look away. "What's going on, Jack?"

"Nothing," I say quickly, walking away. "You're right. We'll ask admin."

She doesn't say anything as I leave. Outside I take out my phone.

> Nance wouldn't give me the roster

Jenna

> Then we meet tomorrow at the admin office

23

Dear Fucking in Love,

It's always nice when someone wants to be more
like me, and yes, I take letters from straight guys
hoping to have more casual sex without feeling
romantic feelings. Hormones are powerful things.
But first off, I want to make sure you want to be this
guy you describe—the guy who sleeps around and
doesn't get attached—because you genuinely think
it'll make you happy, not because TV told you that's
what being a teenaged dude is about. It's okay to fall
for someone and try monogamy and then maybe
break up. It's not for me, but you shouldn't feel bad

about liking someone. You shouldn't feel like you have to be a particular sort of person because you see him on TV.

But, if you really don't want to get attached, you don't have to. Sex and love aren't as connected as everyone says they are. You just need to be like, "Great orgasm, but these feelings—they're about the orgasm, not about the person who gave me the orgasm." We release a whole party of hormones or chemicals when we fuck, and those make us really like the person who gives us an orgasm. I think they're literally called bonding hormones, but ask your bio teacher. And it's not like they don't affect me. The first guy who gave me an orgasm? I plopped down next to him when we were done and I looked over at him, and all the little flaws I'd seen before and had decided weren't quite deal breakers— the weird mole on his neck, the cowlick, the braces— those went from things I was putting up with to things I actively thought were cute. And when he started to snore, I thought that was cute, too. We all get swoony after we come. Now, how did I not curl up and spoon him and then tell him he was special the next day? I remembered the hormones. And then I told myself—I'm grateful he gave me that orgasm, *and I enjoyed it, but I should appreciate it, and his technique in giving it, not him as a person I want to spend time with now.*

I still get that feeling when I look at a guy I just came with. It happened last week—a one-night stand who told me he wasn't interested in a repeat, but he was cute and funny and I was high off orgasm hormones, and so I developed a little crush for a day or two. But the crush faded, and while I had it—I didn't act on it. I didn't ask anyone out.

It also really helps if you're up front with the person you're about to hook up with that there are no expectations of a relationship. Just saying that out loud beforehand helps to keep you from feeling like you want one after. Plus, it's the right thing to do.

But if that's not doing the job, here are my techniques—first, recognize that the orgasm is making you feel what you feel, and thank the person for giving it to you, but don't focus on how cute they are. Focus on how good you feel. Then, don't ask them out. It's cool to have a crush on them for a bit, but remember you're not going to feel this way forever, and you say you don't like yourself in relationships, so focus on that. You

don't have to act on every emotion, after all. I
think it's about how society is always like, "Sex =
love + these chemicals." But any other emotion,
they'd tell you, "Just walk it off." Some bitch says
something nasty, but was trying to be funny? Just
walk it off. Why should it be any different with
sex? It's not an easy task, but in the end it's about
restraint, and selfishness. And it's okay to be selfish
about stuff, as long as you're clear from the get-go
that you're not a relationship guy.

—Jack of Hearts

I feel better at home, at least once all the window shades are down and I know no one is watching me. I take a cold shower and work on my homework and then dinner—a stir-fry. Mom comes home around the normal time, but it feels like I haven't seen her in ages, and it's like we're reuniting at an airport or something. She gives me a hug from behind while I'm at the stove.

"Sorry I've been gone so much," she says. "This lawsuit at work is...complicated."

"That's okay," I say. Because it is. If she hadn't been gone yesterday, I never would have gotten the lead on the papercraft class. But thinking of that makes me think of the note I got—now in a drawer in my desk—and how Mom is in it. I offer her the wooden spoon I'm using to stir and she takes it from me, spinning the meat and vegetables in the pan.

I lean against the counter next to her. "So, how was your day otherwise?" I ask.

"There barely was an otherwise," she says. "What is this, sesame oil?"

"Soy sauce, half an orange, nothing fancy," I say. "Are you having any fun these days, Mom?"

"Fun?" She laughs. "What are you talking about?"

"Are you . . . you know." I shift uncomfortably. I don't want to be having this conversation. "Maybe seeing someone?"

Mom looks up at me and does this thing where she stares so intensely it's like she'll never blink again. It's not aggressive, it's just very curious. "Is this for your column?" she asks finally. "Because I don't want you to mention me in it, if that's okay, honey. I completely support your writing it, I just don't love the idea of my life being out there, for—"

"It's not for the column," I interrupt, because otherwise that's going to go on forever. "I just . . . want you to be happy." It sounds forced as I say it, but Mom smiles, apparently just reading it as awkwardness.

"You're a good kid."

"That's not an answer."

"When there's an answer I feel like sharing, I'll share it," she says. "But I get to have a private life, too, you know. You don't see me asking why all those towels and a set of your sheets were in the dryer yesterday."

"I did some laundry," I said. "What's wrong with that?"

"Nothing, because it's none of my business. But you better have used protection," she adds quickly. "I think this is done." She hands me the wooden spoon, and I take it and poke at the food and taste some.

"Go sit down," I tell her. "I'll serve." I ladle the stir-fry and some rice onto plates for us and bring them to the table. We eat in relative silence, with Mom telling me how good the food is and asking about school, and me giving half-hearted replies. Her not answering my question makes it pretty clear to me she's seeing someone, and if she doesn't want to tell me yet, that's cool, but how does Pinky know? Is he watching her, too? Spying on my whole family just to have more to terrorize me with? The food isn't my best, and I finish quickly and go to my room, telling Mom I have homework.

I have a few texts on my phone. One from Charlie asking if I'm free tonight, and one from Brian asking if I'm angry at him or something. I ignore the one from Brian and text Charlie back that I have homework.

> I got something you can work on

> My mom is home

> Aw, shit. Oh well. Let's meet up again, soon. I'm really liking your column. The way you let that straight girl have it? That was AWESOME 💯

> Thanks. Sorry about tonight

And I am. It would be a great distraction to get laid tonight.

> Don't worry about it

> Here, have a little taste of what you're missing, though

> Feel free to reciprocate

He sends me a great shot of his cock, hard and pressing an outline into a pair of white boxer-briefs. Then he sends me another without the boxer-briefs. I grin but shake my head and put the phone down. I really do have homework.

I work on it for a few hours, until I hear my mom go to bed. Then I Google her to see if anything comes up, but it's all her résumé on the hospital website and medical papers I don't understand. So Pinky didn't get anything that way. How does he know more about her life than I do? Maybe I'm just a crap son who doesn't pay much attention to her.

I close my books and lie down in bed. I take out my phone and look at Charlie's photos for a while, enjoying the memory of the last time we had sex. I try texting him.

> You still up?

No response. I picture him in a jockstrap and think about maybe sending him some photos back. I strip and take a few shots. I've sent nudes before, so this isn't shocking behavior from me. I know it's not cool, and since I'm under eighteen, it could be considered child pornography, but I only send them to people who send me nudes first. I know if anyone shares the ones of me, I can share the ones of them, which I know isn't the best policy—mutually assured public nudes or whatever—but it feels more secure. Because I really don't want my nudes getting out into the world. I can only imagine what new types of gossip they would spark.

I flip through the shots I've taken, and suddenly remember the note in my drawer—the other person who wants nudes. I wonder if sending him these would stop him. Jenna says it would make it worse, but won't not sending them make it worse, too? Besides, maybe he has them already. Maybe he's bugged my phone. My arm starts to twitch and I go run some cold water on it. Then I delete the photos. They weren't flattering anyway.

24

THE ADMIN OFFICE IS A SMALL ROOM THAT SMELLS LIKE
cheap floral candles. There's a desk and one chair, and the carpet-
ing and walls are the same color of beige. There's one window,
but the shade is drawn, so the only light is from the yellow ceiling fluorescent. There's a door to another room, but it's closed,
so we're gathered in front of the desk, waiting for whoever is
going to come in to come in. Jenna is in her professional drag
again—pink slacks and a matching blazer with a white button-
down and black tie, hair up in a bun, chandelier pearl earrings.
Ben and I are less costumed up—Ben in the usual neon polo and
me in an oversized gray cardigan with black jeans and a star-
patterned tank top.

"I hate it when people aren't where you need them to be,"
Jenna sighs, looking at the clock on the wall.

Ben is texting again. It's still cute, but I'm worried it's going to go from cute to annoying soon.

"Other Ben?" I ask him.

"Sorry," he says, putting his phone away. "I know, I'm becoming one of those people. But we were just finalizing plans."

"It's okay," I say. He's not one of those people yet. "Doing anything fun?"

"After school we're going to go to the costume museum at the Fashion Institute. I want to show him some of the stuff. Then we're going to dinner at some Turkish place he loves."

"That's so cute," Jenna says. "You, then him."

"He's kind of a foodie," Ben says. "I'm worried I'm going to get fat. Fatter." He pats his belly. "And then he won't be as into me."

"Stop worrying about that," I tell him, as the door opens and a tired-looking woman with glasses walks out. "If he's into you, he's into you."

"Hi," Jenna says to the woman. "I need a paper copy of my transcripts for a study abroad program I'm applying to for the summer."

"We can email them," the woman says, sitting down and clicking a few keys on the computer.

"They want a paper copy on school stationery," Jenna says, her voice an impressive blend of authority and apology. "They're on a boat in the Mediterranean, so they don't have steady email access, and sometimes the computers go out—they like having paper."

The woman raises her eyebrows. "Exciting," she says. She doesn't sound excited. "Let me bring it up, then. Student ID?"

Jenna hands over her student ID card and the woman takes it

and starts typing. A few minutes later, she's printing out a transcript on fancy paper. She hands it to Jenna, who looks it over.

"There's a mistake," Jenna says.

The woman sighs. "What?"

"I took the papercraft art elective last year? With Nance—um, Ms. McNair. It's not on here." She hands the paper back to the woman, but the woman ignores her, squinting at the screen. She types a few more keys.

"You're not on the roster," she says.

"Are you sure?" Jenna asks. "It's Jenna, not Jen, or Jennifer. Can I see?"

"I can't show you the roster, sorry," the woman says. "But I promise there's no Jenna, Jen, or Jennifer on it."

Jenna crosses her arms and looks at us, motioning with her eyes to get behind the desk. "Then that's a mistake. How do I fix it?"

"Does the papercraft class matter that much to this application?" the woman asks as Ben, who is closer to the edge of the desk, slowly starts stepping behind it. I move closer in, trying to block the woman's field of vision.

"Of course it matters!" Jenna says, sounding offended. "These programs are very competitive, you know. And if I don't get into it, then my chances of getting into an Ivy are smaller. I thought you people cared about your students."

The woman blushes and purses her lips, glancing up at me curiously. She turns back to Jenna. "Of course we care. It's just a little paperwork error. These things happen. We'll fix it—no need to get hysterical. You just need Ms. McNair to fill out a form." She presses a few more keys. Behind her, Ben has his phone out and is zooming in on the screen. He shakes his head— it's not on the roster anymore.

"Wait, before we bother her, just check one more time," Jenna says. "Please?"

The woman sighs, presses a button, and looks at the screen. Ben nods and starts snapping photos, inching closer and closer to the computer. The woman turns around suddenly and glares at him.

"What are you doing?"

"Can I have the form?" Jenna asks, but I can already feel the chaos starting to ripple outward. I take my phone and hold it in front of the screen while the woman stares at Ben, snapping a few more photos. I snatch it back as Ben runs around to our side of the desk.

"What is going on?" the woman asks, standing. The door to the hallway opens behind us.

"Lucy? Everything okay?" We turn. It's Principal Pattyn. He sees our faces and he glares. "What's all this?"

"This student was behind my desk," the woman says. "I don't know what he was doing."

"Ben Parrish," Pattyn says, looking him over. "Detention. Today."

Ben's face instantly falls.

"That's not fair," I say quickly. "You just have her word."

"She's administration. I trust her word. Why is it every time you're around there's trouble, Jack? Or, maybe I should say drama?"

221

"What do you mean by that?" Jenna asks, getting in his face. I, of course, have taken a step back, because I'm a fucking coward and I feel slapped, like he's saying everything—Pinky—is all my fault somehow.

"And you're no better, Jenna. I think you two had better leave before you join Benjamin in detention."

Jenna glares at him, unmoving.

"Come on," Ben says, grabbing us both by the arms and dragging us out of the office. "We got what we came for."

Outside we take a breath. I lean against the wall.

Ben sighs, his head down. "I've never gotten a detention before," he says. He looks up and gives a faint smile. "At least I got the photos, though, right?"

"Yes." Jenna nods. "Sorry about having to cancel on Other Ben, though."

"Oh," he says, just realizing it. "Right."

"Sorry," I say. "Blame it on me. Say I got you in trouble and tell him I'm so, so sorry."

"It'll be fine," Ben says. "We'll just go tomorrow. If the museum is open tomorrow. I think it is. It's definitely open on Thursday. Not a big deal."

"You're way too cool about this. I'd be angry at me," I say.

"You're my best friend," Ben says. "I don't, like, love delaying my date…but this is important. I want to help you out." He sighs. "I mean, if we could put my glasses on you and you could do detention for me, I would want you to do that, but I don't see us pulling it off. So I guess I'll take the hit this time. But you owe me. Big."

I smile at him and give him a hug.

"We have to get to class," Jenna says. "Both of you email whatever photos you got."

"Okay," I say.

"Right," Ben says, and we split up and head for our classes.

I can barely focus again. I keep tapping my toe to the point where I get told to stop by all my teachers. At lunch, it's hard to read the names on our small phone screens so we agree to go over them at home—Jenna can clean up the photos on her computer and let us know the names. And luckily, Other Ben doesn't mind Ben getting a detention.

"He says I'm a bad boy," Ben says, blushing furiously while looking at his phone. Jenna and I look at each other and try not to laugh.

"Maybe he'll spank you," I say, making Ben blush even more.

"Shut up," Ben says.

I look to Jenna for a laugh, but she's staring at the photos on her phone.

"I think this is Jeremy," she says. "Yeah, one of the names is definitely Jeremy Diaz."

I sigh, suddenly not feeling like a laugh anymore. I scan the lunchroom and catch sight of Jeremy, talking with his friends, rapping the table as he speaks—one of his speeches. He catches me staring and shoots me an angry "what are you looking at?" stare, so I turn away.

"Love can make people crazy," Jenna says. "Could be him."

"Could be anyone."

At home, Jenna confirms it's Jeremy. She sends us the whole list:

Rufus Aaronson-Silver

Eloise Bachman

Leo Chu

Peter Das

Jeremy Diaz

Richard Gavallino

Hannah Ling

Kaitlyn Montenegro

Prisha Reddy

Ava Richard-Rose

Thomas Weinstein-Fuller

Parson Woolfrey

Twelve names. Only two of them already on the suspect list. Ten new people to add. I can't imagine what I could have done to them, though. Some of these names I don't even know.

> I don't think I've spoken more than two words to most of these people

> I don't even know some of these names.

> Who's Parson Woolfrey? Or Peter Das? Is this, like, Hannah Ling, annoyed about the non-fourgy I had in her hot tub?

Jenna

I thought the note talked about other guys? Doesn't that mean Pinky is a guy?

Ben

Plus she doesn't have access to backstage

Parson is a sophomore. He does some stage tech, so he does have access pretty easily...but he's also had a steady girlfriend for two years

Jenna

Peter Das is in my French class. Our year. Transfer from Boston. And I think he's bi

But I don't think we should worry about the other names. Jeremy is suspect number one now

I bring up Instagram as I text with them, searching for the names I don't know. Parson looks vaguely familiar, but Peter I don't recognize—though I think I saw his Instagram before, when looking for origami. Now I pay more attention, find a

225

selfie. He's pretty cute, actually. Short hair, parted sharply on the right but kind of messy. Black tank top. Thin but muscular arms.

Ben

But if Peter is into Jack, then that fits the whole 'love from afar turning to obsession' thing

Jenna

Jeremy is obviously more obsessed

But I can bring Peter to a smoke break tomorrow before lunch. We have French right before

Yeah. Do that. I just want to look him in the eye

Jenna

But we agree it's probably Jeremy?

Ben

Honestly—yes

Sorry Jack

I frown at the screen of my phone. I don't like the idea of it being Jeremy, but they're right. He makes the most sense now.

It's hard to imagine I broke him that badly, though. I didn't mean to. And he was the one who broke up with me. Does he really think I'm such a bad gay that he...has to hurt me? That he'd threaten me? I just can't see it. Jeremy was always opinionated—stubborn, maybe—but he never advocated violence or harassment. The worst thing he ever suggested was glitter-bombing a politician.

> Let's meet Peter. Maybe it's him, or maybe he can tell us if anyone in the class is obsessed with me or what

Jenna

Ok. Tomorrow then

> Great. So Ben, did you reschedule with Other Ben?

Ben

We made it Friday. Much more date-night-y

Jenna

And no school the next day if you're...out late

Ben

LOL. I'm not there yet

Jenna

Is he?

Ben

I...don't know

I mean, when do most guys...get intimate?

Jenna

Get intimate? Ew

Don't be mean

And it varies. But if he invites you back to his place, maybe have an excuse prepared if you're not ready

Ben

Yeah. Thanks. I just don't want to fuck this up. How many guys like him are there in the city?

Plenty

But don't worry. You won't fuck it up. Just be yourself

Jenna

And practice giving head on a banana

Ew, no

Ben

That doesn't work?

I mean...I guess?

But every banana is different, so you know, you can't practice for something until you've seen it

Jenna

He means you won't know how his dick fits in your mouth until it's in your mouth

Ben

Thx I got that

I'm going to turn off my phone now. I'm behind on some of my costume work because they wouldn't let me bring a sewing machine into detention

K. C U tomorrow

Night

I put down my phone. Then I pick it up again. I look up every-one on the list and study their faces. I linger on Jeremy's profile pic on Instagram. Little rainbow flag in the corner. His fist up in the air and lit so he could be a propaganda poster from the '30s. Join the Queer Revolution. Join us or die? Join or have your mom spied on? It can't be him. We may have different ideas about who we should be—want different things in relationships—but he never...Whoever is doing this hates me. And I don't think he does. He doesn't like me. He's angry at me. He thinks I'm awful. But he doesn't hate me.

Or maybe he does.

I go and peek outside my window, looking for anyone star-ing up at me, but there are just pedestrians walking under the electric lights. My skin starts to feel like there are worms sliding up and down it, so I take a cool shower and wash my makeup off.

When I towel off, I think about going to bed, but I catch myself in the mirror, and instead I take a few selfies—nude, but showing off my ass, not my cock. They look okay, but I delete them.

Mom doesn't get home until late, and I swear I hear some murmuring at the door before she opens it. I crack open my bedroom door and watch her come in, but I don't see anyone else outside in the hall.

"You're home late," I say from my door.

She stops dead in her tracks and stares at me. "Oh, Jack. Didn't see you there. Why are you lurking in the doorway?"

"I was just about to go to bed, but I heard you come in, so I wanted to say good night. Did you have a hot date?"

Mom smiles her unreadable doctor smile and shakes her head. "Good night, honey."

She goes to her room and closes the door.

I lie down in bed and close my eyes and try to sleep. But all I can think about is Jeremy. Jeremy folding little pieces of pink paper. Jeremy with pink-handled scissors cutting my jacket. Jeremy coming at me with a pink-bladed knife.

I take a deep breath. Then another. In-out-in-out. I count them one at a time. I fall asleep sometime after nine hundred.

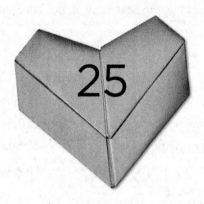

25

Dear Jack of Hearts,

So, I'm a virgin. I'm not, like, ashamed of that or
anything. Until the other night, I hadn't even kissed a
boy, because I wanted it to be special. And I know that
sounds Disney-princess stupid, but it's what I want,
or at least it's what I tell myself I want, because I also
don't think I'm exactly an ideal man or anything, and I
didn't think anyone would be into me, so saying I was
waiting, that I wanted it to be special, always felt like a
good defense—I'm a virgin because I'm a romantic.

But anyway, I've been seeing this guy. And,
girl, he's cute, and I like him, and now it's like

everything I worried about is gone—he's into
me. And I'm into him, and we kissed! And it was
special. But now I'm worried about other firsts. I...
once gave a blowjob to some rando, but it was for
like ten seconds, so it doesn't count. But this guy
I'm seeing—we haven't talked too much about it, but
he's not a virgin. I'm positive. For one thing, he's
so hot—and hot people are never virgins. But for
another, he's said some stuff...he's implied, I guess,
that he's not a virgin. And now we're starting to
get pretty serious, and like, I haven't told him I'm
a virgin, and I don't know what he expects from
me on the third date or whenever, and I don't know
how to tell him I want to take it slow because I'm a
virgin without losing his interest. I don't want him
to think I'm a prude and I won't put out—I totally
will—but I'm not going to strip down and give him
the orgasm of his life any time soon, either. Do I not
tell him and play coy? Do I just put out the moment
he makes a move? How do I do this without losing
this guy? 'Cause I really like him.

Sincerely,
Virgin Territory

I try not to look up at Ben as I read his Jack of Hearts letter off my phone. We're waiting in the park for Jenna and Peter, and

I'm going through the emails, deleting the occasional ones that say fag and hoping there won't be anything from Pinky. There isn't. But the one from Ben makes me smile. I almost want to turn to him and hug him and tell him he's amazing and it's going to be okay, but he wanted this to be anonymous, so I'm going to try to respect that. Instead, I take out my compact and check my eyeliner. No wings today, very subtle lines, but in blue. I look pretty good. Peter could be Pinky, but if he's not, he's still cute.

"How will you know if it's him?" Ben asks. We're on the bench in the park, staring at one of those bouncy horse things. It was yellow but it's chipped and faded now.

"I don't know..." I say. I take out my cigarettes, I don't care that it's not Monday. "I don't know how I'll know it's anyone. I've been getting so paranoid lately. Watching everyone, looking for something in the way they look at me—like I'll know some-how. But I won't." I take a cigarette out of the box and stick it in my mouth, then light it. The smell of the match lingers for a moment before the tobacco overwhelms it. "I used to feel like everyone—well, not everyone, but a lot of people—were talking about me, watching me, to gossip and stuff. And that...wasn't great, but I could live with it. This is..." I inhale deeply and blow out a plume of smoke.

"Are you saying you can't live with it now?" Ben asks, his voice trembling a little.

"I..." I think about what he's saying. "I just want it to stop," I say finally.

"Okay, that's an answer that makes me worry," he says, standing up and looking down at me. "What do you mean?"

"Calm down," I tell him. "I don't mean it like that. I'm not going to . . . how would I, even?" But I know that one. I've known since sixth grade. Pills. Mom has a whole bunch of sleeping pills in her medicine cabinet.

"You promise?"

"Yeah," I say. I think most closeted kids know how they'd do it, but the fact that I remember it now isn't a good feeling. I swallow and lick my lips. It's just because Ben asked. It's not the sort of thing people forget, right?

I look up as I hear the park gate creak open. Jenna is leading in Peter. He looks like his Instagram photos, but now he's wearing a black blazer over an artfully torn green sweater. I can see patches of his stomach through the holes.

"Fellas, this is Peter. Peter, this is Ben and Jack."

Peter extends his hand and I stand to shake it. I look him dead in the eye. His irises are brown, almost bronze. There's nothing malicious in them, and his handshake is warm. But what the fuck do I know, right?

"So which one of them did you want to set me up with?" Peter asks with a smirk.

"What?" Jenna asks.

"The smoke break invitation . . . two handsome gay dudes waiting for me."

"I have a boyfriend," Ben says proudly.

Jenna raises an eyebrow. "Is that official?"

"What?" Ben asks, sitting back down. I turn away from Peter to look at Ben. He looks like Jenna slapped him.

"Sorry," Jenna says quickly. "I just mean...like, putting a label on things usually means you talked about it."

"I guess I just thought..." Ben says. "When should we talk about it?"

"Whenever," I say, sitting down and putting my hand on his shoulder. "Seriously. If you want him to be your boyfriend, you tell him you want him to be your boyfriend, and what that means to you. He's clearly into you, with all these dates you're going on."

"Yeah," Peter says, sitting on the other side of Ben. "I mean, I don't know who this guy is, or what your situation is, but there's nothing wrong with saying you want him to be your boyfriend. Worst case he says he's not there yet."

I look past Ben at Peter, who looks up at me and winks. Like, actually winks. And I hate him, because it's fucking hot.

"Okay," Ben says. "Maybe over dinner on Friday. I'll just ask him if we're there yet."

"Sorry," Jenna says, taking out her e-cig. "Didn't mean to cause a crisis."

"That's okay," Ben says quickly, shaking his head. "I'm just... being dumb."

"Sounds like you're really into him," Peter says. "So I guess I'm here to meet you, Jack."

"I'm not trying to set you up," Jenna says. "And Jack isn't the dating type."

"Neither am I," Peter says, smiling, his eyes still locked on me.

I decide right then that he's not Pinky, because it's pretty obvious we're going to fuck at some point, and I'm looking forward to it, so if he was obsessed with me or whatever, all he'd have to do is what he just did—which he probably could have done whenever, and I'd be heels over head for him.

"Here." Peter fishes out his phone and hands it to me. "Give me your number."

I enter mine and hand it back, and he types something. My phone vibrates. When I take it out I have a text message from an unknown number—just a winky face.

I look up at him and he winks again. Fucking flirt.

Jenna sits down next to me and nudges me with her elbow. I look over at her and she raises her eyebrows in a question. I shake my head, but then shrug. Maybe it is him. I just really hope not. Because the five minutes I've spent flirting with him have Pinky fading from memory really quick.

"So you're the Jack who writes the column?" Peter asks.

"That's me, professional slut," I say. "But not a sex worker," I quickly add. "Not that there's anything wrong with that."

"Wait, are you getting paid? Because if so, Jenna, I'm pretty slutty, too."

"No payment but the pleasure of knowing he's helping the sexually frustrated and curious," Jenna says.

"Sexually innocent," Ben says. "That sounds better."

Jenna smirks. "Sure."

"Well, I think the column is cool. And I loved your rant at the straight girl who wrote in. That was pretty hot."

"Hot?"

"Yeah, just watching a queer dude really lay into someone about their straight privilege…it's hot. I'm not sure what Jenna told you, but being bisexual, I deal with both the straight privilege and the gay erasure stuff. 'Bisexuality is just a phase,' and so forth."

"Ugh, I can't even imagine," I say. "Straight people are the worst."

"Totally," Jenna says. "We suck."

"You're an honorary queer," I tell her.

"That come with a title or a medal or something?" she asks, taking a drag of her e-cig.

"Sure," Peter says. "I dub thee Lady Jenna of the Straight-But-Not-Narrow."

We all laugh. I stare at Peter over Ben's head, and he stares right back.

"We should get back," Ben says. "Class and all."

"Right, right," Peter says. "Educating our nubile young brains." He wiggles his eyebrows, which, again, shouldn't work— and yet. How the fuck have I not slept with this guy already?

We head back to school, where Jenna and Ben peel off for class, but Peter stays with me as I go to my locker for a book.

"So," he says once we're alone. "You want to hang out sometime?"

"Hang out?" I ask.

"Naked," he says seriously.

"Sounds fun," I say, opening up my locker. "I'll text you if my mom is going to be home late to—" My words fade off as a pink note drops out of my locker. It's shaped like a lizard. I quickly bend down and pick it up, then shove it in my pocket without opening it.

"What was that?"

"Just a...nothing," I say. Does Pinky somehow know the moments I'm going to be feeling good, feeling like myself again, and time it so his notes ruin them? Because flirting with Peter, I forgot about Pinky, just for a few minutes, and now all the memories come crashing back like the school is falling down around me.

"Love note?" Peter asks.

"No," I say quickly. I force myself to smile, I grab out for the feeling I had just a moment ago, where I was sexy and fun and slutty and loving it, and not being slowly imprisoned in pink construction paper.

"So tonight maybe?" Peter asks.

"Yeah." I grin and he leans in, really close, like he's going to kiss me, but hugs me instead. His hand wanders south and gives my ass a firm squeeze.

"Looking forward to it," he whispers, and then he's released me and is down the hall. His scent lingers, though. Sort of like a thunderstorm smell mixed with hair product and the smell of sex. I watch Peter leave, but as he does, he passes by Jeremy, at his own locker, who's glaring at me. He catches me catching him and looks away, slamming his locker closed.

I sigh and duck into the closest bathroom, which has some guys in it, so I hide in a stall and pull out the pink note, my back crawling like it's infested with maggots or something. Like I'm the walking dead.

Jack,

Where are my nudes? I hope you're just taking time to make them SUPER sexxxy.

Is your mom as open about her romantic life as you? Do you think her hospital would like to know her the way I know you? Would she like being the talk of the town? Star of gossip? Because I can't decide. I hope she wouldn't get in trouble, because of who her boyfriend is. What do you think? And then there are your friends. Ben has a new boyfriend. Also named Ben—tacky. But did you know his boyfriend Ben has a grindr account? There are some very naughty photos up there. He has a BIG dick. Think if I sent your friend those photos and told him they were sent to me, his boyfriend's OTHER boyfriend, that he would be ok w/that? First love is so delicate. That's why I'm happy I'm not your first, Jack. I know you can handle anything I do to you. But Jenna—I don't know. Do you think if I sent her an alert about a bombing where her mom is that she'd freak out? What if I sent her a bunch of them, all the time? Alert after alert. Your mom is dead. Your mom is dead. She'd know they were fake, right? Or would she wonder if one of them was real? Every day. That could be stressful. This is why I'm so happy we're together, Jack. Because when I think about you, I don't have to think about doing these things. Your photos will make me feel like we're together. So you better send them quick. I don't want to get upset.

And Jack, since you're my boyfriend now, you need to stop sleeping with other guys. Just me from now on, ok? I love you.

26

Dear Virgin Territory,

Your virginity is your business. You don't have to tell the guy you're seeing—ever. Your sexual history—whether a blank page or a rap sheet forty pages long, like mine—is not for anyone else to know unless you want it to be. Not even potential naked buddies. The only exception is if you have something contagious—then you need to tell them beforehand and use condoms and whatever else will make sure you don't infect them. But if you're free and clear, then you don't ever need to tell him you're inexperienced.

*If you want to go slow, you just tell him you want
to go slow. That might be related to your virginity
in your mind, but he doesn't need to know why you
want to go slow—he just has to respect it. And if he
doesn't, he's scum and you should exit, ASAP.*

*But maybe you **want** to tell him you're a virgin.
That's totally cool, too. You can tell him so he knows
you might be a little clumsy the first time (though
maybe not—you could be a natural), or maybe
you're worried you'll come too fast, or not at all,
or some other thing, or you just want to tell him
because you feel close to him and want him to know
about you. People in relationships often talk about
their past relationships once they feel secure.*

*The first time I got naked with another boy, I told
him—but I told him right then. We were down to
our underwear and making out and his hand was
pulling my briefs down and I said, "Just so you
know, I've never been naked with another guy," and
he said, "Do you want to be?" and I said, "Fuck
yeah," and then we were, and I sucked my first
cock and got mine sucked for the first time (and
then we did both at the same time) and it was a lot
of fun and he was extra careful when he heard my
breathing speed up—he would stop and give me a*

minute so I didn't come too quick. But, that's me, and I've never had much interest in going slow.

It sounds like you really like this guy and want to take it easy. So, if you're feeling like you want to tell him—not that you have an obligation to—then I think the right time is when you're alone. Maybe you're kissing, making out a little—but clothes still on. And then you say to him, "Hey, I want to tell you something," and he'll probably say what, and you say, "You're really special to me, but I want you to know I'm a virgin. So I'm kind of nervous about getting naked too quickly." And if he's a decent guy, he'll just smile and say, "That's cool, we can go as slow as you like," and kiss you again, and if he's not a decent guy he'll say, "I was really hoping to get laid tonight, so either take off your pants or I'm going to get on Grindr." Or some variation. If he's a really good guy, he'll try to make sure your first time is special.

Tell him what you need to feel ready to fuck—maybe monogamy, or some specific language for the relationship. He might also wait for a sign from you—you may have to tell him when you're ready to go all the way, because he won't make the first move to take off your pants once he knows.

Just remember, there's always a chance he won't be
into being your first, in which case he wasn't meant
to be your first—but don't compromise on what's
going to make you want to punch that v-card just to
make sure it's him who does the punching.

—Jack of Hearts

I shove the pink note in the drawer of my desk with the other one once I'm home. It could all be lies—why would my mom having a boyfriend make her the talk of the hospital, after all? I've been obsessing over it all day, wondering if Pinky knows something I don't—he seems to think he does—and what it could be. And there are the other threats, too. So maybe Other Ben has a Grindr account with some X-rated photos—so what? But I know if Ben sees them, if they're sent to him with the right note, he could start obsessing, spiraling out of control, feeling like Other Ben is lying, cheating, something. I think I could talk him down from that. It would be bad for a while, but fixable. I think. Ben could still get his fairy-tale romance. The worst threat was probably against Jenna. She doesn't talk about it much, but back in fifth grade, she told me whenever her mom goes away for a story, she checks the internet every day for where she is. She went to a shrink all through junior high because she had nightmares about her mom being killed. A single text saying her mom could be dead would probably stress her out for a week. A barrage of them could easily crack her. Pinky knows us, that's for sure. I don't know what he knows about my mom exactly, but the other threats are scary enough on their own.

I wonder if I should warn Ben and Jenna—if preparing them for their fears coming to life would make them able to handle them. I pick up my phone and think about texting them, but don't. I don't want them to blame me for being targets. It's selfish, I know, but I'll just have to make sure Pinky doesn't do anything to them. I'll just have to find him.

Mom texts me to say not to wait up, so I can't ask her about a boyfriend. I think about going to the hospital, asking her there, maybe spying a little, but if things at work are as crazy as she says, then I'll just get in her way, and when I think about a guy with a sponge in his stomach or dying from a surgery gone wrong, my little pink notes pale in comparison. Could be worse, right?

So instead, I text Peter. Because I deserve some distraction. Because at this point the only real suspect I have left is Jeremy, and I don't want to think about that. I don't want to consider what it is I've done that could have made him like this. And because I don't think Jeremy would actually hurt anyone.

I know the last note said I couldn't fuck anyone anymore, but I can't let him scare me. And besides, how is he going to know? I closed my blinds, and Peter is new. Maybe I'm just helping him with his homework.

Though, in fairness, we haven't really eliminated Peter—my libido has. I just can't imagine someone as smooth as he is doing all this, though. I can't see any plan where this gets him anything he couldn't have gotten so much easier. Unless what he wanted was for me to suffer. But I didn't know him before today. Why would he want that? I text him.

My mom says she's going to be out late

What's your address?

I don't know if it was because of how badly I needed it, or because Peter is just really skilled, but after, as we lie on the floor, I can feel my whole body uncoiling, and the stress that was trapped in it evaporating.

"I think that's all I got left in me," he says, wiping sweat off his face and grabbing a sheet from my bed to wipe himself down.

"Me too," I say. "But I think three rounds is enough."

"For any healthy American teenager, anyway." He grins. I like his grin. He can't be Pinky.

He rolls on top of me and starts kissing down my chest.

"I thought you were running on empty," I say.

"I am, but I still want to appreciate this while I have it in front of me."

"We can do it again, you know," I say.

He stops kissing, rolls back so he's next to me. "You're not asking me out, right? Because I was serious when I said I wasn't a relationship kind of guy."

"So was I," I tell him, propping myself up on one elbow to look at him. "Monogamy, relationships...maybe later, like, after college. But for now I just like sex. And I thought we just did it pretty well. So I am up for a repeat, no strings attached."

"Are you sure?" He narrows his eyes at me. "I mean, I thought that, based on your columns, but someone is slipping little pink origami notes in your locker."

I roll onto my back. "Trust me when I say I wish they wouldn't."

"Ex?"

I let that spin on my tongue for a moment. "Anonymous," I say finally. I look at him. "It's not you, is it?"

He laughs. "I only just met you for real today. I mean, I've seen you in the hallway before, thought you were hot, but... that's not my style. And I'm awful at origami."

"Yeah?"

"Nance may have called me her biggest disappointment."

I laugh. I hadn't considered people being good or bad at origami. Maybe Nance could recognize Pinky from their work? The idea sounds insane, but I file it away for later, anyway. I'd have to find a way to show her the origami without letting her read the note. I couldn't stand it if Nance looked at me the way Pattyn did.

"Where'd you go?" Peter asks, and I realize I'm staring at him. "You're not gazing lovingly at me, right?"

"Get over yourself," I say, smiling.

"It's just...there was this girl in Boston, and I thought we were great—friends who fucked sometimes. And I fucked other people, too, and she seemed okay with it, but it turned out she was only okay with me fucking dudes. She freaked out when she found out I was sleeping with women, too. And we fought and now we don't talk, and it sucks because I liked her—I just didn't want to be anyone's boyfriend."

"Seriously," I say. "I'm the same as you. Promise. I'm only going to be jealous if you're fucking the guy I want to be fucking. And even then I'll just ask for the details after."

Peter laughs, waves me off. "You should just ask to join in."

"Open invitation," I say, and kiss his neck. "I will keep that in mind."

"So you're not a romantic like your friend?"

"Ben?" I grin. "Ben has been waiting for this forever. But my mom, she told me something once when I asked her why she'd never gotten married. I was little, but it's one of those things that stuck with me, and she said she'd never found the right guy at the right time. I like that. She was focused on her career and didn't want to get married. Right now I'm focused on..."

"The D?" Peter suggests.

I laugh and grab a pillow off the bed to hit him with. "My life," I say. "I don't want a boyfriend. Maybe in a decade."

"What if you find the right guy before then?" he asks, looking at me. His eyes have flecks of bright yellow in them.

"Then hopefully I'll find him again in a decade," I say. "Or I'll find some other Mr. Right. There can't be just one."

"I know, right? Whenever people talk about soul mates I actively want to start trolling them with questions about it. I hate that idea so—" He stops as there's the sound of the front door slamming. He looks at me, confused. "I thought your mom wouldn't be home until late."

"Fuck," I say. I look for my phone among the pile of sheets and clothing on the floor. Peter starts getting dressed. My phone is still in my pants pocket. I have another text from Mom.

> Will be home earlier than expected! 💯

I immediately start putting my clothes on.

"Jack?" Mom calls from outside my room. "You home?"

"Just a sec, Mom," I yell back. Peter stares at me, gives me a "what do I do?" look, and I just shake my head. I throw my sheets in a pile on the bed as Mom knocks on my door.

"Mom, I have a friend over," I say through the door. There's a pause. Somehow I can hear the expression on her face. I look over at Peter, who's gotten his clothes on, and shrug apologetically. He smiles—this is funny to him, now that he's dressed. I open the door. My mom is standing right up against it, her expression matching Peter's.

"Hi," she says, her voice innocent. She looks past me at Peter, who waves. "I'm Jack's mom, Ruth."

"Hi," Peter says, and to my relief no one offers to shake hands. Peter hasn't washed his yet. "I'm Peter."

"Nice to meet you. Come on out. I bought groceries, which, I don't know what Jack's told you, but it's a rare occurrence. I'm going to cook. Also a rare occurrence. Stay for dinner." She smiles and walks back to the kitchen. I follow her, Peter behind me.

"That's really sweet of you to offer," Peter says. "But I'd better get home. My mom is expecting me."

"Oh, come on," Mom says, taking a bunch of scallions and chopping them. She still has this look of amusement on her face, and it's almost making me want to laugh, except I'm also mortified. "I'm sure your mom won't mind. And it would be so nice to get to know you better."

"Mom," I almost shout. "He says he needs to go, so he needs to go, okay?" I look over at Peter and try to apologize with my eyes.

"Oh, all right, if you say so, honey," Mom says. "Too bad. I had so many questions."

"I can answer them," I say. Peter is heading back to my room and grabbing his bag. I follow him.

"Sorry," I whisper.

"She's kinda funny, but I don't want to be the prop for her comedy tonight."

"Yeah," I say, not quite getting it. "So . . . goodbye?"

"I'll text you," he says, shrugging his bag onto his shoulder. "We're going to do this again, right?"

"Oh yeah," I say, and realize I didn't whisper that and immediately turn to look out my open bedroom door. My mother is chopping vegetables with feigned innocence.

I walk Peter to the door, where he smiles at me and waves goodbye to Mom.

"So nice meeting you, Peter," Mom says in a syrupy voice. I sigh, and Peter looks embarrassed for me as he leaves and I close the door behind him.

Mom is now setting a pot of water to boil and a steamer over it. I walk over to her and glare.

"Not fun having your love life interrogated, is it?" she asks without looking at me.

"That's what that was about?"

"Oh, come on," she says, turning and grinning. "I wasn't that bad at all. I could have been so much worse. Asking how long you've been seeing each other, saying I was so happy to meet your boyfriend—"

"He's not my boyfriend," I say quickly.

"Or I could have asked you about this in front of him." She pulls a pink envelope out of her pocket. Suddenly the sound of the fire under the pot of water gets loud, like, furnace, blowtorch, burning-city loud. That and the beating of my heart are the only things I can hear. My mom's mouth is still moving, though. And it's like the burning, beating sounds are in an echo chamber—they're way too loud and my hands are shaking-crawling-covered in bugs.

"Where did you get that?" I ask. I realize a moment later I've interrupted her.

"It was taped to the door," Mom says, shrugging. "Secret admirer?"

"N-no," I stammer. "You haven't read it, have you?"

"Of course not." She frowns at me. "I would never. I guess whoever wrote this for you must like you a lot to tape it to the door, though. I thought all kids did today was text. A real written love letter…" She takes a wooden spoon out of a drawer and stirs the water with it, then taps it on the side of the pot. "Anyway, it seems special, is all I'm saying. May be worth it to try to make something more long-lasting with whomever sent it."

She holds the letter out to me and waves it in the air when I won't take it.

"Oh, come on," she says. "Romance isn't all bad."

I snatch the letter from her and put it in my pocket in one quick motion. Every part of me is twitching.

"I'm going to take a shower before dinner," I say.

"Probably a good idea." She turns back to the pot and starts pouring rice into it. I run back to my bedroom. A note on the door. I can't decide if opening or not opening it is better. I take it out of my pocket and hold it in both hands, but just with my fingertips, because I don't want to be in too much contact with it. Pinky was at my house. At my front door. Maybe—probably—while I was having sex with Peter. Did he hear us? Did he like it, or did it make him angry? Is he going to terrorize Peter now, too?

I feel my brain flooding with more questions, more fear, and they crawl out of my ears like bugs. I tear open the envelope. The pink note inside is shaped like a flower, but flattened. And there are two photos, too. Pictures of my mom, walking with some guy in scrubs. They're holding hands. She looks really happy. The photos look like they were taken near her hospital, on the street. She's holding an iced latte—she drinks those even when it's cold. In the second photo she's sipping from it and the guy is also really happy. He's younger than her, a big guy, with brown hair. He looks nice. This should make me feel good, but these photos are worse than just a note. I can hear my heart pounding as I unfold the flower. On one side is a typed note:

Jack
I'm sorry. Maybe I'm coming on too strong for you. But I really like you, Jack, and I know we're meant to Be Together. That's why I need you to stop sleeping with other boys. To stop ignoring my request for photos of you. When you do that, it makes me so angry, and I do things, like cut your jacket. It's really your fault for making me so angry. How can I help it, when I love you so much? I don't want to have to get mad, Jack. I love you so much. Please stop making me mad, and send me the photos. Then I can forgive you.

But then, on the other side, scribbled in pen, is another message:

I CAN HEAR YOU.

With Peter, I assume he means. He heard me and Peter having sex. We weren't exactly quiet about it. And now...I don't know what's going to happen. There's nothing in either note about the photos. They're just there, proving how he knows something about my mom that I don't. Something he's going to act on now that I've "cheated" on him with Peter. I can feel my heart racing and I make myself take a large gulp of air, but it doesn't feel like enough. My skin is crawling again, too—bugs racing over it.

I throw it all into the drawer with the others, and shove them to the back, so you can't see them when you open it. Then I stand under the cold water in the shower until it calms my body down, but it doesn't help my brain. How could he have gotten in? We have a doorman, but he lets in delivery guys without buzzing us. Maybe Pinky had a plastic bag of food and pretended to deliver something. That's how I'd do it. There's a camera in the lobby, too...but if I ask to see the footage, the doorman will tell Mom, and then she'll ask why and she already saw the note and isn't dumb, so she'll figure it out. Then she'll ask questions, and I don't want that. I don't need her knowing that she's being stalked because of me.

And the worse question: How is he going to punish me?

"Jack? Dinner's almost ready." Mom knocks on the bathroom door. I'm shivering. I don't know how long I've been in here. I turn the water off and take a deep, slow breath. I look in the mirror and towel off. I look pale, and my makeup is running, so I wipe it off and quickly put some eyeliner on, just so Mom doesn't see how...wrong I look right now.

I feel like there are two Jacks. Jack before the notes, and Jack now, and they feel so different, I don't know how Mom hasn't noticed.

I go out into the kitchen and Mom is spooning the rice into two bowls.

"All right," I say, sitting down, trying to sound normal. "What gives? Why are you home so early, and why are you cooking? That's my job."

Mom laughs. It's easy to impersonate old Jack. I was him, after all. I can't blame her for not noticing when I'm so good at hiding.

"I thought I had a meeting, but it was rescheduled, and because I'd planned for it, I got out so early...I just thought it would be nice."

I smile, eat some of the food. I can tell it smells good, tastes good, but the flavors don't bring enjoyment like they should. "Well, it is nice," I say. "Though you need more salt."

"I'm watching my sodium," she says. "I'm not a teenager."

"Fine," I say. "Want to watch TV?"

"Sure, honey." We turn on the TV and flip channels until we find an old black-and-white screwball comedy, and I lay my head on Mom's shoulder as we watch and eat, plates in our laps. She doesn't ask about the note, which I'm grateful for.

"I'm glad you could come home early," I say.

She strokes my head. "I'm glad, too, honey. You all right?"

I want to tell her everything. It's on my tongue and about to pour out of me like melted ice cream. But I remember the photos and how she could get in trouble in ways I don't understand, and I don't want her to know about it. I need to keep her safe from all this.

"I'm just tired," I say. "I should go to bed."

"Okay," Mom says, and kisses me on the forehead. I go into my bedroom and turn out the lights. I strip for bed, but then, instead, I take a few photos. I use shadows to cover my dick and my asshole, and I tilt my head, so it's also obscured, or in profile—a photo where if you knew it was me you'd recognize me, but where if it got out, someone who saw it might go, "Is it him?" and look at it a while before deciding it was. I try to make myself pose sexy, too, like those classy nudes you see in fashion magazines, and not straight-up porn. I go through them and pick out my three favorites. They're not the best nudes I've ever taken—I look dead in the eyes in all of them—but they're good enough.

I send them to Pinky.

Then I go to the bathroom and spend a good few minutes throwing up.

27

Dear Jack of Hearts,

*I think something is wrong with me. I don't want to
have sex. With anyone. And it's all everyone talks
about. Which boy is cute, who's done what with
whom. It freaks me out. I feel like I'm missing a
piece, or maybe I'm broken or something. I want to
want people—guys, girls, I don't care. I just want
to want sex, to see why everyone else is always
talking about it. But I can't seem to make myself. I
look at movie stars, and porn, and I can objectively
acknowledge these people are attractive, but the
thought of doing anything with them? No, thank
you. It's not fear, to be clear, it's just sort of like*

*light revulsion. Like eating spiders. I don't want to
do that. I suppose I could, but I seriously doubt I
would enjoy that. But everyone around me is eating
spiders or talking about spiders they want to eat or
something, and I just sit there, alone, and I feel like
I'm not even a real person because of it. How do I
fix this?*

—Wanting to Want

I don't tell Jenna and Ben. They ask if I hooked up with Peter and I tell them I did, and pretend to be old Jack, and wiggle my eyebrows and bite my lip when they ask me how it was.

"So he's off the table as—" She cuts herself off with a yawn. "Sorry. Didn't get much sleep last night."

"Why not?" I ask, my heartbeat a heavy thud.

"I got this text around eleven—it looked like a news alert, but I didn't know the number. And it said there'd been a bombing at the embassy where my mom is doing her interview, so I, of course, get thrown into a panic. Dad is with Mom right now, too. So I check the news, and call her, but she doesn't pick up, so I call her work, and the hotel, and it takes, like, an hour, during which I'm just panicking, freaking out, ugly-crying hard. But then Mom called back. No bombing. Everything was fine. But of course, after that it takes me another few hours to get to sleep. It must have been a bad alert or something. Someone better get fired for it, anyway."

I purse my lips and stare at her. This is clearly Pinky, but I don't know if I should tell her. Is it better or worse if she knows she's a target?

"Anyway," she says. "You're sure Peter isn't Pinky, then?"

"Yeah," I say. "There's no way."

"You have proof?" Ben asks.

I look down. The note being taped to the front door is proof.

"What is it?" Jenna asks.

I bite my lip, but don't say anything. I know they've been helping me, but photos on the door is a new line, and I don't want them crossing it with me. I don't want them to know I sent Pinky the photos.

"Jack, what happened?" Jenna asks. I also don't want to be alone with it, though. I can feel my old-Jack face slipping.

"Pinky left a note on my front door," I say. Fuck, I am so selfish. May as well be *asking* Pinky to keep torturing them. "While I was with Peter. He couldn't have done it."

"What?" Jenna slams the table. "And you weren't going to tell us?"

"It had pictures of my mom...with some guy. Her boyfriend, maybe?" I can feel my voice shaking. I focus on trying to be old Jack, smiling Jack, but it's not working. "And the note was... different. Like, apologetic, almost. But it didn't mention the photos." I don't talk about the other side of the note—"I CAN HEAR YOU"—or how my fucking Peter is probably why Jenna was terrorized last night. It's Pinky showing he's not afraid to follow through on his threats. I'm not telling her, I realize. I'm not

259

going to tell her because I can't let it happen again. Just telling them this much was cruel.

"This is too far," Jenna says. "We're going to the cops."

"No," I say quickly. "If the guy Mom is with is someone who can get her in trouble at the hospital, then the cops will definitely fuck that up for her. I don't want her relationship screwed because of me. She looked really happy in the photos."

Jenna crosses her arms, and I can feel her glaring through the sunglasses.

"Then what are you going to do?" Ben asks. "Just...what, send him photos? Give in? Confront him?"

"Who?" I ask.

"Well, it has to be Jeremy, right?" Ben says. "There's no one else on the list. Unless it's a girl."

"A girl would have to be pretty insane to think she could blackmail him into being straight or whatever," Jenna says.

"Maybe if I do give him the photos..." I say, wondering how they'd react if they knew I already had. Ben looks away and Jenna's face goes hard.

"Absolutely not," she says, leaning forward. "This is too much. And I love you. And even if you hate me, I need to protect you. So, you'd better talk to Jeremy or whoever, and get this to stop. Because I'm going to tell my dad, and we're going to go to the cops."

"Please," I whisper. "If you go to the police, he'll win."

"No," she says. "Everyone will lose. Dad gets home this weekend. I'm talking to him then. I get what you're saying about your mom, and I like your mom. But I like you more."

260

I look down at the lunch table. I know Jenna means well, but it feels like she's turning against me.

"Wait," Ben says. "Is Peter going to be okay? Will Pinky target him?"

"I thought about that...but I don't know how to ask. Pinky knew when I fucked Charlie, too. I...could text him."

I take out my phone and text Charlie.

> This is going to sound weird, but you haven't gotten any pink origami lately, have you?

I stare at my phone, but there's no immediate response.

"Do you have any plans?" Jenna asks.

"I'm going to talk to Nance," I say. "I should have done it last period, but I didn't want to in front of people. I'm going to ask her who could create origami so nice. I have the flower from last night in my bag."

"But it's pretty obviously Jeremy," Ben says. His phone beeps, but he ignores it. "Why don't you want to admit that?"

"You can text Other Ben," I say. I can tell he wants to, but he keeps staring at me with big puppy eyes. "I just don't think it's him."

"You haven't really spoken with him since freshman year," Jenna says. "You don't know him anymore. You don't know who he's turned into."

I sigh. I look down at my meal—a bottle of water. I'm not hungry at all. Ben takes out his phone and texts something, smiling.

I watch him, and I feel this angry jealousy, which I hate myself for feeling. But there's Ben, getting everything he wants. Maybe I should have been like him, should have been a good gay boy, who never kissed on the first date and...no. I can't think like that. I look up at Jenna, who's watching me stare at Ben.

"This is Pinky's fault," she says, reading my mind.

"So..." Ben says, looking up. "Can I ask something non-Pinky related?"

"Of course," I say. "Please. There's nothing talking about him is going to do except make my skin twitch."

Jenna leans back in her chair and bites into a carrot stick.

"Are we going to the party at Evie Kurtz's this weekend?"

"I..." I'd forgotten. "If you want."

Jenna and Ben look at each other, and I can't tell exactly what they're thinking. "What?" I say. "I shouldn't go to parties? You told me I had to make him mad—keep writing the column, get him to send me more notes, don't be afraid, live your life, Jack!" I'm yelling a little, so I take a large gulp of water.

"You're right," Jenna says. "You can't ignore him till he goes away...but you shouldn't be afraid of him, either."

I am. But I don't say it.

"Can Ben come to our pregame meet-up?" Ben asks.

"Sure," Jenna says. "We'll do it at my place since Evie's place is downtown, right?"

"Yeah," I say. "Sure."

My phone buzzes in my pocket. I take it out—a reply from Charlie.

> No pink origami, sorry. Unless that's like a sex thing?
> You asking me to come over in my uniform and fold your
> legs?

Ben reads over my shoulder. I sigh. At least that means I'm the only target.

> Sorry, no

"You're turning him down?" Ben asks.

"I have a lot of homework."

Ben and Jenna exchange a look again and I stand up. "I'm going to go talk to Nance," I tell them, and walk away before they can respond. I know I'm being a bad friend, walking out on the conversation, but Jenna is threatening to tell the cops, which would be awful, and Ben is so wrapped up in his new love life. And I keep involving them in this by telling them what Pinky does.

I need to get away from them. For a little while, anyway. And maybe it would be better this way. They wouldn't be targets if they weren't my friends.

The art room is empty and the lights are out. It smells like clay and glue, which is sort of nice, musty and warm. I set down my bag and sit on one of the stools, looking at the paint- and glaze-stained wooden tables. I take the origami flower out of my bag and study it. It's crumpled, but the creases are sharp and it folds back into place easier than it should. A pink flower. In another life, I would have thought it was gorgeous. Might have tried wearing it in my hair, or at least pinned to a jacket.

The lights are flicked on and Nance walks in. She's in a gray pinstripe suit with clay stains around the sleeve cuffs, and a black T-shirt for a metal band I don't know.

"You just had art," she says. "Did you forget something?"

I hold out the flower to her. "Do you know who could have made this? It...it was better before I undid it, and it's been in my bag all day. But it was a really nice flower."

Nance tries to take it from me, but I pull it back—I don't want her to read it. She looks me up and down. "What is this about?"

"I just...I need to know who made this. I think it was someone in your papercraft class. Was it Jeremy? Can you tell?"

Nance looks down at the flower. "The folds are crisp, exact...." She shakes her head. "I don't know, Jack. Why are you asking me this?"

I put the flower in my bag. I should have known this would be a dead end. Who can tell who folded paper?

"Jack," Nance says, and then she reaches out and delicately puts her fingers under my chin and raises my head so I'm looking at her. She has the hands of a sculptor—they're forceful but gentle. "Jack," she says again. "What's wrong?"

And I don't know what it is, maybe just too long living with this, maybe Jenna's ultimatum, or how Pinky tortured her all night and I didn't tell her, or maybe it's the feeling that my friends can't help me anymore, but the story starts to spill out of me. The first note, the second, the third, the email, the jacket, the note on the door. I don't talk about my mom, or that I sent the nudes, but I tell Nance how Pinky demanded them. I tell her how Pattyn won't do anything. I tell her that I don't want to tell the police because the police would never believe a slut like me.

"Pattyn knows about this?"

I nod and wipe my eyes. I'm crying. I don't know when I started, but my hands come away with smeared eyeliner, and I hardly put any on this morning.

"That asshole," she hisses. Then she looks back at me, and she hugs me close, for a long time. I don't think a teacher has ever hugged me before. It's probably considered inappropriate behavior. But Nance's hug is like her hands, and I feel my emotions being molded, calmed. I take a deep breath and she lets me go.

"I . . ." She tilts her head. "Go to the bathroom, clean yourself up, fix your makeup," she says. She grabs a piece of paper and a marker, writes FREE SCULPT, and pins it to the door. "I'll be back in a bit," she says to me, and then she marches out.

I watch her go with an empty but relieved feeling. And then I go to the bathroom. I wash my face. I examine myself in the mirror and take out my eyeliner. I hear voices that I recognize in the girls' bathroom next door. Apparently the reprieve from Jack gossip has ended.

"I saw him talking with that new student, the one from Boston, in the hall."

"Well, he's barking up the wrong tree, then. Peter hooked up with Hannah Ling a few months ago."

"He's been wearing so little makeup this week. I barely recognized him."

"Maybe he's trying to butch up for a new boyfriend."

"He doesn't have boyfriends, Kaitlyn."

"Maybe he does now."

"I'll believe it when I see it. What I want to know is what his friend—the little one—is designing for us to wear onstage. Maybe all three of us will match."

"We're just in the chorus, Ava, calm down."

"Still, I want to look good out there. They should get Jack to do our makeup."

"Stage makeup is different. You have to be able to see it from the back row."

"So not so different for you."

Laughter from two voices.

"Don't be a bitch, Kaitlyn."

"You know I love you, girl."

"You think he's going to fuck Peter? I bet he's slept with straight boys."

"Are they straight if he sleeps with them? You can't be straight and have sex with guys."

"It's called conversion."

"Gay people aren't in a cult, Kaitlyn."

"They kind of are. I mean, have you ever been in a gay bar? It's amazing. All these hot guys with their own language, and then drag queens. I got up onstage and tried to dance with a drag queen, but she pushed me off, and everyone booed. I think they don't like real women."

"Or maybe they didn't like your dancing."

Laughter from two voices.

"Now who's being a bitch?"

"Don't dish it out if you can't handle it."

"Why were you there, anyway? Was Jack there?"

"No. It was too butch for him. Though maybe now that he's not wearing makeup...no, still too butch for him."

Laughter.

I tune them out, and I dig through my bag for spare eye shadow and gloss, and give myself the most fabulous makeover I can. Curlicues coming off my eyes. And when they leave, I tell myself, I'll leave, and glare at them in the hall. I can't make Pinky stop, but I can sure as fuck do something about them.

Except before they leave, the loudspeaker cranks to life.

"Jack Rothman, please report to Principal Pattyn's office."

They all stop talking and then burst into giggles. I sigh, and march out and to Pattyn's office. His secretary's eyes widen at me, but she tells me to go in.

Inside, Nance is standing, facing the door. Waiting for me, I realize. She smiles. Pattyn, sitting at his desk behind her, frowns.

"You see?" he says. "This is what I mean."

"This has nothing to do with it," Nance says, turning around quickly. "We have a student being stalked and harassed on campus. We need to do something about this."

"Let me see this note you claim was put in your locker." Pattyn puts his hand out, looking down his nose at me. I take the flower out of my bag and hand it to him.

"This one was actually left at my house," I say.

He sighs and looks up at Nance. She folds her arms. He turns back to the note and reads it.

"And do you have proof this is from a student here?" he asks.

"No," I say.

He looks at Nance again, but she doesn't budge. He hands the note back to me.

"I'll make sure security has your schedule," he says finally. "And...we have a speaker coming in for an assembly about bullying. I'll make sure she talks about notes in lockers. Maybe that will set your admirer straight." He pauses. "Though that won't be for six weeks."

"Really?" Nance asks.

"What else do you want me to do, Nance?" Pattyn asks. He turns to me. "Should we call the police?"

"No," I say quickly. "Please."

He looks back at Nance. "Then my hands are tied. The security is the best I can offer." He looks at me. "But maybe if you stopped that column of yours, Jack, you wouldn't attract so much attention.... And maybe you could...try to blend in more."

Without saying anything, Nance turns and marches out of the office. Pattyn stares after her and sighs, then looks at me.

"Well, I guess that's it, then," he says. "But you really ought to think about stopping the column, Jack."

"I will," I say, and I mean it. That is what started all this, after all. Maybe stopping it will stop Pinky, too.

Pattyn looks at me until I follow Nance out of the office. She's not in the waiting room, but I find her in the hallway outside.

"I'm sorry I couldn't do more," she says when she sees me. "Are you sure you don't want to go to the police?"

"Yeah," I say. "You saw how Pattyn looked at me. He thinks this is my fault. The police won't be any different."

Nance looks down. "Yeah. They're not exactly great with queer people." She kicks at the floor. "Let me see that flower again?" I pull out the origami and give it to her. She studies it, unfolds it, refolds it. "Okay, this is good work. I don't know for sure if it's someone from the papercraft class, but if it was, there were only four students who were good enough to do this: Hannah Ling, Rufus Aaronson-Silver, Kaitlyn Montenegro...and Jeremy Diaz. That's the Jeremy you were asking about?"

I nod. I can't say anything. I don't want to believe it, but every sign is pointing right at him.

"So you think it's him."

"I don't want it to be him," I say, much softer than I meant to. "He's my ex...but I didn't think it...He's not a bad guy."

"There was this guy I knew in college," Nance says, putting her hand on my shoulder. "I thought we were good friends. Like, best friends. And then one night, he tries to make a move. And I push him off and tell him he means a lot to me, but not like that. And suddenly, it's like this switch flips. Says he deserves to be with me because of how nice he's been. Says he did everything right—that he's a good guy. He got so angry he punched a hole in the wall. After that, he started harassing my friends, telling them I was a bitch, thought I was too good for everyone...." She lets go of my shoulder and leans against the wall. "My point is, you never really know other people."

"So you think it's Jeremy, too."

"I don't know," she says. "But I think it's worth talking to him. People like that, who try to scare you from the shadows, who try to control you and tell you how to be who you are—they lose their power when you know who they are. When you can look them in the eye and say fuck off. So...talk to him. That's what I'd do. But, in a public space with other people around. And maybe record the conversation on your phone—if you get him to admit anything and show it to Pattyn, he'll have to do something."

"Yeah?" I'm not sure I believe that.

"You tell him otherwise you'll put the whole story on Jenna's website, and tell the press."

"I..." I would never do that. But it's a good idea. I nod. She pats me on the back.

"Okay. You missed most of whatever class you just had, but I'll write you a note. Why don't you come sit in and punch some clay?"

I don't see Jeremy for the rest of the day, but that's kind of a relief, because I don't know what I'd say to him if I did. When Nance told me I needed to talk to him, confront him, it sounded right, and kind of easy, but when I think about actually doing it, I'm not even sure where to start.

I see Jenna and Ben when I'm leaving school. I think maybe they're waiting for me. Jenna waves when she sees me leaving, and Ben smiles in a way I haven't seen from him before. Like I'm delicate or something, and I need to be treated carefully. It's the smile you give a crazy person.

"Did you talk to Nance?" Jenna asks.

"Yes," I say, walking to the train. "She says it could be Jeremy. So . . . I'm going to talk to him."

"Talk to him?" Ben asks.

"Yes. I'm going to talk to him, and ask if it's him, and ask why he would do it. And I'll record the whole conversation, so if he confesses, I can go to Pattyn."

"That . . . I don't know, Jack," Jenna says. "He'll probably just deny it. You could make him angrier."

"Nance says if you tell someone you know that they're terrorizing you, then they might back off, because being secret is where their power comes from." That's not quite what she said, I know, but it sounds good.

"So you told Nance everything?" Ben asks. "Is that why you were called to Pattyn's office?"

"Yeah," I say. "But he wasn't helpful, at all."

"Of course not," Jenna says.

"Anyway, I'll talk to Jeremy tomorrow," I say.

"What are you going to say?" Ben asks.

"I don't know."

We're silent for a moment as we walk.

"At least it'll be over," Ben says. "Then we can party!"

"Yeah," I say.

Jenna is quiet, but in a way that makes me think she has something to say. Probably something about how we need to go to the cops, or be careful, or something I don't want to hear. So I don't say anything. We split off at the subway station, Jenna heading downtown, and Ben just texts Other Ben for a while, so I get to walk in silence, which I like. I say goodbye to Ben at my place and go upstairs, looking forward to just being alone, trying to figure out what to say to Jeremy, what could have made him like this, what I did—but when I open the door, Mom is there. She has a glass of wine and is sitting on the sofa, with the TV off. Not a great sign.

"Hi, honey," she says.

"Hey, Mom," I say, closing the door behind me. "You're home early."

"Your principal called me at work. To talk about your stalker."

Fuck.

"Stalker might be overselling it," I say quickly. "I've just been getting some notes in my locker."

"And they're bad enough that Pattyn thinks a security guard needed to be told?" She's talking really calmly, which is freaking me out.

"The notes haven't threatened me, or anything." I still haven't moved from the door. I'm doing some calculations in my head—I never told Nance or Pattyn that Pinky threatened my mom. Or that I sent the nudes. So Mom can't know, either.

"He said some article of clothing of yours had been cut up?"

"That...yes," I say softly. I walk toward the sofa. "But I think I know who it is. I'm going to talk to him tomorrow."

"Was the pink envelope on the door a note, too?"

"Yes."

Mom sighs. "And you didn't say anything." She takes a long sip of wine. I notice the bottle is half empty. "I know you're a teenager, and I know you want privacy, and I try to give that to you. I try to let you live your life, Jack. But things like this— notes on the door to OUR home. Destruction of property? You need to tell me."

"I just...I didn't want to worry you."

"Oh, screw that," Mom says, rolling her eyes. "That's my job. To worry. I'm going to worry all the time. This is just...something else to worry about. You're not piling on."

"It just...it feels like a prank," I say, which is a lie, but sounds believable. "A prank that's gone too far. Someone thinking they're being funny, but really not."

"A prank," she says, deadpan.

"Yeah. I mean, the notes are stuff like 'I love you,' and they're in weird handwriting.... It's just a prank." I let the lie play in my mouth a little as I say it, sink into my teeth.

Mom shakes her head. "Who is it you think is doing this?"

I bite my lip and look down.

"Jack, tell me."

"Jeremy," I say.

Mom considers this. I don't know how much she remembers Jeremy. He was over here a lot for those few weeks freshman year, but never after that. She drains her glass and sets it on the table, then stands.

"I'm going to call his mother."

"What?" I rush up close, hoping it will stop her. "No."

"Jack."

"I'm going to talk to him tomorrow." I take a step back. "Please. Just . . . let me handle this."

She sighs, and sits back down. "You haven't handled it yet."

"I've been trying to figure out who it is," I say, sitting next to her. "I don't need you to swoop in at the last second and save me—or make it worse."

Mom pours herself more wine. "You're going to talk to him?"

"Tomorrow," I say.

"All right. You'll tell me how it goes tomorrow. And if it isn't fixed, then I'm talking to his mother. And then the police."

"Please, Mom, no cops. I don't want that. Jeremy was a nice guy once. Maybe he just needs help."

"The only reason I didn't call the cops the moment the principal hung up on me is because he asked me not to. Said it would make your situation worse. Worse for the school, he means, of course, like I couldn't see that—what a little dipshit he is." She takes a deep breath, and her eyes refocus on me, like lasers. She doesn't say anything for a while. I can see her tasting my lies, like I just did, rolling them around on her tongue. She drinks

274

deeply from her wine. "One day, Jack. Less. Text me tomorrow the moment you're done talking with Jeremy. If it isn't settled… well. I'll go on the mom warpath. No promises about who I won't tell. You don't get those, after everything you've been keeping from me."

"Okay," I say, finally. And it's like we're standing across the room from each other, even though we're up close. Like we're across an empty runway.

"Good. Let's order a pizza."

28

Dear Wanting to Want,

Oh, honey, there is nothing to fix. Yes, I know, the world is obsessed with sex. Not just people our age, either—sometimes it seems like "adults" are even more obsessed than we are. But sexual desire is a personal thing, and sometimes to drum it up, it requires very specific things—and sometimes it doesn't exist at all. And none of those things are wrong. Asexual people exist, and I am willing to bet they get so much more done than sluts like me. Seriously. If I could think about, like, schoolwork instead of all the times I'm thinking about sex, or doing something to have sex, I would be a straight-A prodigy by now, I'm sure.

So maybe you're asexual, but that is not at all bad. I know it feels bad—you're pretty much in your own version of the closet, trying to figure it out. I've been there—I thought my liking boys was a phase I would grow out of if I just ignored it, and also that it was more about people thinking I was gay because of the way I acted (I was a little flaming stereotype, even back then), so I worked hard to avoid being a certain way, because then people would look at me and think I was gay, and that would make me gay, or at least make me an outsider. It was . . . so much work. Exhausting.

I know it's not the same—gay and asexual—but I want to tell you as someone who thought they were broken, and everyone was staring at them and knew, that you are not broken. Plus, you might not be asexual, you might just not be interested in sex now, or only be interested in sex with people once you know them and have a bond with them, or maybe you're only turned on by a very particular kind of sex or fetish that you haven't discovered. But as long as everyone is consenting, there's nothing

wrong with your desire, or with your not having
desire. We're all wired differently.

For now, try finding some online asexual
communities and try to acknowledge to yourself
that maybe you're not into anyone yet—and maybe
you never will be—but also acknowledge that that
doesn't make you broken. Maybe one day you'll
wake up craving dick or vag. Maybe you won't. But
figure out what a happy life looks like for you—sex
or no sex—and try to achieve it, and I'm sure you
can. I wish you so much love—because love has
nothing to do with sex.

—Jack of Hearts

I wait at Jeremy's locker before school starts the next day. I still haven't worked out exactly what I'm going to say, but I have questions—so many questions—about what I did that could possibly deserve this. How is it that my being me is so offensive to him?

When he shows up, he's not alone, which is okay. He's with other members of the GSA—Eloise Bachman and Sonya Shiniski. I know them both, and we're friendly. Sonya has a buzz cut and wears suits and carries a briefcase with patches on it—rainbow, gay rights, "butch dyke," and more. I've always liked her, even though we don't talk much. I like to think she likes me. She always gives me that chin-based bro-nod in the hall. She gives it to me now when she sees me. And Eloise smiles. Jeremy says something to them and they walk to the other side of the hall and he comes up to me. They can still see us, though. Which is good. It should be in public, I remind myself. I reach into my pocket and tap record on my phone.

"What do you want?" Jeremy asks, already super aggressive. Or maybe defensive. "Am I doing something wrong?"

"You were the one who told me I was doing something wrong last time we talked," I say. And I'm already off track. I was going to come at him all sweet, and now we're fighting.

Jeremy sighs and starts undoing the lock on his locker. "You're right. I'm sorry. You're right. And you were right when I yelled at you in the lunchroom."

"You didn't yell," I say. "You lectured."

"Yeah." He smiles, but kind of sadly. "I do that, right?"

"It's okay," I say. "We both always loved drama." It's funny how easy it is to be like a couple again. To be aware of how close he is, how much body heat he lets off—he always ran warm—and I kind of like it. We haven't really spoken in so long. Just lectured, yelled.

"I'm trying not to," he says, looking away from his locker at me. "Drama gets in the way of change."

"Sometimes it causes change," I say.

"Yeah, but that's not good for us. People already think we're all drama queens. We have to be twice as professional as straight people, and twice as charming, just to get them to listen to us."

"I know," I say. "And I know that's why you don't...like me."

"I just...I want you to be yourself," he says, looking back in his locker. "I just want us to be treated fairly, you know? And I don't think we will be. Ever. And when you don't seem to care..."

"I do care," I say. I almost reach out, put my hand on his shoulder. This is not going how I thought it would.

"I guess we just have different ways of showing it." He frowns a little, and I can tell he didn't mean to sound so bitchy, but he's not going to take it back.

"Look," I say, "I have to ask you something."

He takes a book out of his locker and studies me. "Sure."

"Have you been sending me notes? Pink notes, in origami?"

He looks at me like I'm crazy. "What?"

"I've been getting these notes."

"What kind of notes?"

"They..." I'm not sure how much to tell him, but he's staring at me intently. "Asking for things. Telling me how to behave."

"How to behave?" He shoves his book in his bag, then looks at the floor and sighs. "I'm really sorry about what I said in the lunchroom, Jack. Seriously. I know I get...weird. I just don't want people to look at me and see a stereotype. And I just worry that..."

"When they look at me they do, and if they see one of us acting this way, we all must. I know," I say. "I've known that's how you've felt forever, and I wish I could convince you that you didn't have to."

"I don't think anyone can," he says. "But I am trying to be angrier at them—and not angry at you. You get to be who you want. I...don't get to tell you how to behave. No one does. I didn't send you any notes. Were they awful?"

"Yeah," I say, kicking the floor.

"What did they ask you for?"

"Photos," I say.

He stares at me, and as his eyes narrow I can see him figuring things out. He was always smart. Really, really smart. It's why he gets angry at me—because he knows he can't change all straight people. But one gay guy—maybe he can fix that.

"Nudes," he says. It's not a question. "And telling you how to behave. Sexually? What's going on?"

"It's just, if it is you—"

"It's not." He slams his locker. "I...look. I don't love how we broke up, and I know we have our differences, but I haven't sent you any notes. Why do you think it's me?"

"Nance said you were good at origami."

He holds up his hands for me, and spreads his fingers. "No paper cuts," he says. "You can ask Nance about that. I always got terrible paper cuts when I did origami. We all did."

I study his fingers. Not even a scratch.

"These notes aren't good, are they?"

"No," I say.

He turns his face away from me like he's been slapped. "You really think I hate you that much? Or that I'm that terrible a person?"

"I don't know," I say. "I didn't think so, but someone pointed out you could be obsessed with me, and then there was that lecture."

He closes his eyes and rubs his temples, and for a moment, he looks really angry, but then he sighs and looks really sad. He opens his eyes and stares at me. Then he moves toward me. I back away, but I realize he's not going to hit me—he's hugging me. I let him. I even lightly hug him back.

"I'm sorry I've been...I'm sorry that I've done anything that would make you think that of me." He lets go. "Seriously. And I'm sorry that when we broke up, I tried to hide behind politics instead of just telling you I wasn't ready."

"You weren't?" I ask. This is news to me.

"Oh god, no." He laughs. "You didn't figure that one out?"

"No—I thought you hated me for being a slut, working against the cause."

"I..." He sighs. "I can see why you'd think that. But we each work for equality in our own way. I'm more Harvey Milk. You're more...Robert Mapplethorpe."

"I think of myself as more Bruce LaBruce," I say.

He rolls his eyes. "You should come back to the GSA."

"Maybe." I laugh. "Always recruiting."

"That's me. Making an army." He grins, but then his face turns serious. "Have you told Pattyn about this? About the notes?"

"Yeah. But he's not doing anything. Some assembly on bullying in a few weeks. Security watching my classes. And that's only because Nance made him."

"Figures. He's so useless. And remember when he made you take off your 'Make Hetero Illegal' T-shirt? I knew right then that he was one of those corporate types who say they have no problem with gay people, as long as the gay people never kiss or hold hands or talk about their boyfriends, and just fade into the background."

"Yeah," I say. "Well, I've never been good at that. He's trying to get me to take the column down—says then all this will stop."

"Oh, fuck that," Jeremy says, shaking his head. "You were totally right the other day. We all get to be the kind of queer people we want to be—and your column serves a purpose. It shows people we are sexual beings, and that we have autonomy over our own bodies and lives. And it sounds like that's exactly what this note-writer is trying to take from you. Don't let some paper-folding coward tell you who you have to be. And don't let me do it, either."

"Thanks," I say. I mean it. I feel…stronger for a moment. But then I realize that I still have no idea who's doing this to me. Maybe it's not someone from the papercraft class. Maybe it's someone who just knows origami really well. The moment fades as I go through suspects in my head, and realize I have none left. That I literally haven't got a clue.

"I better get to class," Jeremy says. "Later."

He walks off, and I watch him and his friends go. I don't believe it's him. Everything he just said reminded me of who I knew freshman year—and who I cared for. Still care for. And I don't believe that person could do what Pinky is doing.

But that means I'm stuck. And I still have Jenna's time limit before she goes to the cops. And Mom. I take out my phone and text her.

Talked to Jeremy. Everything is going to be ok. Just a stupid prank gotten out of control. Stand down

I don't get a text back, but I'm not expecting one. I go to my locker to get out my books before class. Jeremy was right. I can't let Pinky tell me who to be. Except... what other choice do I have?

When I open my locker, a note falls out. The same pink as always, and folded into a frog.

Jack,
Thank you for the photos. They are SO HOT. I jerked off to them. And don't worry. I won't show them to anyone else. And I forgive you for fucking that Boston boy. I won't call your friend again and tell her that her mom is dead. I won't do anything bad, as long as you stay my boyfriend. Just mine. That means no more columns, too. Those stories make me jealous, and when I get jealous, I get mad. So no more stories, no more column. Just you and me. We'll be together forever. Love you.

29

Dear Jack of Hearts,

I think I'm a bad person. I like girls. I mean, I like girls sexually, and I've had sex with a few of them, and I've liked it, but what I really want to do—what I really get turned on by—is the idea of hurting them. Not, like, beating them or anything, but spanking them, slapping them, making them wear collars and ball gags, and ordering them around. I fantasize about that—a lot. But I'm also a woman, and a feminist, and violence against women is wrong and awful, and making them servants to fulfill my wishes is bad. Like, these desires are wrong. If anyone told me to bend over because I'd

been a bad girl, I would smack them in the face. If
someone hit me during sex, I would push them off
and go to the police. But I want to do these things.
Is this, like, the patriarchy inside my head? Am I
just a sociopath? Should I just join a nunnery so
that I never do any of these things? I feel like I'm a
terrible, perverted person. I feel like I should be in
jail. How do I fix this?

—Bad Feminist

Is it weird that Pinky's love notes don't bother me as much now? I'm getting used to them, which is on some level great, because I don't get the same flush of panic that makes all my hairs stand on end and my makeup run and my face feel hot in a really unsexy way. But, it's not great because...I'm used to them. This is part of my life now. But if I think too much about that, I start to get queasy.

I don't even look for Pinky in the crowd anymore. I just accept that he's watching. And I don't know who he is. And maybe I never will. I just know he's there.

My skin still feels like it's covered in twitching insects, and I still want to take a cold shower every five minutes, but I don't, because I know it won't really help, in the long run. Pinky is my boyfriend now. My first boyfriend since freshman year.

I go through the rest of the morning like I always do now—only half paying attention, and tired in ways that have nothing to do with sleep. I want to fight this, like Jeremy said. I want to control myself and not be controlled, but I don't know how. I have no idea how.

At lunch, I tell Ben and Jenna about my conversation with Jeremy, but not about the note. There's no real point. Another note doesn't make much difference.

"You're taking no paper cuts as evidence?" Jenna asks. "He could just wear gloves. He could have gotten better."

"It's not him," I say without much conviction. I don't want to argue. I don't want them involved with this now. They're targets, and I need to get them away from that.

"He could be two-faced, a liar," Jenna says, louder, like she's getting angry at me for not getting angry. "Who else could it be?"

"What does it matter?" I ask. If I don't care, maybe they won't care, and then they'll drop it. Then Pinky will leave them alone.

Ben is staring at both of us, wide-eyed.

"What does it matter?" Jenna slams the table. "What the fuck is wrong with you? If it's not Jeremy, you have to figure out who it is, Jack, or I'm going to the police."

"They won't believe you," I say. "They'll need proof, they'll need me to say something. Pattyn won't let them in school. . . . There's no point, Jenna."

She gets really quiet. I can't see her eyes behind her sunglasses, just my reflection. I forgot to put on makeup today.

"Then what do you want to do, Jack?"

"Nothing," I say. "There's no point."

Jenna sighs and, without saying anything else, gets up and leaves. I don't follow her.

"Jack," Ben says softly. "Are you sure you're okay?"

"Sure," I say. "Just fine."

"And we're going to the party this weekend, right?"

I think. Pinky hasn't said I shouldn't go to the party. "I guess," I say.

"Good. I want you to meet Ben again." He pauses. "As my boyfriend." He breaks into a grin.

"You talked with him?" I ask, genuinely happy for him.

"Yes." He nods. He's so happy. I can feel it like warmth through a cold window.

"That's great," I say. "I'm so happy for you." And I am, but I'm worried, too. This is just one more thing Pinky can destroy.

"Thanks," he says. "Anyway, you can meet him at Jenna's on Saturday. So you should go talk to her."

"There's nothing to talk about," I say. "I'm so tired of this mystery. I don't have it in me to do this anymore."

"I...understand that," Ben says, reaching out and squeezing my shoulder. "But this is your life. You can't live in fear. And Jenna feels like you're giving up. I...agree."

"It's my life, like you said. I can give up on whatever I want."

"Let's go talk to her. She's probably in the park, smoking."

I shrug. "I wouldn't know what to say."

"Say you get why she's angry, but you're tired. You're not letting him win, you just need a break from it being your whole life."

I tilt my head and take a deep breath. I am letting him win.

I don't say that out loud. But it's true. I've done everything I can think of, I've gotten nowhere, and now I'm going to let him win. I'm going to be Pinky's boyfriend, if only so everything will stop. What does "boyfriend" even mean, anyway? It's meaningless. It's all meaningless.

Ben's eyes search my face. "You're not letting him win, right?"

"Let's go talk to Jenna," I say. I don't want to let Ben down. I don't want Pinky to win. But I don't want to fight him anymore, either. "Make sure she still wants to go to the party with me."

"Good." Ben nods. "Good. Going to a party. That's very Jack."

"Sure," I say, and stand up. I haven't eaten much, but I don't feel hungry. I think about what Jeremy said, about how I shouldn't let someone else decide who I'm going to be, but he didn't really understand.

It's not even about the nudes getting out. I mean, I don't want that—people's gossip would go through the roof—but I could live with it, if all this would stop. The constant barrage of notes. The being watched, evaluated. The fact that any moment of joy or relief I feel is always cut short.

We walk out to the park, where Jenna is smoking, the air already heavy with the smell of roses. She looks up at us and sighs.

"Sorry for storming out," she says.

"Sorry for not..." I look at Ben. What did he say to tell her? "I'm just really tired, Jenna. I don't know how to fight this anymore."

"You fight it by standing up," Jenna says. "You fight it by letting us help you. You fight it by going to the cops."

"I'm just afraid that'll make it worse. And my mom—"

"Your mom would gladly dump her boyfriend to save you from this," Jenna says. "I have no doubt. And we don't even know what Pinky has on her. Let's just go to the cops. Please. Or at least let me call my dad."

I sit down next to her. "Okay," I say, and saying it, I feel a little better. Maybe there's some non-cop solution her dad can come up with. Maybe he can fight for me. "Ask your dad. Tell him. But no cops without my permission."

"Really?" Jenna asks. I nod. She hugs me. "Great. I'll pitch it to him as a hypothetical. Then he can't go to the cops. But at least we'll know something."

"Right," I say. Her hug feels strange, and then I realize that it's that I'm feeling anything. That the numbness is fading just a little. "That's something. That's a good idea."

"Good," Jenna says. "I'll ask him when he gets home tomorrow. Then I can tell you about it before the party."

I nod.

"We're going to have so much fun at this party," Ben says. "We're going to forget all about Pinky."

"Yeah," I say, nodding. But I'm not sure that's possible.

The rest of Friday goes quickly. I'm focused on wondering what Jenna's dad will say. Mom texted me back **good** so I guess she isn't worried about the notes anymore. If I do end up going to the cops, though, she'll probably be pissed about me lying. But it's not Jeremy. I don't think. It just doesn't make sense to me.

But then, neither does anything else.

We help Ben pick out his outfit for his date that night (he has photos of the choices on his phone) and then I go home, and I sleep. Saturday I spend choosing an outfit. I look at each piece of clothing and consider if I'd mind if it gets cut, or burned, or whatever else Pinky could have planned. That's how I think now. My outfit is boring. My makeup is pretty dull, too. But I look okay. It's not like I'm going to get laid, right? I mean, if I do, then Pinky will be mad, and I don't want that. I don't want Mom or Ben or Jenna to suffer just because I wanted to have fun.

What if he shows himself and says I have to sleep with him? Or maybe just meet him at some truck stop and suck an anonymous cock through a glory hole. I might do it, if it would make everything stop.

I would definitely do it, if it would make everything stop.

Jenna isn't super dressed up, either, so I don't feel bad for my bland outfit. She's in a cute skirt and a long-sleeved shirt with billow sleeves and occasional sequins. Ben, though, is in a full three-piece suit. He looks like he's going to a wedding.

Jenna has a silver platter of cucumber sandwiches, and I eat one, but I'm more excited for the pot and champagne. Maybe greedily excited. The first hit of the pot floods through me and makes my body feel jellylike and calm, relaxing muscles I didn't realize were tense—almost painful.

Jenna waits until we're buzzed before she tells us what her dad said. About the hypothetical stalker.

"I told him it was for an article," she says, and sips her champagne. "He says..." She sighs. "He says these are hard cases. Especially when there's no suspect. And he says if you go to the cops they might help, but all they can really do is keep track of the harassment. They're probably not going to put a detective on it until the notes become overt threats on your life, or if..."

"If I die," I offer cheerfully. I take another long drag on the blunt and drain my glass of champagne.

"Seriously?" Ben asks. "They can't do anything?"

"They'll assign someone to the case, but my dad felt skeptical that anything would come of it until there was real danger or lawbreaking."

I laugh. "Well, Pinky does have some inappropriate photos of a teenager," I joke. I take another hit of the blunt—greedy, I know—before handing it to Ben, who just passes it to Jenna. Except Jenna isn't looking at him. She's staring at me.

"Did you send him photos?" she asks.

Oh, right. I never told them that. I motion for Ben to hand me the blunt instead, and he does, and I take another hit, then reach for the bottle of champagne, but Jenna snatches it away.

"Jack," she says, her voice a long warning.

"Yes," I say. "I thought it would make him stop. And he sent me a note thanking me. Says I'm his boyfriend. So it worked, right? Everything is cool." I reach for the bottle but she pulls it back.

"You don't have boyfriends," Jenna says.

Since she won't hand me the bottle, I take another drag on the blunt. I'm such a fucking stereotype, I know—teenager dealing with bad things with drugs! Scandal! But it's not about dealing with the bad things. It's about feeling good. And the bad things make that harder, is all, and pot and booze make it easier again. It's not like I'm trying to erase the pain of my situation, or forget it or whatever. That's not going to happen.

"What does it matter?" I ask. "They weren't even full frontal."

"Were they full back-al?" Ben asks.

I raise my eyebrow at him. "Kinda."

"That doesn't matter," Jenna says. She sighs and puts the bottle down. "Now you have no case. Now even if we catch Pinky, they can claim you sent the photos, you were in a relationship, you consented."

"Well," I say, snatching the bottle. "I did. Because I wanted all this to end. And it didn't, but I don't think he's going to cut up my jeans tonight—and even if he does, they're, like, my fourth-best pair, so it's okay. Come on, let's just pretend things are normal! Let's just enjoy ourselves."

Jenna glares at me, and I offer her the blunt. She takes it, and now that both my hands are free, I pour that champagne.

"This is bad, Jack," she says. "You've fucked this up."

"It's not happening to you," I say, and drink. We probably look like we're enacting some Elizabeth Taylor movie. I feel a melodramatic sort of drunk flowing through me.

"Guys," Ben says. "Calm down. Jack sent the photos under

duress—blackmail. That's a crime, right? He was blackmailed for photos of him—underage and nude. Crime, right?"

"Why would you do that?" Jenna asks. "When we're trying to help."

"Because trying isn't enough," I say, and it sounds mean when I say it, and I feel bad almost immediately, but then Jenna narrows her eyes at me, and I don't want to take it back.

"Guys," Ben starts, but then the doorbell rings.

Jenna sighs and gets up.

"Just...relax," Ben says to me in a whisper. "We just want to help. We know we haven't fixed it yet. But...we just want you to be okay, Jack."

"I don't know if that's possible," I say, and down my glass of champagne.

Ben frowns, but then breaks into a huge smile. I look behind me, and Jenna is walking in with Other Ben. He's wearing a sports jacket and a tie with a plaid shirt, which...he's trying, bless him. He grins at Ben and they go over to each other and kiss. Loudly. Normally I'd look at Jenna now, and we'd roll our eyes, but when I glance over, she's looking away from me, her arms folded.

"So," Ben says, when they're not kissing anymore, "guys, this is my boyfriend, Ben!" He takes Other Ben by the hand and leads him over to the sofa. They sit down together, super close, though there's plenty of room.

"We've already met," I say, smiling.

"Yeah, but now you're meeting my boyfriend," Ben says. Other Ben laughs.

"So, you guys normally do this?" Other Ben asks. "It's so fancy." He reaches out and grabs a cucumber sandwich and then nibbles on it daintily.

"We're very fancy people," I say, raising my glass slightly. I think my words might be slurring a little. I should probably have another cucumber sandwich myself, but I don't want to reach for it.

"I can see," Other Ben says. "Thanks for letting me crash."

"Of course," Ben says.

"Did you guys have fun at the museum yesterday?" Jenna asks.

"It was really cool," Other Ben says. "Lots of…glamour. Do you guys like clothes as much as Ben?"

"We like fashion," Jenna says, forcing a smile.

"As long as no one is cutting it up," I say, and laugh. Jenna shoots me a look. I roll my eyes.

"Do you smoke up?" Jenna asks. "I can relight the joint."

"Oh, no, thanks," Other Ben says. "That stuff isn't for me." He stretches his arm out and Ben leans into it, like a baby bird. I giggle as I picture Ben with feathers.

"Sorry," I say. "I'm already drinking too much."

"That's okay," Other Ben says. "I'm just nervous about meeting you guys. Ben says you're his best friends. That he probably wouldn't have been able to deal with being gay if it weren't for you."

"Really?" Jenna asks.

"Well, yeah," Ben says, like it's the most obvious thing in

the world. "I was already a weirdo...being a gay weirdo....I thought I would be alone, like, forever. But you guys took me in. You're my family." He smiles at us with such love that I'm not mad at anyone anymore. "You too," he says to Other Ben, and kisses him on the cheek. I turn to Jenna, to roll my eyes again and smile at how ridiculous but sweet they are, but she still won't meet my eyes. Not even after that. Well, fine. Fuck her.

"We should get going," I say, standing up. "We're out of champagne."

"Already?" Ben asks.

"We'll talk at the party, don't worry." I wave him off. "But let's go get drunk!" I raise my glass. "Drunker."

30

I OPEN MY EYES AND IMMEDIATELY REGRET IT. MY HEAD hurts, the light is bright, my mouth is dry. I've had hangovers before, but this one is bad. Really bad. My phone beeps. I sit up. I'm dressed—still in my shoes—in my own bed. I don't remember anything from last night. No, that's not true. I remember getting to the party. Dancing. Drinking. More drinking. Ben and Other Ben were joined at the hip. Jenna wouldn't talk to me. Brian kept grinding against me. More drinking. After that, I'm not sure. I check if I'm still wearing my underwear—I am. So I don't think I got up to anything too regrettable.

I pick up my phone. A lot of texts, and even a few missed calls. All from Jenna and Ben.

Ben

Are you ok?

Jenna

Are you ok?

Jack, seriously, I know you're mad, but tell me you're okay and then we can go back to being angry

Ben

Jack, please. I'm afraid you're dead or in a dungeon or something

Jenna

Are you ok?

More like that.

I'm fine, aside from this hangover

Ben

Oh, thank god

Jenna

Not cool

> Sorry. I don't really remember last night. Why are you so worried?

Ben

You were really drunk

No vomiting, either, which Ben says is worse. Alcohol poisoning

Jenna

And you were being weird

Peter was there, and you danced, and he asked if you wanted to go back to his place, and you said you couldn't because your boyfriend wouldn't like it

I sigh. Well, fuck. There goes sex with Peter becoming a regular thing.

> Was he angry?

Ben

Confused. Thought you were kidding

Ben

Then Jeremy came up and said you were just drunk and you needed to get home

And before we could do anything, he was taking you out of there

Jenna

We thought he was Pinky, and he was kidnapping you

Ben

But he just put you in a cab. We watched.

Jenna

But then we thought maybe he'd told the cab driver some weird location, and you were being held hostage or something

I laugh at that. I look around the room. Everything seems normal.

No

Home

> Hungover

> Sorry you were worried

> Sorry I got so drunk

Jenna

You're going through a lot. It's not our place to judge how you handle it

So...sorry about that

> Sorry for letting you down

Ben

You didn't let us down

We just want you to be okay, and it feels like you don't want to be

> I'm fine. Just hungover

Jenna

That's not what he meant

I put down the phone and stumble to the bathroom, where I take a cold shower. I feel a little more human afterward, and go out to the living room, where Mom is browsing on her tablet.

"You okay?" she asks. "You were home late."

"A little sick, I think." I pour myself a glass of water. Mom glances up at me and we both know what "sick" is code for. She thinks for a moment, then decides to let it slide.

"Poor baby," she says. "Well, come sit next to me. We can watch some movies. That sound good?"

"Yeah," I say, and go sit next to her on the sofa. She takes a blanket out and puts it over me and then has me lie down with my head in her lap, which feels so silly, but I do it, because her lap is super comfortable. You wouldn't think so, with her legs being so skinny, but she plays with my hair and it feels nice.

"Do we need to have a talk about drinking again?" she asks, but nicely, no warning bell in her voice.

"No," I say.

"I can tell you're hungover, honey."

"Yeah," I say. I think about telling her why I drank, and how it's the only thing I can do now, until Pinky tells me to stop, but I take a deep breath, and I keep it to myself. "It was a stupid mistake," I say instead. "I didn't realize how strong the drinks were until I'd had too many."

Mom nods, still playing with my hair. "I've been there. But now you know, right? One drink, see how it affects you, plenty of water?"

"Yeah, Mom."

"Good." She puts on a BBC mystery and I close my eyes and when I open them, I feel better, and hours have gone by.

I sit up and drink the whole glass of water, then get up for another, but Mom takes the glass and refills it for me. She sets it down and then sits and puts her arm around me, pulling me back down and playing with my hair again.

"So," she says when I'm nearly asleep. "There's something I want to tell you." I turn so I'm on my back, looking at her. She smiles down at me like she's about to tell a joke. "Your deductions are correct. I am seeing someone."

"Who?"

"His name is Hank. He's a nurse at the hospital."

I sit up and narrow my eyes at her. "Is that allowed? Aren't you, like, his boss?"

Mom looks back at the TV. "I am technically in a position above him, but I'm not his immediate supervisor."

"So it's okay?"

"Well . . ." She shakes her head. "Don't worry about it."

"So it's not okay," I say, sighing.

"We need to inform HR. But we haven't yet, because we've been taking it slow. I wanted to tell you . . . in case things move a little faster."

"You mean you want to bring him home."

"Yes."

"But not so we can all eat around the table and share stories?"

"Don't be a smart-ass. I'm just saying, you might meet him soon. I'll try to make sure there's a formal introduction."

"But you're going to tell HR, right?"

She narrows her eyes at me. "Eventually. Why do you care?"

"I don't want you to get in trouble," I say. Plus, Pinky won't have that piece of blackmail anymore.

"I'll be fine," she says.

"Please, Mom. Tell HR."

She looks at me like I'm being silly and brushes my hair out of my eyes. "Okay. I'll talk to Hank tomorrow, and if he's okay with it, we'll go to HR. Strange demand coming from my son who refuses to get a boyfriend."

"Well, if he's important enough that you want me to meet him, it feels like he's your boyfriend."

Mom grins. "Yeah, I guess he is."

"Are you happy?"

Mom looks surprised by the question, but her face turns a faint pink and opens into a look of joy, like the one in the photos from Pinky. "Yes. I am."

"Good," I say, and lie back down in her lap. At least she'll be safe now. "How did it happen? Was it like on all the hospital shows where they make eyes over a dead body and then fall into bed right after?"

"No." She laughs. "Just a little flirting at first. Then coffee in the cafeteria. Then he asked me if I wanted to get lunch somewhere outside, and I said yes. It wasn't even really a date. Just two people who enjoyed each other's company. Friends. We talked a lot. For months. Then, one night, when we were both working late and had run out for a coffee, he told me he found me attractive, and wondered if he could kiss me."

"He wondered?" I laugh.

"He's very respectful," Mom says. "And he's a bit younger, and there's the job thing, so he was being careful. Relationships should always be handled carefully. Sex is one thing—throw your bodies together, wake up the next day—but if you want to really know someone, it's best to remember that while you look like skin, people are glass on the inside. You have to be careful."

"That sounds exhausting."

"It can be. Which is why you should only bother if you want to."

"I don't want to," I say. "Not yet. That's okay, right?"

"Of course!" Mom scratches my head. "Look how long it took me. And I wasn't exactly chaste before now. But it's a different thing."

"Don't say 'chaste,'" I say. "Makes you sound like a nun."

"Sure, Sister Rothman. That makes sense."

"Mother Superior, I'd think."

"That I like, actually. You should just call me that anyway."

I laugh, and we watch the TV for a minute. "Have you ever had anyone who liked you, but you didn't like them? And they didn't get the message?"

"Sure. Everyone has that eventually."

"How did you tell them?"

"I was as kind as I could be. I told her that she was one of my greatest friends, and I loved her, but I didn't want to change our relationship. I wanted her in my life in the way she was."

"But she was your friend, like Hank."

"Yes."

"So why didn't you want her like that?"

Mom shakes her head. "I don't know. It was just a feeling. She was gorgeous, but I didn't want her like that. I wanted her to be my friend."

"And did she stay your friend?"

Mom sighs. "No." She shifts slightly and I sit up and drink from my glass of water. "You want to order lunch? Chinese? Pizza?" She stands and goes around to the kitchen and opens the menu drawer. I've told her a million times she can order on her phone now, but she keeps the menus anyway.

"Chinese," I say. "Soup."

"Sounds good." She picks up the phone and starts dialing, but then stops and looks over at me. "You're a good kid," she says. I shrug, and she just goes back to dialing.

I feel better by Monday, but I'm still wearing sunglasses in the hall. I guess "better" isn't the word for it. I mean, I still have a little hangover, but I'm also just worried about what I did at the party. Turning down Peter, getting blackout drunk, fighting with Jenna, being sloppy in front of Ben's boyfriend, dressing casually. That's not me. I don't like who I am now.

I like it even less when a perfect origami heart falls out of my locker and I instinctively catch it before it hits the ground.

Jack,

I WAS so happy when you didn't go home with that Boston guy because of YOUR boyfriend. You meant ME! You get it NOW—it's you and me forever. No one else. I'm going to take such good care of you. I'm going to be the BEST boyfriend. I won't ever hurt you, or cut you with scissors, or destroy your clothing or books or friends. Not as long as we're together. No more sleeping around for you. But don't worry, you can send me photos of you. Maybe videos, too. I can send you little presents for you to play with in your videos. But just for me—your boyfriend. Forever.

I swallow and put the note in my pocket. Even with Mom telling HR, I know I'm still under Pinky's thumb. I know he's capable of horrible things—maybe even hurting me, or people I care about. Even if this one bit of blackmail is off the table, there are others. He'll find more. He's everywhere. He sees everything. And I'm his boyfriend now.

"Hey." Jenna is suddenly next to me, leaning on the lockers. "What's up?"

"Nothing," I say. "Hungover."

"Yeah, I'll bet. I'm sorry if I said anything that made you want to . . . you know. Overindulge."

"You didn't." I shake my head. "I just needed it."

"Did you text Peter yet?"

"No." What's the point? I have a boyfriend. I'm not allowed to screw Peter anymore.

"Well, you should. He was kind of weirded out. I know you weren't, like, going to start going out, but I thought you two liked each other."

"I do," I say. "I'll text him."

"Okay." She looks me up and down suspiciously. "You okay? You're holding your body weird."

"Weird how?"

"Weird like when we were in sixth grade and you used to slump and rub your legs together."

I look down. I am slumping and my right leg is currently lifted, rubbing at my left calf, where my skin is twitching. I force a laugh. "Hangovers bring back bad habits, I guess." I put my foot down, try to straighten my back out. "Anyway, I'll see you at lunch?"

"Yeah. I have an idea for trapping Pinky."

I smile, but don't say anything and turn away. There is no

trapping my boyfriend. He's trapped me. I'm not allowed to sleep around anymore. I don't know who he is, but he's always watching. It's like being in the closet again—no sex, always afraid of stepping out of line, doing something that will make Pinky slice up my clothes or hurt someone.

At least it's only for the next year and a half. I can handle having a boyfriend that long. I hope he won't follow me to college. Then that's another four years. By then I probably won't have any other friends, either. Jenna's going to keep getting mad at me for not stopping Pinky, and Ben is going to go live happily ever after with Other Ben. Just me and my boyfriend. It'll be over in college. Or maybe after college. It'll have to be over by then. I'm sure of it. I think. I'll have to handle it until then. At least it's not like I'm being beaten to death, or burned or tortured in some redneck's basement, right? It could be worse.

31

At lunch, Jenna lays out her new plan—a home DNA test. I nod politely. It won't do anything. She suggests writing an article about it, too—but anonymously. Talk about the situation and how the school isn't handling it.

"No," I say. "That'll just make him mad."

Jenna frowns. Ben texts Other Ben. Life goes on. The test will take a week to show up, and then who do we even test it on?

At home, I close my bedroom door and strip naked, and then, holding the camera up high, I kneel on the floor and look up for the photo. I'm exposed in it, completely, my soft cock almost central to the image, but it's the position—subservient, docile— that I hope will make him happiest. I have to keep my boyfriend happy, after all. I think about one or two of them a week will do it. I send the photo to Pinky, and then I do my homework. I don't hear anything back the next day, or the one after that. That's good. It means he's happy.

At night, Ben texts me. And Jenna. They talk, but I don't answer. I just don't know what to say. I don't go to any parties that weekend—I tell them the idea of alcohol still makes me sick. They don't say anything, but they know as well as I do: Their friend Jack is pretty much gone. I'm just Pinky's boyfriend now. Pinky. That's funny. I don't even know his real name. I should come up with one just to use in my head. Something sexy. That'll make it easier. Johnny? Desmond? I always liked young 007 Sean Connery with his furry chest and well-muscled thighs. Sean isn't a great name, though. Connor, I decide. I try it in my head. My boyfriend's name is Connor, and he sends me pink notes telling me what to do, and I do it, because otherwise bad things will happen. But we'll break up when I get to college, and then I can go back to being Jack, not Connor's boyfriend. Or maybe after college. We'll see. Whatever makes him happy.

"He got blackout drunk at the party last weekend—maybe he didn't want to go out this weekend 'cause he was afraid of, like, dying from alcohol poisoning."

"It wasn't that bad."

"Did you see him, Kaitlyn? He could barely stand."

"He was just being dramatic. Gay guys are dramatic."

"Whatever, it wasn't cute."

"He said he had a boyfriend, too."

"I know, can you imagine? Jack settling down."

"He must be pretty special."

"Or really good in bed."

Laughter.

"Sad that his boyfriend wasn't there when he got so drunk, though."

"Maybe he got drunk because his boyfriend wasn't there."

"Or maybe his boyfriend was the one who helped him to the cab—the angry one? Jeremy? They dated freshman year, right? Maybe they got back together."

"No, Jeremy isn't his boyfriend."

"You seem pretty sure about that."

"I am. They're just not compati—ow!"

"What? Are you okay?"

"Sorry, just a cut."

"Another one. Jesus, Kaitlyn, look at your hands. What have you been doing?"

"They're just paper cuts. I have a lot of paper—textbooks, and stuff."

"Since when do you open your textbooks?"

Laughter.

I take a deep breath. My cigarette is still dangling over the sink, and I suddenly realize all the smoke is hovering in the air and about to set off the alarm, so I wave it quickly out the open window with my hands and then throw the cigarette in the sink.

Kaitlyn. Really?

I feel weirdly light, like I'm floating to the ceiling, but like I could also get tossed against the wall by a passing breeze.

It doesn't make any sense, except that it does. She was one of the four who was good with origami. She's in the musical. But...she's also not a gay man, as far as I know. And it's not like I've ever done anything to offend her—maybe that column was confrontational, but that was after the notes started showing up.

I go over the facts in my mind. She was at the party where my jacket was cut. She knows origami, she has cuts on her hands, so she's probably been doing it. I take out my phone and find her Instagram. I flip through the photos, realizing I don't know anything about her. She's one of the trio of girls who talk about me. That's it. I've never spoken to her, except when it was all of them. Which...kind of lines up with what Ben suggested—someone watching me from afar, obsessed.

Her Instagram is a lot of selfies, fashion shots, and a lot of really pretty photography of the city. Nothing incriminating. This is a stupid idea, I tell myself, still frantically swiping through her feed. Why would she do this?

And then I see a photo of my bedroom window. It takes me a moment to recognize it. At first it looks weirdly familiar—it's a building, another of her pretty city shots, #viewfrommywindow. Some filter to make it softer and bluish. And one of the windows on the right side is my bedroom. I recognize my wall, my Tom of Finland print. She has a view into my bedroom? How did I not know this?

313

I pull up the student directory on my phone. She lives across the street from me. With her view, she can probably see the front door of my building, too. Easy to see my various paramours come and go. Easy to see my mom with her boyfriend.

But I still don't understand why. Why would anyone—especially some straight girl I barely know—do this to me?

32

Dear Bad Feminist,

Okay, so the first thing you need to ask yourself is—do you want to smack women during sex who consent, or not? Because if you're turned on by the idea of someone genuinely saying, "Please don't hurt me" and you hurting them, then you should probably go talk to a shrink about that. But if you want to role-play with a partner who says, "Please don't hurt me" but has told you beforehand exactly what they're into—face slapping, spanking, handcuffs, whatever—and has a safe word for when you go too far, then that's perfectly fine. Kinky, BDSM sex can be fun. I've never gone quite as far as you want to, but I've used handcuffs, blindfolds, engaged in some light spanking, and "Oh, no, please don't hurt me" role-play.

The most intense it got was with a guy I met on Grindr. He was a bit older, but I didn't ask how much older. Before we met up, we talked about what he wanted to do, and what I liked and didn't—we set boundaries. Then, when we met up, he tied me to the bed and blindfolded me, and I pretended I had woken up like that and didn't know what was happening—that was his fantasy, and I was pretty into it. He told me beforehand to use the traffic light system, which I didn't know about—but green means you're enjoying yourself, yellow means you're becoming uncomfortable and he should dial it back, and red means stop immediately. I was supposed to say those words depending on how I felt. So I, of course, did an Oscar-winning performance of "young man waking up tied to bed and blindfolded" by asking where I was, what was going on. He told me I was his now, and I was going to be his slave. It was pretty hot. He straddled my chest, made me suck him off, then flipped me and spanked me a little. Then he said he was going to paddle me. I said "yellow" to that—the spanking was fun, but bringing a paddle into it sounded too intense. But

yellow means slow down, not stop, so he went back
to spanking me, to which I said "green," and then he
fucked me.

But then he put his hands around my neck. I said
"red" to that real quick—choking is scary and we'd
*never talked about what to do if I couldn't **say***
"red"—and he immediately stopped, and untied
me. He apologized and said he should have checked
beforehand if that was something I was into. I told
him it was okay, and we relaxed for a bit, then went
back to fucking, and then we even cuddled, and it
was great sex. He never called me or anything—I
think I was too tame for him—but I always felt in
control. Dominated, used, a sex toy, but still able to
stop everything if it went beyond what I wanted.

You want to be the dom, not the sub, and that's
okay. You just need to find yourself a sub. Talk
about what you want to do beforehand—with hard
limits—work out a system for stopping or slowing
down, lay ground rules about what you're into and
if you can leave marks (and what kind of marks, and
how long they last) and all that.

Then have fun. And don't worry about it being
un-feminist. You are two women exploring your

desires and both of you are consenting. That's pretty
fucking feminist. So go find a sub (which, admittedly,
might be hard in high school, but ask around, you
never know) and have some good, kinky fun.

—*Jack of Hearts*

I text Jenna and Ben. I need someone to tell me I'm not crazy.

> I know who Pinky is. Maybe

Ben

> What?!

Jenna

> Who?

> I'll be in the park. I need to tell you all my
> evidence, and then you tell me if this is insane

Jenna

> Be there in a few

Ben

> I have French. But fine, I'll be late

I probably have class, too, but at this point, I don't care. I walk out of the building to the park. My body feels jittery, like I just got a hit of something. Like I'm waking up, maybe?

It feels like I have glitter in me. Like I used to have glitter in me—my blood and skin and hair and eyes—and I was special, because I fucking sparkled. And then it drained out, and I forgot to refill it for a while, but now it's back. I took a big hit of glitter. And now I'm sparkling again. I know, I know, it's super gay. But so am I.

As I walk to the park, I take out my phone, and without thinking too much about it, I call my mom. She picks up after a few rings.

"Honey?" she asks. "Is everything okay?"

"Yeah," I say. "Yeah." It might be true, too. I feel so...me again.

"Is there some emergency at school? Why aren't you in class?" Her voice is getting higher and higher, and I wish she was here and I could hug her and tell her to relax.

"I have a free period," I lie. "Mom—can I ask you something?"

"Oh...of course. You're sure you're okay?"

"Yeah, yeah. I just...that story you told me the other day. The friend who wanted to be more than friends."

Mom is quiet for a while. I stare at my shoes and kick the pavement.

"What about it?" she asks.

"I guess...you said you weren't friends anymore. 'Cause she wanted more than that. And...did she ever get...mean, I guess?

When you weren't friends anymore. Did she ever say something nasty to you, maybe try to get you to be more than friends that way?"

"Is this about Jeremy?" Mom asks. "Is he still bothering you?"

"No." I almost laugh, because it's the truth. "I was just thinking about it."

"Oh." She takes a breath. "Well, maybe once. She sent me a letter—we were both in medical school, and this was before computers really, and she sent me a letter. And it wasn't very nice."

"What did it say?" I'm at the park now, but I stay just outside the fence marking its official border, wrapping my free arm around myself, 'cause it's a little chilly.

"Oh... nothing you can't imagine. That we were meant to be. That I'd made a mistake."

"What did you do?"

"I tore it up," Mom says simply. I smile, thinking of the note I tore up, the pink fireworks outside my locker.

"And that was it?"

"I... I was sad for a while. I'd lost a good friend. But, then, maybe we hadn't really been friends? Maybe I'd thought we were friends, and she thought we were something else."

"So you never tried to change to be her friend? Tried to make yourself want that relationship?"

"No. If she cared about me, she would have loved me for whomever I was, not just who she wanted me to be. What she maybe thought I was. Relationships are always made up of these

320

little perceptions of relationships, you know. What you think is friendship is something else to someone else. You can never really know what's in someone else's mind, no matter how much you love them."

I nod, then say, "Yeah," because I realize she can't see me. I think of the distance between us, and how maybe there's that distance between all of us, because she's right, I can't know what's in someone else's head. And just like that, I can feel the distance close—snap like a rubber band. We were never really far apart, maybe. It just looked that way.

"Thanks, Mom," I say.

"You sure you're okay, honey?"

"Yeah. Just thinking, I guess."

"All right. Well, maybe focus on studying instead. I'll try to be home early tonight. We can order sushi."

"Okay. Love you, Mom."

"Love you, too."

I walk into the park and sit down on one of the benches. I'm smiling. I feel like I can see my life again, and it's my life. Unless I'm wrong about everything, of course. Unless it's not Kaitlyn.

I take out my compact and fish through my bag for makeup. I'm not wearing any today, and that needs to change, because I'm me, and me wears makeup and looks amazing in it. I find some blue eyeliner and sparkly translucent eye shadow and apply them liberally. By the time Jenna and Ben show up, I'm looking like me again. Though if they tell me my theory is crazy, I will probably want to wash it all off.

"So?" Jenna asks, taking out her e-cig.

"Kaitlyn Montenegro," I say. Jenna and Ben exchange looks. They think I'm crazy.

"Why?" Ben asks. "I mean, she's gossipy and not the nicest person, but it's not like she has a chance with you. It's not like you've done anything to her—have you?"

"I don't know," I say. "And I don't know why she'd do it. But her window looks into mine."

"So?" Jenna asks. "New York is a small town. We all look into, like, fifty people's windows."

"Just..." I take a deep breath. Maybe this is the dumbest idea ever. They're right. It doesn't make sense. Except. "Listen," I say. And I run down all my evidence. Her being one of the top origami artists, and in the musical, and with paper cuts, and as I tell them that, I think about the conversations I've heard, too—how when they talked about me, she was the one who suggested I have a boyfriend, but also the one who said it couldn't be Jeremy. She's the one who talks about wanting to fuck me.

"And she was at all the parties we've been at," Ben says.

"She's at all the parties because she's at every party. All three of them are. Most of the school is."

"But she saw me throw my jacket on the bed," I say.

Jenna inhales on her e-cig thoughtfully.

"I'll buy it," Ben says. "She's obsessed with you because she can't have you, so she decides no one can. Very melodrama."

"I think it's more complex than that," Jenna says. "And I'm not sold on the idea of it being her. But I think you should tell

Nance. And then if she agrees, she can talk to Pattyn. Then, at least, they'll be suspicious."

I nod. "Yeah." I start walking back to school. "I'm doing that now." Ben and Jenna hurry to follow me. We practically march to the art room. I push open the door, and they flank me, like a small army. Nance looks over at us from the front of the room, where she's demonstrating how to spin a plate to a group of freshmen. She raises an eyebrow that stops me in my tracks, and I wait until she's done with her explanation and walks over to us.

"I get that what's going on with you is important, Jack," she says. "But I still have a job."

"I know," I say. "I'm sorry. I just...I think I know who it is, and I need you to back me up when I tell Pattyn, because..." I flounder.

"He needs an advocate," Jenna says.

"Seems like he has two," Nance says, crossing her arms and looking at Jenna and Ben. "I'll take care of it from here. You're both late for class."

"Yeah," Ben says. He gives my arm a squeeze. "I'll see you at lunch. Good luck."

"Thanks," I say, and he runs off to class. Jenna stays, folding her arms. "Go," I tell her. "It'll be weird if we go to Pattyn together."

"Fine. But I expect a full debrief," she says before stalking off.

I look at Nance and shrug.

"So who is it, then?" she asks.

"Kaitlyn Montenegro," I say.

Nance narrows her eyes, then tilts her head up. She sighs. "Lord save me from straight people," she says. "Okay, why?"

I explain, and when I'm finished ten minutes later, she turns around to the class and tells them to free-sculpt until the end of the period.

"And no throwing clay at each other!" She turns to me. "Okay, let's go see Pattyn."

"Now?"

"No better time."

Pattyn leans back in his chair and rolls his eyes. I let Nance explain to him that it was Kaitlyn.

"So this is based on... paper cuts? And things that happened off school property, where it sounds like there was a lot of under-age drinking?"

"It happened on school property, too," Nance says. "I'm not saying you punish her. I'm saying you call her in. Ask her about this. She's being accused of stalking and bullying, and the school has a strict anti-bullying policy. Bring her in and let her speak for herself."

Pattyn takes a deep breath and then looks at me. He's glaring. He doesn't want to do this and thinks it's all my fault. My fault for being the sort of person who attracts this attention. My fault for wanting to fight against it. Well, fuck him. I cross my arms and glare right back.

He leans forward and pulls a mic out of his drawer, presses a button, and speaks into it. "Kaitlyn Montenegro, will you please report to the principal's office?" There's a weird static-y feedback shriek, and he turns off the mic and puts it away.

"You know," I say, "you can just say 'my office.' We know your voice."

Pattyn glares at me a moment, and Nance puts her hand on my shoulder. We wait in silence. After about ten minutes, just as I'm wondering if Kaitlyn has made a run for it, the door opens and she comes in. She's in a short gray skirt and a matching cardigan over a lavender T-shirt, and she's nervously twisting her small gold cross necklace in her hands—which have a pair of short lavender gloves on them. She steps in and first sees me, but her face doesn't change at all. Then she glances over at Nance, and then finally at Pattyn.

"Kaitlyn," he says. "Thank you for coming. Please, sit down."

Kaitlyn pulls one of the chairs out and sits next to me. "Did I do something?" she asks. Her eyes are large, and a little watery. She's so pale when she looks us over, so worried-looking. She pushes her white hair back behind an ear and pats her skirt over her legs. She's practically a child's doll. I'm starting to wonder if I got this all wrong.

Pattyn clears his throat. "Kaitlyn, Jack here has accused you of bullying."

"Bullying?" Kaitlyn asks. "I'm just a girl. I don't bully."

"Girls can bully," Nance says. "We don't mean you're beating people up—but Jack has been getting notes in his locker. Notes threatening him, and telling him to do things he doesn't want to do."

"Notes?" Kaitlyn asks.

"Origami notes," Nance says.

Kaitlyn nods as if she understands now. "So you're bringing in all the students who took your class?"

"Can we see your hands?" I interrupt.

"Jack," Pattyn says. "Let us handle it."

"I just want her to take off the gloves," I say.

Kaitlyn, still wide-eyed, looks at Pattyn.

"Only if you don't mind," Nance says, managing to make it sound like an order.

Kaitlyn frowns and takes the gloves off. Underneath, her hands aren't what I was hoping for. I was expecting hundreds of cuts, making her hands pink, swollen, literal red-handed evidence. But she just has a few paper cuts. Pattyn looks at me like I'm wasting everyone's time.

"I didn't put any notes in anyone's locker," she says. "I don't even really talk to Jack."

"You talk about me, though," I say.

She frowns at that, turns to look at me, glaring. "I couldn't say."

"Gossip isn't bullying, Jack," Pattyn says. "If you don't want people to say unkind things about you, it's best to make yourself less conspicuous."

"That's the lesson you're teaching?" Nance says.

"Can I go?" Kaitlyn asks. "You should call in the next origami-maker, right?"

"Why would you do this?" I ask Kaitlyn.

She looks at me and lets her eyes rove over my body, possessive, amused. In that moment I feel certain. These are the eyes I've been feeling on me that I couldn't find in the crowd. These are the eyes that were always judging.

"I didn't do anything, Jack. You did this." She stands up and looks at Pattyn. "I can go, right? I have chemistry."

Pattyn nods and waves her out of the room, then turns back to me. "See, Jack? It's not her. You can't throw around these ridiculous accusations."

I get up before he's done talking and dart out of the room. Pattyn and Nance call after me, but I ignore them. I catch Kaitlyn when she's just outside the waiting room, in the hallway, and I grab her arm.

She turns to me, and smiles without showing her teeth. "Like it rough, Jack?"

"Why?" I ask.

"It's not very nice of you to listen to private conversations, Jack," she says, pulling her arm back.

"The bathroom echoes, I can't help it."

"A good boyfriend would find another bathroom," she says.

"You wouldn't know the first thing about being a good boyfriend, Kaitlyn," I say. "I'm done. Blackmail, threaten, whatever. I know it's you, and anything you do I'll just trace back to you."

"After that performance?" Kaitlyn raises an eyebrow. "No. You'll look like the bully." She starts pulling her gloves back on. "You're done when I say you're done. You're going to be my boyfriend. This doesn't change anything. I'll show the whole school those photos. I'll ruin your friends' lives. I'll tell your mother's boss about what she's doing with that nurse."

"You need help."

"Aw, Jack…see, that's you being a good boyfriend. Worrying about me." She reaches out and pats me on the cheek. "Keep that up and maybe I'll let you decide what makeup you're allowed to wear next week."

"You know no matter how much you harass me, I'm never going to fuck you, right?"

"You don't fuck me, Jack. I fuck you. That's what a good boyfriend does. A good boyfriend pays attention. A good boyfriend listens to people who care about him. I care about you, Jack. But you make bad choices. I'm going to make the good choices for you from now on."

"What? Like no sex, no column?"

"Well, you sleep with the wrong kind of people." She shakes her head, frowning in a way that could be fake, and I can't tell if she's thinking all men are the wrong kind of people or if she has some weird checklist or even if she's just playing at this—playing at being some mentally unbalanced person from a bad movie. "And that column…it's tasteless, Jack. People will think less of you for it. No, you need to settle down. Behave."

"Why me? There are plenty of other gay guys or slutty guys in school. Why are you doing this to me?"

"I like you." Her expression turns almost sweet, and she shrugs. "I used to watch you get dressed through your window. You never noticed. And the way Ava and Emily talked about you . . . it was like a story. The shy girl and the popular boy, across the street from each other, he never notices, she longs for him . . . and then one day, something happens, and he sees her, and they wave at each other through the windows and kiss a little after that, and then they live happily ever after. I always liked you. But . . . well, you never noticed. So I took matters into my own hands. And now we're together." She smiles, a big grin, and she clasps her hands in front of her. She steps closer to me and sighs—her breath smells like peppermint. "I'm so happy."

"You're fucked up."

She ignores me, and keeps smiling. The way she looks at me is strange, like I'm not really there, but at the same time I'm all that she can see. "At least this will make things easier. I can just tell you to your face what I want. So send me some more nudes, Jack. Try to get hard for at least one of them this time. A limp dick doesn't do it for me. Oh, and wave at me from your window before you go to bed."

She leans forward, like she's going to kiss me, and I pull back in horror. She laughs, turns, and walks away.

I take a deep breath, take out my phone, and click stop on the recording. Then I walk back into Pattyn's office and hit play.

"What did Pattyn do?" Jenna asks. It's lunch, and Jenna and Ben are around me. I've invited Jeremy, Ricky, and Peter to sit with us, too, and I'm telling them the story.

"He hemmed and hawed. But then Nance said if he didn't expel her based on their no-bullying policy, then she would call the cops. And the papers. And then he agreed."

"Awesome," Peter says. He seemed especially happy when I explained to him that the boyfriend I mentioned was a stalker.

"Then Nance said it wasn't just Kaitlyn doing this to me. She said it was the culture here. And she glared at Pattyn, and Pattyn turned red, and then Nance just left, so I followed. Totally badass."

"She's right," Jeremy says. "It's not just the culture here, too. It's straight culture everywhere telling queer people the right way to be queer. That's why Kaitlyn felt like she could do that to you."

"Way to make it sound like a culture war," I say.

"Fuck you," Jeremy says, but he's smiling as he sips his coffee.

"Is it that bad?" Ricky asks, a little worried-looking.

"No," I say. "And I think she was probably just unstable and focused on me 'cause I'm hot."

"But seriously, why would she do it?" Jenna asks. "Is she just, like, mentally unwell? Some childhood incident, some genetic... whatever brain thing?"

"I don't know," I say. "And why did you need to respond to me saying I'm hot with 'but seriously'?"

Jenna laughs.

"I'm telling you," Jeremy says, "she might be off—but that off-ness manifested the way it did because of the heteropatriarchy." I successfully resist rolling my eyes. "You should come to the GSA, Ricky. We talk about all this stuff."

"You want to write an essay about that for my website?" Jenna asks. She looks quickly at me. "Don't worry, nothing about this—but about queer culture in high school?"

"I'd read that," Ricky says, probably to get out of going to the GSA.

"Me too," Ben says.

I look at Jeremy. "You should."

"Okay," Jeremy says.

"Great," Jenna says. "We'll make it a regular column."

"No," Jeremy says quickly. "Just one."

"We'll see," Jenna says, a familiar smile on her face. I'm about to say something snarky when I see Ava and Emily a few tables away, glancing over at me, nervous, then whispering to each other. When they catch me looking, though, Ava stands, chin up, arms crossed, and marches over, Emily behind her.

"Hey, Jack," Ava says. Everyone around me is very quiet. "What's going on? Kaitlyn was called to the office, and then we saw her outside with her parents, crying. She wouldn't talk to us. We saw you in the office with her."

"You don't know?" I ask.

They shake their heads. Ava purses her lips. "Did you do something to her?"

"No," I say. "She did something to me."

"Does she have psychological problems?" Jenna asks suddenly.

"What?" Ava asks. "No."

"Does she hate gay people?"

"No," Ava says again, putting her hands on her hips. "Her cousin is gay."

I roll my eyes.

"Although she did say she didn't think he was going to last long out of the closet," Emily says. "I thought that was kind of harsh."

"Emily, shut up," Ava says, and marches off. Emily shrugs at us, and follows her.

"So they don't know," Ben says. "I don't know if that makes me happy or sad."

"At least they weren't in on it. I don't need three stalkers," I say.

"It's hard to imagine her keeping a secret like that from them, though," Jenna says. She turns to me. "So, what are you going to tell your mom?"

"Nothing," I say. "I don't...She finally finds a guy she likes and someone uses it as blackmail? I'm not telling her that. No chance. She'd never date again. She can think it was Jeremy playing a bad prank."

"Thanks," Jeremy says, rolling his eyes.

"You can deal with it. You'll come hang out sometime just to show how over it we are."

"I'm just so happy it's done," Ben says. "Now you can go back to being Jack. Not... whoever you've been."

"That bad?" I ask him.

"Girl, I couldn't take it. I could barely look at you. I pretty much just cry on the phone with Ben about it. I think he's going to break up with me."

"He's not," I say. "And yes. I'm back to me. Anyway, I just thought you all should know."

"Thank god," Jenna says. And she reaches out and grabs my hand and squeezes. "Now you get to go back to your real life."

Real life, we all decided, was retail therapy that weekend. I didn't find a new jacket, but I did find a great T-shirt with a pair of leather daddies on it, and some skintight black pants with purple pinstripes that I'm obsessed with. And some great new blue lipstick. Afterward, Ben took us to a fabric store and we all picked out stuff for him to make clothes for us—a flowy dress for Jenna, a new jacket for me, and we bought Ben the fabric for him to make himself an amazing houndstooth suit, as a thank-you. Then I took everyone out to dinner. Or I guess, I should say, my mom did. But she was there, and we were all pretty well-behaved.

Mom brought home her boyfriend, too, a week later. He seems pretty nice. She asked me not to tell him about the column, though. She said, "It would be weird if my boyfriend was getting sex advice from my son."

"Does he *need* sex advice?" I asked.

She just glared, but I laughed for a while.

I still don't know why Kaitlyn did what she did. Or even what she wanted, really. Did she think we'd be a couple? That forcing me back into the closet would turn me straight, like one of those conversion camps? I still wonder about it sometimes. I have bad dreams, where I'm cut by a thousand pink origami notes, raining down like hail, and I can't move as they slice me. But then I wake up, and I remind myself that it's over, and I have my life back.

Maybe she had a condition, or she really thought we had some sort of relationship, or maybe, like Jeremy says, she was just doing it because she could. Because that's what straight people do to gay people. Not all of them, of course, but more than just one. Or maybe that's just an idea I like, because I don't want to think I'm alone in what happened. Even if I won't really ever understand why it happened.

Whenever I wake up from one of those nightmares, I have a ritual: I go through the Jack of Hearts emails, and I pick one and I start to answer it. It makes me feel a lot better, and I fall asleep with people's sex questions in my mind—which makes for some delightfully naughty dreams sometimes.

Maybe, like Pattyn said, if I were more "subtle," blended in, I wouldn't have attracted Kaitlyn's attentions in the first place.

But I think he had it backward. It's not about making myself less amazing so I blend in—it's about making sure everyone around me sparkles with their own shade of glitter, that they feel as amazing as I do. And once I tell them that—and yeah, I tell them that through sex advice, but it's still what I'm telling them—then I can get back to sleep.

33

Dear Jack of Hearts,

*So, you seem to have a lot of experience with sex—
lots of men, lots of positions, lots of . . . stuff. But
is there anything you haven't done that you really
want to? How do you make stuff like that happen?
How do you ask someone to fulfill a fantasy?*

—Can't Make It Happen

"Okay," I say. "Now you kiss him."

Peter grins and leans forward to kiss Charlie. I pull off my shirt.

"And you two," Peter says.

Charlie presses his mouth against mine, and I can feel his tongue licking my lip. His arm pulls me closer into him. Peter starts kissing my neck from behind me. I let out a soft gasp and a laugh of pleasure. Not because I'm about to have my first threesome. Well, not just because. But because, though I know sex isn't everything, it's still a lot of fun, and not being able to have sex, not being able to do what I want (consensually) with who I want... that would take away *me*. And right now, in the moment that our pants come off and our bodies press together, and we moan and kiss and fuck—in that moment, I get to be me.

And if you don't like that, fuck off.

BONUS COLUMNS FROM JACK

Dear Jack of Hearts,

The other day, some friends and I were hanging out, just sharing a joint and talking about shit, and we got onto hot girls we're thinking of going after. When we get like this, we normally all make fun of each other's choices—nothing mean about the girls, just about, like, how the girls we like are out of our league, how we'll never get them, shit like that. But we get to me, and I say the name of the girl I like, and they all start laughing and calling me gay. Turns out, the girl I'm into is trans. I didn't know. And I tell them, and they laugh and call me a cocksucker and stuff, and then we move on. It wasn't mean, it was the same as what the other guys got. But I can't stop thinking about it. I still think the girl is hot. Does that make me gay? Should I go for it with her anyway?

—Maybe Gay

Dear Definitely Not Gay,

A few things are going on here. The first is that your friends are assholes. I don't know how they made fun of each other, but making fun of you for liking a trans girl by calling you gay is rude to you, rude to trans people, and rude to gay people. It's not right, and you know it, which is why it's still bothering you. There's a massive difference between saying, "That girl is out of your league, loser," as a way of teasing, and, "That girl is a man 'cause she's not cis," and you need to sit your friends down and tell them that. If they realize what they said wasn't okay and apologize and don't do it again, then fine—we all deserve a chance to become better people. But if they keep insisting that being into a trans girl makes you gay, or if they keep saying it was just a joke and you're taking it too seriously, dump them, 'cause they're transphobic assholes, and no one needs people like that around.

Now, as for whether liking this girl makes you gay: No. A girl is a girl. That's the whole story here, but let's address what people talk about when they talk about being into trans people and sexuality: what's in their underwear. As though that's all that defines a person. But we're told to worry about that, so maybe that's what's worrying you—and it's definitely what your friends were teasing you about when they called you a cocksucker. She might have had surgery, or maybe not, that's her business. But it doesn't matter, because not all girl parts look the same. I've been with a lot of boys and their various parts—big, small, and some detachable. Fucking a couple of trans guys (sadly not at the same time, yet) doesn't make me even mildly straight. I'll admit, I felt a little out my element my first time with a trans guy, and I told him so, and I asked him to tell me what he wanted me to do to him—but I do that with most guys. "What do you like?" He talked me through it, same as most guys do, and it was a delightful time. He even let me pick out which cock I wanted him to use when he fucked me (I love a bespoke experience). But him being trans was just a difference— like cock size, or ass size, or hair color, or whatever. Some guys like anal, some like oral, some just like to rub bodies together until everyone orgasms. Touch here, rub there, suck this to get him off. This guy was no different, in that he was different from every other guy—unique. But that didn't make him not a guy.

As for whether you should go for it with this girl—I don't know. She's hot, cool. Did you just want to fuck her? Date her? Has she shown even the slightest interest in you? There's no harm in maybe asking her out for coffee, seeing where it leads if she says yes. And yeah, if you get to the point with her where you're both naked, her body is going to be different from the body of the last girl you were with—but that would be true of any woman. What's important to you and your question is that they are parts on a woman, and so they are girl parts, and having fun with those parts is decidedly straight.

Now, yes, some people are really into what's in the underwear. They want that perfect cock, the perfect pussy, some weird porn-star ideal. They jerk off to "hole pics," where you can't see the person's face. If you're one of those guys, then maybe getting naked with her will be an issue, I don't know. But most of us are into other stuff than just genitalia—eyes, mouth, face, shoulders, butt, chest, or— more likely—the combination of everything. The sum of the parts, so to speak. If you think her lady parts not being your idealized lady parts are going to be a problem, though, don't ask her out. You don't want to put her in a situation where you're getting naked and you run out of the room because her parts aren't to your exact standards. But if you already think she's hot, it sounds like you don't care about her individual parts, 'cause the sum of her parts is making your parts stand on end (I mean she gives you an erection). In that case, go for it. But be honest—you're into her, but you've never been with a trans girl before and you might need some guidance. Guidance can be fun. But if you do want all that, remember to talk to your friends beforehand, and get them to realize they were being assholes. It's not cool to her for you to, like, date her but be embarrassed by her around your friends or keep her a dirty secret. You're into a girl—which is the definition of straight, and anyone who tells you otherwise needs to go, and the ashes of that friendship get tossed in the ocean. Never forget that—if people have an issue with who you're into, you shouldn't hide or be ashamed of it. You should say fuck them, and find better people to hang out with.

—Jack of Hearts

Dear Jack of Hearts,

So, I've been out since I was fifteen. I'm a hardcore dyke, wear
a tie to school, buzzed hair, haven't worn a dress since I could
dress myself. Coming out was easy because I feel like I had always
been out. No one batted an eye. And then, I started working
backstage on the school play, and there was this new kid, and he
was cool, and we started talking, and hanging out, and then we
ended up having sex. I really liked it. I like him, too—I like that
he doesn't ask me to change my style or act all girly or anything,
and I like his body, which is shocking to me. I'm still into girls,
don't get me wrong, but now maybe I'm into guys, too, or at
least this one guy? And...I don't know how to tell people! It's
so embarrassing because I already did this—I came out, I'm a
super-lesbian, and now I have to go back and be like, "Turns out
I'm a super-bisexual!" or something. Am I betraying my lesbian
sisterhood by doing this? Am I just another confused bisexual?
Why is this so hard?

—Coming Out Again

Dear COA,

I actually have gotten several letters like yours, so first of all:
You're not alone. I think a lot of queer folks, when they first
come out, come out loud—you were a super-lesbian, you were
into girls, and damn anyone who stands in your way. So coming

out again, as bi or pan or homoflexible or whatever, feels like a step backward. Like you're putting a foot back into the closet. But you're absolutely not. You're just coming out of a new closet you didn't know you were in. When I came out, it was like I had shed so much bad stuff, like I was free of everything that being in the closet made me feel. But that's not how it works. You have to constantly come out—new people need to be told you're gay, like people at work and people you'll meet at college. It's a process, and every time I have to casually mention a guy is hot or something around a new friend, I feel a slight uptick in my nerves before I say it. That almost flight-or-fight response where my hair stands on end as I casually mention my enjoyment of Chris Hemsworth's ass. Even when I know everyone must have figured it out by now. The closet leaves scars. And realizing you're in a new closet brings all that trauma back up.

But you got this because you've done it before. And you didn't do it wrong or anything. It was right for who you were then. Sexuality isn't neat little boxes. It's fluid and can change over time, and maybe this is the only guy you're ever going to be into, but if you want to pursue a real relationship with him, then your friends have a right to know. And he has a right to be your public boyfriend or whatever. So just tell them: "Hey, so, I know I'm this big ol' lesbian, but it turns out there's at least one guy who does it for me. I'm still queer, I'm still very into ladies, but for now, meet my boyfriend." If any of your friends—queer or straight—give you a hard time for being into this guy, they're

*absolutely not your friends. You are not betraying queer people—
even if you end up marrying this guy and never fucking a girl
again, you're still queer, and you're not betraying us. Anyone
who says differently isn't your friend—that's not friendship, it's
assimilation. But if people could handle you coming out to them
the first time, then the second time should be easy. You're not
going back into the closet—liking boys is not the closet. Not being
open about liking boys is. And you're stepping out of that. So
just be honest. Because you already know how horrible the closet
can be, and there's no point hanging out in one just because you
managed to come out of another already.*

—*Jack of Hearts*

Editor's Note: A version of the following column originally
appeared on Attitude.co.uk as an "Ask Jack" column. The question came from Noah Grimes, of Simon James Green's Noah
Could Never book series.

Dear Jack,

*As a shy British teenager who can't even say S-E-X but has to
call it "bow chicka wah wah," what do you think I could learn*

from you? Also, can you pre-warn me what subjects you might tackle, in case I need to prepare a cold flannel? Um...someone, not me, was wondering: If you are gay, how much do you have to do before you're definitely not a virgin anymore?

—Noah Grimes

Dear Noah,

Well, I don't know if there's a huge difference between shy British teenagers and shy American teenagers, but if you're hoping that by reading my column you'll go from not being able to say "sex" to having a Grindr profile with photos modeled after Olly Alexander's Paper *photospread...well, probably not. I'm just a seventeen-year-old American boy after all, not a god, but I do hope reading my column will make you more comfortable not just with saying "sex," but with wanting it. And those are the topics I'm most curious about. What turns you on but you're afraid to say out loud? Besides the word "sex." But as to your big question: virginity. Virginity is such a straight-person concept, isn't it? "Ah yes, now that my penis has gone into your vagina and caused bleeding, we have proof that you were heretofore (I'm trying to sound more British here) a virgin, and so an undamaged item, and now I own you and don't have to return you to your father," or however it worked. The fact that it's still an idea is sort of ridiculous. Like, why do we care? I can get you may want to tell someone if you've never done something before*

if you're about to do it, but there's a wide range of naughty things
we can do for the first time beyond trying to make a hymen break.
Especially when neither of us has a hymen.

This is sort of one of the joys of being queer, I think. We get to
redefine everything.

So I think when it comes to virginity, the best way to redefine it
isn't as a switch that's been turned on, or a cherry that's been
popped, but more as a wish list:

- *gotten jerked off*
- *jerked someone off*
- *given a blowjob*
- *gotten a blowjob*
- *topped*
- *bottomed*
- *played with a sex toy*
- *been blindfolded while someone went down on me*
- *threesome*

Etc. So on and so forth. For me, the first thing on my list was
having someone else jerking me off. When it happened, in my
mind, I was no longer a virgin. I was jerking him off at the same
time, too, but that seemed like the second thing on the list. Your
list might be totally different, though! The great thing about
thinking of it as a list is it becomes less about "what you've done"

as some sort of proof of something—your hymen being intact enough so that now your husband can continue to stay married to you and own you, for example—and more about what you want to do. And the emphasis there is on WANT. Things you've fantasized about or that you're curious about. Not stuff other people or society or terrible teen movies tell you that you should be into. So I'd recommend making that list. Maybe you're not a "given head" virgin, but you're still a "getting it in the ass" virgin. And maybe you don't want it in the ass—that's cool, too, and never doing it doesn't make you a virgin forever. Your virginity is yours to define. So make your list, then start checking it off.

—Jack of Hearts

Dear Jack of Hearts,

So, every year I go to a queer summer camp, and, darling, it's AMAZING. But this year, I'm worried it might be a little different. You see, my best friend, the Vera to my Mame (though I'm sure he would say it's the other way around), is going all butch for a boy. There's this boy at camp he's had a crush on forever, and this boy is "Masc4Masc"—you know, straight-acting and butch and only into the same—and me and my bestie...well, we can rock some sequins, and we're amazing actors, but "masc" is a stretch, even for talented actors like us. But my friend is really going for it. He's been studying straight boys all year, and he says he's going to cut his hair short! I'm not even sure if he's going to sign up for theater this summer! All to play a part and win this boy, make him fall in love with him, so he can then reveal his true self. It all seems like a ridiculous mistake, darling, and I just don't know what to say to him. He must be headed for heartbreak, right? What do I do?

—I'm Happy to Be the
Vera, Too

Dear Vera,

I had to google to get those references—sorry, not a theater queen—but you and your friend sound awesome. And his plan sounds...crazy. Masc4Masc boys are usually brimming with enough issues that I don't go near them, no matter how hot they are. But this is your friend's plan, not yours. If he were asking me if all this was worth it for some boy, I'd say no, or if his plan would work, I'd say, "Who knows?" But he's not writing me. You are. And he's your friend. So all you can really do is support him, right? I mean, you can try telling him it's not worth it, or you don't think it will work, or you're worried he'll lose himself...but *will he listen? All you can do is tell him, "I'm here for you, but you'd better not ditch me," and if he starts to ditch you, or turn into someone you don't know, then you pull him aside and say so. But you can't stop him, it sounds like. So just support him.*

And keep us informed. Sounds like it's going to be one crazy summer....

—Jack of Hearts

DISCUSSION GUIDE

1. At the beginning of the book, Jack lives by the motto "could be worse" when it comes to homophobic instances (page 97). Do you agree with him? Why or why not?

2. What symbolism might there be in the pink origami blackmail notes? Is there significance behind their color or their shape?

3. Jack says, "I've always wanted to live my life openly...but maybe there's such a thing as too openly" (page 76). What do you think Jack means?

4. While Emily, Ava, and Kaitlyn's bathroom conversations are clearly harmful to Jack, they never perceive themselves as being homophobic or toxic. Why?

5. Jeremy claims that he and Jack have a duty to be "respectable" and "not slutty" in order to combat stereotypes of gay men in the media (page 136). Why does Jeremy think this, and why does Jack disagree with him? When it comes to minority representation in the media as a whole, whom do you agree with more, and why?

6. In the Jack of Hearts column, Jack is very open about what happens in his sex life, but there are rarely any sex scenes in the story. Why? What might the author be trying to say about Jack's narrative control?

7. Throughout the book, Jack is often angered by Jenna's desires to punish Pinky publicly. Although Jenna does not intend to hurt Jack, are her actions misguided? Where do her attempts to help her friend cross a line that Jack doesn't want her to cross?

8. Eventually Jack begins to follow Pinky's demands and isolates himself from his friends. What compels him to make this choice even though it causes him pain?

9. Why was Jack blackmailed? What do you think the motive was behind this "relationship"?

10. Which Jack of Hearts column was your favorite, and why? What insights might it have given you into relationships, sex education, and identity?

11. What makes a queer novel "queer"? In some books a character's queerness does not affect what the book is ultimately about, while other books celebrate queerness for the sake of queerness. How does *Jack of Hearts (and other parts)* contribute to this conversation and continue to expand these definitions of queer narratives? What other books do you define as queer literature, and what do they do similarly to or differently than *Jack of Hearts*?

12. At the end of the book, what does Jack learn about himself and the way toxic straight culture affects the LGBTQIA+ community? How can you endure, cope with, and fight against microaggressions and homophobia?

TURN THE PAGE FOR A PREVIEW OF

PUTTING THE "OUT" IN THE GREAT OUTDOORS

CAMP

L. C. ROSEN

ONE

The smell wraps around me like a reunion between old friends when I step off the bus. That dark soil smell, but mixed with something lighter. Something green that immediately makes me think of leaves in rain, or trees in the wind. I love this smell. I love it every summer. It's the smell of freedom. Not that stupid kayaking-shirtless-in-a-Viagra-commercial freedom. That's for straight people. This is different. It's the who-cares-if-your-wrists-are-loose freedom. The freedom from having two seniors the table over joke about something being "so gay" at lunch.

Several tables are set out next to the parking lot, a big banner hanging over them: WELCOME TO CAMP OUTLAND.

This year, I admit, it smells a little different. Maybe not quite as free. But I knew it would be like this when I came up with my plan. This smell, I hope—slightly less pine, a bit more grass, the barest whiff of daisy, which I could be imagining—this is the smell of love.

"Keep it moving, keep it moving," Joan, the camp director, calls out to us as we step off the bus we've been traveling in for the last several hours, waving her hands like a traffic cop. "Tables are by age—find your age, go to that table to register."

I look for the table that says 16 and wait in line. I run my hands over my newly shortened hair. Until two days ago, it had been chin length and wavy and super cute, if I do say so myself, but I needed to lose it for the plan to work. The line of campers moves forward and I'm at the front, staring down at Mark, the theater counselor—*my* counselor. I think he's in his forties, gray at the temples, skin that's a little too tan for a white guy, wearing the Camp Outland polo, big aviator sunglasses, and a pin that says THEATER GAY in sparkly rainbow letters. This will be the big test. He looks up at me, and for a moment, there's a flash, like he recognizes me, but then he squints, confused.

"What's your name, honey?" he asks.

I smile. Not my usual big grin; I've been working on changing it. Now it's more like a smirk.

"Randall," I say. "Randall Kapplehoff."

"Randy?" He practically shouts it, looking me over again as he stands up. "Oh my god, what happened to you?"

"Puberty," I say, now smiling my real smile. I look around, bring it back to smirk.

"Honey, you were a baritone last summer, this isn't puberty," he says. "I barely recognized you."

Good, I think. That's the point.

"I just thought it was time for a change," I say.

"Were you being bullied?" he asks, concerned eyes peeking over his sunglasses.

"No." I shake my head. "Just...wanted to try something new."

"Well," Mark says, sitting down. "It's certainly new. I hope you haven't changed so much you're not auditioning for the show this summer, though."

"We'll see," I say.

He frowns and flips through the pages on his clipboard. "Well, at least you'll still be hanging out with us. You're in cabin seven." He takes a name tag label out from the back of his clipboard and writes a big *R* on it before I think to stop him.

"Actually," I say, putting out a hand, "it's Del now."

He peeks up at me over the sunglasses again. "Del?"

"Yeah." I nod, chin first. "I'm Del."

"Okay," he says like he doesn't believe me, and writes it out on a new name tag sticker and hands it to me. I press it over my chest, rubbing it in, hoping it will stick. "Well, I'm going to have to talk to my therapist about this later," he says to himself. Then he glances at his watch and turns back to me. "Flagpole meet-up is at eleven. So, go pick a bunk and be there in twenty minutes."

"Thanks," I say.

"Later...Del," he says.

I walk back over to the bus where our bags have been unloaded and pick up the big military surplus bag I bought online. The purple wheely bag with the stickers of cats wearing tiaras on it wasn't going to work this summer. Neither was having my parents drop me off. I think that made them a little sad. Camp Outland had been their idea four years ago, after I came out. Not many other twelve-year-olds were talking about how dreamy and cute Skylar Astin was in *Pitch Perfect 2*, and how I hoped my boyfriend would look like him someday, so they thought it would be good for me to meet some other queer kids, and they found Camp Outland—a four-week sleepaway summer camp for LGBTQIA+ teens nestled in the woods of northern Connecticut.

And let's be honest. It was an amazing idea. Every summer has been better than the last. But this summer is going to be the best. Because this summer, Hudson Aaronson-Lim is going to fall in love with me.

I hoist the military bag onto my shoulder, not flinching as the scratchy, cheap canvas brushes my ear, and follow the other campers down the path through the woods. The camp is built like a waterfall feature. At the top is the parking lot, then follow the stairs down and you end up at the administrative section—Joan the camp director's office, the infirmary, the big meeting hall for movie nights. Then another flight down and you have a big open field lined with cabins. The tier below that is the last one—the real camp—and has the dining hall, pool, drama cabin, obstacle course, capture the flag field, arts and crafts cabin, and a boathouse next to the river. I stop at the cabin-lined field, surrounded by the woods. There's a flagpole in the center of the field for morning camp-wide meet-ups and evening bonfires. Breakfast is at nine, lunch is at one, and dinner is at six, then lights-out at ten. Otherwise, we pretty much make our own schedules. Sign up for pool time, sports, waterskiing, or just drop by the arts and crafts cabin and spend all day gossiping and weaving friendship bracelets. My favorite thing every year, though, has been the drama cabin. Mark puts on a show, and you have to audition but it's not like school where the pretty blond girl lands the lead every year. They don't care about gender or appearance when casting, they just want everyone to have fun, and we always do. Last year, I was Domina in *Funny Thing*, and I got a standing ovation after "That Dirty Old Man."

But this year, no theater. This year...sports. I manage not to shiver as I think about it.

"Hey," a voice behind me says. A voice I know. It's low and a little breathy. I turn around and there he is, Hudson Aaronson-Lim, in all his glory. Tall, with muscular arms bulging in his white tee, and equally appealing bulging in his black gym shorts. He has a broad, square face, shadowed by prominent cheekbones and a little stubble. His short black hair is swept to the side, but messy, like he doesn't care. He is, without a doubt, the most attractive man I've ever seen in real life. And more attractive than half the men I've seen on-screen. He's got a killer smile, and he unleashes it on me now, crooked and a little sleazy, but only enough to make it sexy. I get that feeling I get around him, like I'm filled with stars and can be anything I want, do anything I want— conquer the world. Checking in on his Instagram never really gives me the same feeling. It's a high I've missed all year.

"Hi," I say after too long a silence. I hope I'm not blushing.

"You new?" he asks.

I smirk. He barely noticed me before, so it's not surprising he wouldn't recognize me. Now I have his attention.

"You could say that," I answer, not wanting to outright lie.

He steps closer. I coordinated my outfit perfectly for this meeting. Brown flannel button-down with short sleeves, untucked; olive-green shorts; yellow sneakers that pick out the yellow in the flannel. I've also lost twenty pounds, cut my hair off, and studied the "bros" at school all year. I am, I think, Hudson's dream boy. A masc fantasy. Sure, I watch everything I do now, and I won't be able to be in the show this summer, but it'll all be worth it for love.

I smell him as he steps closer—this sort of faded lightning

smell, like day-old deodorant and maple. I work hard to keep my knees from shaking.

"I'm Hudson," he says.

"Del," I say, keeping my voice low.

"So, what cabin are you in?" He's really close now. I can feel the heat off his body and I wonder if he can feel it off mine, like we're touching.

"Seven," I say.

"Oh." He raises an eyebrow. "So, did you pick that?"

"It's my lucky number," I say.

"Well, I'm cabin fourteen," he says. "So maybe your luck is changing."

"Something wrong with seven?" I ask.

"Nah, they're good people," he says. "But I think you'd have more fun with me—in my cabin. Folks like us." He waves his finger back and forth between us, almost like a question, a "We going to do this?" and I have to take a deep breath to keep from nodding.

"Well, it's just where I'm sleeping, right?" I say.

"Yeah," he laughs, and reaches out and gives my shoulder a squeeze. This is the first time he's intentionally touched me and it's something I've wanted for years and it's hard not to melt right away, but instead I just lock eyes with him and smile. Remember, I tell myself, you want him to fall in love with you. If I just wanted to screw him, I could probably do that right now—but I'm going to be the guy who finally gets Hudson to commit. No one else has done it, but I will. Because I have a plan.

"Well," he says, dropping his hand, his eyes closing just a little, like he's curious, "I'll see you around, I hope."

"I hope so," I say, and he grins, and I wonder for a moment if it was too much, but no, I think, as I turn around and head for my cabin, that was just enough. I look back after a few steps and he's still watching me and smiles when he sees me watching and then heads for his own cabin.

Okay, I say in my head, walking slowly, breathe in, breathe out. My legs feel like jelly, my heart is racing. Okay. Okay okay okay. Step one, done. It worked. IT WORKED. Maybe this whole thing could work? Maybe I didn't give up carbs and cut off my hair and spend hours working on my walk and voice and learning not to talk with my hands or quote a show tune every sentence for nothing. Maybe I can really win my dream guy.

I walk into the cabin and George starts screaming. "OH MY GOD," he says, giving me a hug. "I was watching from the window, and I almost didn't recognize you—I mean, I saw the photos on Snapchat, of course, darling, and everything you texted me, but I didn't think you'd really be going through with the wardrobe and styling changes." He reaches up and pets the air where my hair used to be. "Poor hair," he says solemnly. "But you just talked to him, and he totally checked out your ass as you walked away! Could you feel his dark, sexy eyes just burrowing into you?" He wiggles his eyebrows.

"Hey," Ashleigh says from her top bunk on the side of the room, where she's flipping through a comic.

I let my bag drop, and I take one long dramatic breath.

"I think it's going to work," I say.

George screams again, one big drag queen shriek.

I grin, and look them both over. My two best camp friends. Two best friends, really. It feels sad saying that about people I only see for four weeks out of the year, but we e-mail and text, and watch *Drag Race* together while in a group chat, and it's not like I have other queer friends. There's not even a GSA at my tiny school in eastern Ohio. Like, I'm sure there are other queer kids, and maybe they're even out, a little, like I am, to a few friends and their parents, but no one is talking about it. Once you start talking about it, other people join the conversation, and in eastern Ohio, they don't always say nice things.

My transformation at school didn't go unnoticed, though. I was still a theater kid (always the chorus, never a lead—there, anyway), but suddenly the girls were looking at me differently, asking me to hang out. I pretended to be sick a lot. My parents gave me weird looks a lot, too, and asked if everything was okay, but I just smiled and told them things were great. It was definitely strange. But worth it if I can go back to school with my phone lock screen as a photo of Hudson and me making out.

"So," George says when he's done screaming, "what's the timeline on this? You're still going to be able to hang out with us, right? Mark says they're going to do *Bye Bye Birdie* this year, and I am so excited! Darling, you know I'm going to cut some bitches to play Kim, so don't even think of going up against me."

George spreads his fingers out in front of him, his nails painted in green and gold to spell B CAMP @ CAMP. I've been so focused on my own physical changes over the school year, I guess I didn't notice his on Snapchat and Instagram. He doesn't look that different. He's still "stocky," as we call ourselves (well, called, in my case, I guess), but his face is a little more angular, and the stubble and chest hair peeking out from the collar of his purple V-neck give his sandy-colored complexion more maturity. His black curly hair is still shaved at the sides and big on top, but it looks less like a kid's haircut and more like a man's. He's gone from looking too young for his age to looking a little older than the rest of us. And he's wearing it well. Ashleigh hasn't changed at all. Same denim cutoffs, same black-and-white flannel wrapped around her waist and black tank top. Same rough-looking undercut, one side of her head shaved, the other side's unwashed wavy hair falling over her thin, pale face. She's the ultimate theater techie. Lights, sound, stage managing—she does it all, way better than anyone else.

"I don't know if I can be in the musical," I say, trying not to sound as sad as I feel about it.

"Darling, no," George says, shaking his head. "I know you have this plan and all, but there's always time for the-ater!" He does jazz hands.

Ashleigh looks up from her comic, a worn-out copy of *Deadly Class*. "You're giving up theater for this guy?" she asks. "Really?"

"That's the plan," I say. "And he's not just some guy. He's Hudson. THE Hudson. The perfect man." As I say it, a few more old friends come into the bunk—other theater kids. We say hi, give each other hugs, some tell me they like my haircut. Jordan does a double take and says, "Whoa, didn't recognize you. Cool look, though," with slightly worried eyes before grabbing a bed. I take the bunk next to George's, under Ashleigh.

"I thought you'd be taking the top bunk with that new hair," George says.

"Calm down," I say. "It's just a haircut."

"And no theater," Ashleigh says.

"What are you going to do all summer?" George asks.

"Sports, I guess," I say, not really sure which ones I mean. "Obstacle course stuff, arts and crafts."

"Well, at least we'll have that," George says.

"I just don't get this, Randy," Ashleigh says. "Like, I get you have a crush on the guy, but—"

"It's more than a crush," I say. "He makes me feel...different. He's special."

Ashleigh sighs above me, and I see George stare up at her, exchanging a look.

"And call me Del now," I add. "At least in public."

"Del." George tries it out. "I don't hate it."

"I do," Ashleigh says. "It's not your name."

"It's the other part of Randall," I say, taking out my sheets—plain gray this year, not the rainbow unicorn sheets I usually bring—and making my bed. "It's fine. I'm not forgetting who I am. I'm just changing the way other people see me."

"To be more masculine." Ashleigh says it with disgust. She hops down from her bunk and helps me tuck the corners of my sheet in. "As if that means anything. Gender essentialist nonsense."

"It's a type," George says, shrugging.

"It's what Hudson likes," I say, sitting down on my made bed and smoothing out the gray sheets. They're high thread count, at least. They may look different, but they feel the same.

"And you're sure all this is worth it?" Ashleigh asks.

"Absolutely," I say.

TWO

We gather around the flagpole in a semicircle, staring up at Joan, who's looking at her clipboard and making that face she makes all the time, with her mouth twisted to one side. I sit next to George and Ashleigh. I can still be friends with them—that won't hurt the plan. I decided if he didn't like me being friends with them, then he wasn't the guy I thought he was, the one who believes we're all special and can do anything. He might not know how we're old, close friends, but that's not important. Besides, I'm going to need their help.

I spot Hudson on the other side of the circle and he waves at me. I smile. Next to him is his best friend, Brad—tall, lanky, shaved head, and dark skin. He's like Hudson, in that he's into sports and doesn't wear nail polish, but strangely,

Brad has never been one of Hudson's conquests. No one is sure why—it's one of the great mysteries of camp, like whether someone really died in cabin three, or why the cabins aren't gender-exclusive but the changing rooms by the pool are.

"I'm going to need you to show me the tree later," I tell George and Ashleigh.

"You've seen the tree," Ashleigh says. She's already been down to the arts and crafts cabin and raided it for string and is weaving a bracelet.

"Randy has," I say. "Del hasn't. Del needs to see the tree while Hudson is watching so I can say I'd never want to be with a playboy like that."

"Playboy?" George says. "Darling, this isn't the sixties. We don't talk like that."

"I'm more worried about how he talked about himself in the third person, and as two different people," Ashleigh says.

"It helps me distinguish," I say. "Del is like a role."

"Method actors," George says, his voice dripping disdain. "All right, all right, I'll help you out—but I don't know how you're going to get him to eavesdrop on us."

"Just take me to see the tree when I ask you to, okay?"

"Attention, please!" Joan is standing at the flagpole in the center of the cabins, holding her hand up. "When the hand goes up!" she says.

"The mouth goes shut!" shout about half the campers in

response. Some people keep talking, but Joan keeps her hand raised and eventually everyone quiets down.

"Thank you," Joan says. Joan always seems like she hasn't gotten enough sleep. She's maybe in her fifties, with short curly hair and big plastic glasses I swear she's had since the seventies on a chain around her neck, always in the purple camp polo and cargo shorts. "Hello, and welcome to Camp Outland!" she says with half-hearted enthusiasm and a smile that would probably be big if she had the energy. "I'm Joan Ruiz, and I run the camp. I'll be leading meetings here every morning at eight, and I handle our LGBTQIA+ history activities on Monday nights. Otherwise, you're probably only going to be hearing my voice if you get in trouble, so let's talk about how not to do that. First—no cell phones, no computers, no smart watches or belts or whatever they have these days. We have boom boxes in each cabin, if you need music, but otherwise, no technology. If we catch you with a phone or anything else, you'll be put on kitchen cleanup for a week, and we will confiscate the phone. You won't get it back until you go home. It'll be dead by then, so you won't be able to immediately get on the Internet, where I know you'll want to be. That also means you have to write letters—Real Mail, I call it—if you want to talk to your friends or family back home. Next: food! You have to be at all three meals a day. If you're vegan or vegetarian or kosher or halal, you should have told us already and we're prepared for you, but if for some reason you didn't, come see me after flagpole. You eat what you're given. It's not so bad, I promise. Yes, you can be sent candy and snacks from home, but only things that follow the rules—nothing with peanuts or sesame seeds or anything anyone is deathly allergic to—your counselors have a list. When you get food from home, your cabin counselor will go through it to make sure it meets the rules. Don't leave food out! That's how you get ants. More ants. And if you're going to gamble with candy, just do it over cards. No betting on who's going throw up after eating too much or who's going to drop the egg during the egg race. That's just mean. No drinking! If we catch you with drugs or alcohol, you'll be kicked out. Same if you're caught outside your cabin after curfew."

I pluck the grass as Joan goes on, stealing glances at Hudson, who I'm pleased to see is stealing glances at me. We lock eyes once and I grin. This might be going too smoothly. The issue now is making sure he knows I'm not just going to be another conquest. That's what he does. A different boy every two weeks at camp. A week of wooing, a week of holding hands and sneaking out to the Peanut Butter Pit, and then, inevitably, a breakup with some tears.

They always stay friends, though. Hudson is the master of staying friends—and that makes sense. He's nice about it, he never cheats on them, they always just...consciously uncouple.

But I'm going to knock all those other bitches out of the water. 'Cause Hudson is going to stay with me all summer.

And beyond that, too. We're going to be boyfriends and share a tent on the canoe trip the second-to-last weekend of camp.

When Joan is done talking, she introduces the nurse, Cosmo, a skeletal man in his sixties with long gray hair to his shoulders.

"Just stay healthy, everybody," he says by way of his speech. "Like, water, sunscreen. You know." He waves at us and walks away. Joan frowns a little, then hoists the big rainbow flag on the flagpole, running it up to the top, where it starts flapping in the breeze. Everyone watches in silence, but with smiles. I admit, I grow a little teary-eyed at it every year—can you blame me? This is our special home. The scent of the wind rushes back, heavy with that smell— definitely freedom—and I close my eyes. I can't tear up this year. Hudson is watching, and butch boys don't cry in public.

"Okay," Joan says, after the flag is raised. "Go unpack, make your schedules with your bunk counselors, then there'll be some group time, some free swim, and then dinner. After dinner, the counselors are going to put on a talent show for you folks. Go with pride!" she shouts, the official dismissal.

Everyone scatters up and heads back toward their cabins, but I see Hudson coming in my direction. George and Ashleigh look at me, as if waiting for something.

"I'll see you at the cabin," I say. George gives me some side-eye as they walk away.

"Hey," Hudson says, arriving just as they leave. "So, your bunkmates showing you the ropes?"

ACKNOWLEDGMENTS

When I first wrote ninety-nine pages of this, I was wary of continuing with it, because I thought it would be unpublishable. I liked it—I was just afraid continuing on with it would ultimately be a waste of time. Plus, I have this rule: Write one hundred pages and you have to finish the book. So, I showed it to Alvina, as a friend, just asking her if it was at all worth continuing on. I think my exact words were "this is probably a terrible idea." But, to my surprise, she liked it, and told me to officially submit it, and when I did, she fought for it at Little, Brown, and has been fighting for it ever since—to make it the best it could be, and to let it be a loud, authentic voice that a lot of people don't want young adult readers to hear. So, none of this would have happened without her. This book would still be ninety-nine pages tucked away within a series of folders in my computer, probably never to be seen again.

I am always forever grateful to my agent, Joy. I genuinely cannot thank her enough for pretty much everything ever. She knew this book was crazy, but said we should go for it anyway and never asked me to tone it down or told me not to do it because it could ruin my career. She's championed me at every opportunity.

The whole team of readers at LBYR who went over this book were invaluable, and I'm very grateful to them for their perspectives and advice: Kacen, who was especially wonderful not just in their reading, but in their answering of all my inane questions, and Nikki and Michael, whose thoughts helped me shape the story into its best possible version.

Endless thanks to Victoria, Holy Be Her Name, Our Lady of the Tentacles, not just for being wonderful, having some of the most perfect taste ever, and being a great friend, but for all the work she's done on this book with libraries and schools. And of course many thanks to her excellent team, Michelle and Christie.

So many thanks to Kristina for all her hard work getting this book into the right hands, not to mention managing me.

Karina put up with a lot of my thoughts on the cover and the interior design of the book, like maybe more thoughts than I should have had—and definitely more than I should have shared—and turned out an astounding, beyond-expectations cover and design, for which I am very grateful. She's just so fucking good. And of course, she couldn't have done it without our Jack, Angel, and our photographer, Howard, not to mention Stephania, Riley, and Patricia. Also thanks to Michelle for swooping in and helping to pull together the interior design and Sasha for helping Karina at the shoot and being so welcoming to me. Karina also chose an amazing artist to create the notes and origami within the book—he actually created the origami and unfolded it so the notes had the right wrinkles on them. So thank you for that, Neil—it's amazing.

I am grateful to Eva, my Sluttiness Authenticity Reader, not just for her excellent critique and insight, but also for her encouragement, especially when I was feeling anxious about the subject matter.

And to sex-pert Allison, who talked out Jack's columns with me over milkshakes, making sure the sex advice wasn't terrible and awful.

I am also grateful to Teri for her incisive read and encouragement, and Molly, who may not actually be a human, but a critique robot, considering how quickly she was able to read the book and how accurate and helpful her comments were.

I had many friends who helped me come up with the letters written to the Jack of Hearts column: Ray, Emily, Miriam, Melanie, and Patricia. I didn't use all of your letters, but they all helped me think about what sorts of topics I should approach—and a lot of them were on standby in case we decided some were too risqué. And special thanks to Ray for giving me some genuine teen perspective.

I had an amazing, supportive sculpture teacher in high

school, and though Nance isn't based on her, she is in honor of her, so I owe a lot of thanks to Nancy Fried, not just for the inspiration, but for everything else she did for me.

And thanks to my various queer male compatriots for the encouragement: Richard, Matt, Jack, James, Andy, and all the others who I feel I don't know well enough to actually name without it feeling creepy, like I think we're closer than we are. Don't worry, I don't, but you're all still special and just by being you, you helped me with this book. Except that one guy. You know who you are.

And of course, I'm supremely grateful to my parents, who aren't as mortified by this as I thought they would be (or are hiding it very well). Without their support in everything I've done, I don't think I ever would have had the nerve to write this book. And special thanks to Mom, because she gave me feedback on it. I told her she didn't have to, but she said she wanted to. So, I'm thankful not just for her critique, but for her willingness to walk into that particular fire for me. And all the other fires, too.

And Chris, for being Chris.